Trengillion's Jubilee Jamboree

Daphne Neville

ISBN: 978-1-326-71806-0

PublishNation, London
www.publishnation.co.uk

Other Titles by this Author

The Ringing Bells Inn
Polquillick
Sea, Sun, Cads and Scallywags
Grave Allegations
The Old Vicarage
A Celestial Affair

2012

Chapter One

"The village looks really dark tonight without the Christmas lights," said John Collins as he walked into the kitchen of the Old Vicarage on his return home from work at the beginning of Epiphany. "I know, I'm not a great fan of Christmas illuminations, but even I have to admit it looks a bit grim without them."

Anne smiled. Her husband was usually the first to complain about the extravagant use of electricity at the beginning of the festive season and had always reminded her that back in *their day* even humble fairy lights for Christmas trees were a rare occurrence.

"If you think Trengillion's streets look grim, wait 'til you see the big room," sighed Anne, taking cherry scones from the cooling rack and placing them in the cake tin. "I took down the decorations today and it seems very dark and gloomy now the lights and tinsel have returned to the attic. Far worse than other years."

John removed his work boots and placed them by the back door. "Hmm, but then you did rather go over the top with the decorations this year, or should I say last year. Some of the beams were hardly visible beneath the huge swathes of coloured foil and holly."

Anne sighed. "I know, but, well, I wanted everything to be perfect because all the family were coming to dinner. Sadly, it doesn't often happen now, and goodness only knows when we'll all be together again. Anyway, it was worth it, because it did your mum and my dad, good to be with everyone. Poor dears; neither of them seems to be coping very well with living alone."

"Yes, sadly you're right. But it's early days yet and at least they both have us all living nearby, not that we can be any substitute for a long-term partner." John reached beneath the chair on which he sat and pulled out a pair of sheepskin slippers: a Christmas present from his mother. He sighed. "I think Mum will be alright though, after all Dad's been gone for almost a year. But your poor old dad, well, it's not even two months yet, is it?"

"It'll be a two months next Wednesday. Mum died on November the eleventh." Anne half smiled. "Easy to remember really, the eleventh of the eleventh, twenty eleven. Mum always did like things to be evenly balanced."

Inside Rose Cottage, Ned Stanley sat beside the coal fire watching the television. After the News he watched *Great British Train Journeys* and then swapped channels for *Emmerdale*: not because he liked it; once upon a time he had even ridiculed it. He watched it simply because Stella always had and to see the familiar faces made it feel as though she was still around.

During the commercial break the back porch door opened and Ned heard someone enter the kitchen. "Coo-ee, it's only me, Dad. Don't get up."

Elizabeth entered the living room clutching a large tin of unopened chocolates and toffees. "I thought you might like these," she said, bending to kiss the thick, grey hair crowning his head. "At least I hope you will. We had tons of sweets and chocolates this Christmas and if I eat any more I'll start to look like one. What's more, I've put on half a stone since the beginning of December. Even Greg commented on my inflated spare tyre this morning and he usually pretends not to notice when I moan. It's awful. I look and feel like an enormous dumpling."

Ned chuckled. Elizabeth smiled. Much laughter had gone from her father's life since he'd lost Stella, his wife of fifty nine years. Her death was not sudden. She had been ill for several months, but Ned really struggled each day to come to terms with his loss. He often felt lonely and frequently berated himself when recalling the rare times he and Stella had not seen eye to eye.

"Well, you know I'm not over fond of sweets, Liz. Your mother was the chocoholic. The hard toffees glue up my dentures and I don't much care for the fruit filled softies. But I'll help out if it'll make you happy and I can always hand them out to visitors."

Elizabeth put the tin of toffees on the settee beside her father and then sat down on the hearth rug. "Oh, it will, it will. And if you put those you really don't like to one side, I'll get Greg to eat them. I'm sure he'd rather do that than see them go to waste. You know what a fusspot he is over wastage."

Ned nodded. "And quite right too. I suppose he's back at work now."

"Hmm, he went back on Tuesday, and so did Tally, so everything's back to normal now."

Ned raised his eyebrows. "Tally's back at school already. But Tuesday was only the third of January, that's rather an early start for the new term."

"I agree. The school here in the village had an extra day and didn't go back 'til Wednesday. But if you remember they all broke up early. It was a good week before Christmas."

"Yes, I suppose so. I must admit I'm sorry Christmas is all over and done with. It did me good seeing all the family together and your sister did us proud with that lovely Christmas dinner. Family get-togethers are so precious, Liz. Which reminds me: did Wills and his sweet wife - I can't remember her name - get back to London alright? I meant to ask you last night when you rang, but forgot."

"Lydia," said Elizabeth, "Wills' wife is called Lydia, and yes they both got home safe and sound."

"That's good to hear. I think it was very brave of Lydia to travel such a long way in her condition, especially at this time of year when the weather is so unreliable."

Elizabeth smiled. "She's a fit and healthy young woman, Dad, and Wills' car is very comfortable, so I don't think it was too much of an ordeal. Anyway, I'm really glad they made the effort as it was lovely to see them both and I think they'll make excellent parents. They seemed so blissfully happy."

"Yes, I'm sure they will. When's the baby due again?"

"Next month," said Elizabeth, averting her eyes from the sweet tin, "the third, February the third. I'm so excited."

"I'm sure you are and I expect the house seems empty now they've gone. I know your mother and I were very much aware of the quietness all those years ago when you were teacher training and then working up-country. Anne was always so quiet and even a little subdued when you were away."

Elizabeth giggled. "Yes, I can imagine she was, after all she had no big sister to argue with, did she? But don't forget, we still have Tally at home so there's not just the two of us yet."

"Of course. Does Tally enjoy teaching?" Ned asked. "She seldom mentions it."

Elizabeth wrinkled her nose. "To a point, but I don't really think it's her forte in life. I think she'd be a lot happier doing something over which she has more say. You know, her own business, something like that. She's let it be known on several occasions that she envies her cousin Jess."

"Yes, I can see her point, but then I loved teaching and never once regretted it. But Tally isn't me and things are so different today, especially when it comes to discipline, but let's not go down that road."

Elizabeth agreed with a swift nod of her head.

Clive Lewis twitched his nose as he walked through the door of his home in Coronation Terrace. Something smelt good. Inside, his wife, Jess, and their seven year old daughter, Florence Anne, were busy in the kitchen; Jess was unloading the dish washer while Florence Anne was laying the table.

"Whatever you're cooking smells absolutely gorgeous," Clive said, removing his jacket and hanging it on the back of a chair in the dining area.

"It's chicken fajitas," said Florence, meticulously checking the cutlery was straight, "and I helped Mummy cut up the peppers."

"Good girl," said Clive, tickling her under the chin. He turned to Jess, "Fajitas, eh, you certainly know how to get to a man's heart.

He kissed her cheek and then dipped his fingers in the salsa. Jess slapped the back of his hand. "They're so easy to make, I thought I might put them on the Pickled Egg's menu this summer. Jim Haynes grows lovely peppers and it would be a good way of using them, you know, local produce and all that. What do you think?"

Clive pulled out a chair and sat down. "Good idea, if they're pretty easy to make, but don't take on too much, Jess; the Pickled Egg gets dreadfully busy at times and you struggled last summer without Janet.

Jess laughed. "Don't I know it? But Janet will be working again this year, unless she breaks the other leg, of course. And Valerie Moore was asking if there would be any jobs going this summer. I naturally said yes, because I like her, so I'll have plenty of reliable helpers."

"Val: now that is a good idea. Trevor was saying only last week how she's a bit lost now the kids are older and out all the time. And there's a limit to the amount of times Gerald can be walked. I reckon she'll be a great asset, especially living next door."

Jess nodded, as she put a plate of tortillas in the microwave to warm. "She makes a mouth-watering ginger cake too, and she's agreed to let me put it on the afternoon tea menu as long as she can make it at home and keep the recipe secret."

Clive screwed up his face. "What is it with women and the hush-hush approach to recipes? Sounds potty to me."

"It was her gran's concoction apparently," said Jess, giving the pan of aromatic peppers, onions and chicken, a final stir, "and she was sworn to secrecy at a very early age."

"I think everyone in Coronation Terrace must be a good cook," said Florence. "At least Mummy, Granny Gert and Mrs Moore are, but, um, I'm not um…"

"But you're not so sure about the Tilley twins," grinned Clive. "Don't worry poppet, neither are your mum and me. But judging by the size of Trish's ar…."

"...Clive, that's enough," scolded Jess, lifting the pan from the hotplate, "it's not polite to pass derogatory comments about the size of our neighbour's posterior."

Coronation Terrace consisted of just four houses. All had originally been owned by the local authorities, but over the years their occupants had purchased them and so now all were privately owned.

Valerie and Trevor Moore lived at Number One with their two teenage daughters and their twelve year old black Labrador, Gerald.

Number Two was occupied by widow, Gertie Collins, who had lived in the house ever since she moved there as a bride with her husband, Percy, shortly after the houses were completed in 1952.

Number Three was the home of Jess and Clive Lewis and their daughter, Florence Anne. Jess and Clive had bought the house following the death of Meg Reynolds, widow of Sid, who had died eight years earlier. The house, on Meg's demise, went to their two children, Diane and Graham, who both lived and worked away from Trengillion, hence the sale.

Number Four was the residence of thirty five year old twins, Wayne and Trish Tilley. Neither was, or ever had been married. They'd lived in the village for only two years, but in that short time had very much made their presence known.

Wayne was an artist. His work, mostly land and seascapes, was traditional, very realistic and extremely popular with both locals and visitors to Cornwall. He displayed and sold his paintings in Trengillion's beach café, the Pickled Egg, and at a popular gift shop in Polquillick.

His sister, Trish was a market trader. She sold jewellery, new and second hand, at car boot sales and indoor markets.

Trish and Wayne, while not identical, were very much alike in looks and height. Trish, however, was considerably stouter than Wayne, partly because she ate considerably more than her brother and partly because she was adverse to any form of exercise. Both had red hair, at least this would have been the case if Trish had not regularly dyed hers a rich chestnut brown. Likewise, both were fair skinned, but again Trish hid her naturally pale complexion and faded freckles beneath thick layers of make-up. However, when it came to character the twins were chalk and cheese. Wayne was quiet, pensive and content with his own company, and it wasn't until he'd had a drink or two that he became in any way loquacious. Even then, only the subject of art roused a reaction, especially if someone had the audacity to, in his opinion, argue the justification for and validity of modern art for which Wayne had no time whatsoever.

Trish, on the other hand was naturally outspoken. She took pleasure in meeting people, loved a good gossip, and enjoyed vodka with lashings of Coke, hence for that reason she was often to be found in the Jolly Sailor where she would chat to anyone about anything except sport.

During the afternoon of Friday, January the thirteenth, as Ned finished the crossword in the daily newspaper, a large vehicle pulled up on the road outside the house next door. Subsequent loud noises and jovial voices emanating from the street thus caused Ned to put aside his newspaper and look from the window in order to establish the cause of the commotion. Unable to observe much, he went upstairs to peer from his bedroom window. Outside two men were standing beneath the back doors of a large removal van. Ned watched as they lifted a cumbersome dining table and maneuvered it over the garden gate posts of Ivy Cottage and then along the path towards the front door. He felt a sudden pang of sadness. It seemed not long since his dear friends, George and Rose Clarke, had moved into that cottage, now sadly, both were gone, the house had been sold by George's nephew, the inheritor, and bought by people with whom Ned was not yet acquainted and of whom he knew absolutely nothing.

Ned stepped away from the window in case he was seen and went back downstairs to the warmth of the living room. With the crossword finished, he wondered how best to spend the remainder of the day.

"That's the worst of living alone," he muttered. "No-one to talk to, not even about the most humdrum of subjects." Ned grinned. Stella would have been very excited about having new neighbours. But then again, would she? She was, after all, devastated by the death of, first George, and then six months later, Rose.

Ned sat down on the settee and picked up Dan Brown's *Da Vinci Code,* loaned to him by Anne. He had not yet started it but knew he was in for a good read as both his daughters and his sons-in-law had read it with great enthusiasm. However, before he had reached the bottom of the first page, he heard the porch door open and close, a gentle rap on the back door followed and then someone called as the door creaked open. "Don't get up, Ned, it's only me."

Ned lay down the book, clearly amused. The caller was his old friend, Gertie Collins, no doubt come to visit to find out as much as she could about his new neighbours.

Gertie bustled in, removed her coat, tossed it on a stool and then warmed her hands by the fire. "I've just been out walking to get a bit of exercise and as I was passing I thought I'd call in to see how you're doing."

"That's nice, it's always good to see you, Gert. Would you like a cup of tea or coffee?"

"Ooh, tea would be lovely. I feel quite chilly, but don't you get up, I'll make it, the doctor says you're not to overdo things and get stressed."

Ned laughed. "I don't think I'd be over exerting myself putting the kettle on, but since you're offering, please go ahead. You know where everything is."

Gertie waddled into the kitchen, put on the kettle and took two matching mugs from hooks on the Welsh dresser.

"There's lemon drizzle cake in the tin if you're feeling peckish, Gert," Ned called. "Our Jess made it and it's quite delicious."

Gertie paused. Jess's lemon drizzle cakes were mouth wateringly scrumptious: they were also calorific. She paused for a whole ten seconds before reaching for the tin on top of the fridge.

"I shouldn't, Ned, I had a pasty for lunch, but then again, why should I care. What's another pound or two, eh? I was a mere stripling of eleven stone, you see, when poor old Percy died, but I weighed myself yesterday and the silly scales said I was over twelve stone."

"Really," said Ned, "you weigh the same as me then."

Gertie entered the living room with a tray laden with two mugs of tea, two plates, the cake tin and a knife.

"Hmm, well, knowing I weigh the same as you makes me feel better then, because you're actually still quite lean. Mind you, you've got to be a good eight inches taller than me, but we'll ignore that fact."

Gertie neatly cut two thick slices of cake and then sat down on the settee beside Ned. "Right," she said, glancing towards the window, "I see there's a removal van outside Ivy Cottage, so what exciting little titbits can you tell me about your new neighbours?"

Inside the living room of Ivy Cottage, retired Police Sergeant, Nick Roberts, stood in the hallway and instructed the removal men into which rooms each piece of furniture needed to go, while in the kitchen, his wife, Jill, made coffee for the workers and attempted to put away kitchen utensils as she unpacked them.

Nick and Jill had discovered Ivy Cottage was for sale whilst browsing through property on the Internet, having decided they wanted to start a new life in Cornwall following Nick's retirement just before Christmas in 2011. After making a short list, and receiving full details in the post from the estate agents handling the most promising properties, they spent a weekend in Cornwall during September seeking out their future home. Ivy Cottage was their favourite from the moment they first set foot on the garden path.

It was dusk when the removal men finally finished their work, but before leaving Trengillion they decided to go for a meal at the Jolly Sailor prior to making their way back to Bristol. Nick and Jill, relieved to have everything safely indoors before darkness fell, sat by an electric fire in the kitchen, eating microwave meals and congratulating themselves on their good fortune.

"Have you fathomed out how to work the central heating yet?" Jill asked, buttoning up her cardigan. "I feel quite chilly now I've stopped dashing around."

"Not yet, but I did check to see how much oil there was in the tank and to my delight found it's half full."

"Excellent."

"Fancy a glass of wine?" asked Nick, scraping the last smear of sweet and sour chicken from his plate.

Jill looked at her watch. "Shouldn't really, there's still loads to do and after one glass I'd be too relaxed to do anything more. We haven't even got the bed up yet."

Nick grinned. "We have. I managed to get it done while the chaps were taking the bedroom furniture upstairs."

"But you've not made it."

"No, but only because I'd no idea where you'd packed the bedding."

Jill laughed. "It's inside the pink ottoman so should be upstairs somewhere."

"Ah, I see. Yes, the ottoman is in the spare room surrounded by bulging black bin liners, if I remember correctly."

"In that case," said Jill, rising, "I'll go and make the bed while you sort out the heating and pour the wine. I must admit, I'm feeling shattered, and more in the mood for celebrating than doing any more work."

"That's my girl," said Nick, hugging her tightly. "I'll take the wine into the living room so we can sit in a bit more comfort."

Jill grinned. "In which case we'll have to turn a blind eye towards the disorder in there and you'll need to move the boxes of ornaments and pictures off the settee."

"No problem," said Nick, reaching for the central heating manual lying on top of the boiler. "Don't be long."

The heating was on and Nick had already consumed a glass of wine when Jill returned to the living room. She found him seated on the settee with feet resting on a box marked books.

"Sorry, I was so long," she said, snuggling down beside him, "but I just had to have another look round upstairs. I really love this house and I'm sure we're going to be tremendously happy here."

Nick handed her a glass of wine. "You don't think you'll miss Bristol, then?"

Jill firmly shook her head. "Not one bit. I shall miss our friends, but not the city. From now on I'm going to be a country girl. Well, woman, anyway, but girl at heart."

"Good. And I have every intention of enjoying country life too. In fact, I think once we've got ourselves sorted out, we must go to the pub for a meal tomorrow night and get to know the locals."

Chapter Two

January ended much as it had begun, mild and damp. On the last night a rain shower passed through just before the midnight hour, after which the temperature dropped to near freezing and at dawn Trengillion's inhabitants woke to witness the first frost of winter.

Elated by the sight of a dry, bright morning, conveniently accompanied by a gentle breeze, several women emptied their dirty washing baskets, loaded up their machines and soon delighted in watching their lines full of clothes and bed linen drying for free in the February sunshine.

Looking from the landing window at the top of the grand staircase inside the Penwynton Hotel, Linda Stevens gazed down onto the back gardens, her thoughts deeply focused on the approaching holiday season. During breakfast she'd overheard two guests discussing the Queen's forthcoming Diamond Jubilee and after thoughtful consideration, decided it might be a good idea for Trengillion to do something in the way of a celebration. The question was what? A street party was always popular but that was very reliant on good weather. Admittedly, if Trengillion celebrated with the rest of the British Isles then the chosen dates were between the second and the fifth of June. June ought to produce good weather of course, but one only had to recall Wimbledon tennis fortnight before the installation of the roof on Centre Court to realise it could not be relied on. Linda laughed, recalling her wedding day in June 1976 when the rain had fallen relentlessly from dawn 'til dusk. No, she didn't think a street party was the best idea. Determined to pursue the subject further she made her way down to the Hotel's reception desk to ask the opinion of Anne Collins.

Anne agreed the village should do something and eventually both women decided the best solution might be to put up notices around the village telling of a meeting to discuss the subject in more detail. If, at the meeting, villagers were in agreement and wanted to celebrate, then a committee would be formed to deal with the finer points regarding planning, finance, publicity and preparation.

They decided the village pub would be the best place to hold the meeting if landlord, Justin, was in agreement, and so Anne, who lived quite near the Jolly Sailor, volunteered to call in that evening to tell him of their proposal.

The Jolly Sailor was quiet when Anne, along with husband, John for moral support, arrived to see Justin. A few lads were playing pool in the games room, and a party of four were eating by the fire in the snug. Only dentist, Ian Ainsworth, and plumber, Larry Bingham, occupied seats in the public bar.

Justin welcomed Anne and John as they approached the bar and sat on stools side by side. Morgana, his wife, tipping pound coins into the till, turned and smiled. After buying drinks Anne put forward Linda's suggestion regarding Trengillion and celebrations for the Queen's Diamond Jubilee.

Justin laughed. "Tell Linda that great minds think alike because I was only contemplating when I was in the shower this morning whether or not we ought to do something. Isn't that so, Morgana?"

Morgana nodded. "And I told him I think we should. So have you come up with any ideas?"

"Not really," said Anne, sipping white wine, "and for that reason Linda thinks we ought to hold a public meeting, invite everyone along and see what the villagers come up with. Then if there's enough interest we'll form a committee and get things moving. What do you think?"

Justin nodded. "Absolutely, that's an excellent idea. I'm all for it and you can have the first meeting here if you like. February is a pretty quiet month and so we'll even put on a few nibbles."

Anne gleefully clapped her hands. "I'm glad you've offered because it saves me asking. Linda thought this would be a good venue, you see. So, when would be best for you?"

"Monday, Tuesday or Wednesday of next week, ideally," said Morgana, "because the week after that is half term and we should be a bit busier then."

Justin nodded in agreement.

"In that case we'll go for the Wednesday," said Anne. "That'll give us a whole week to spread the word around."

Morgana picked up a book from beside the till. "I'll put that in the diary. Wednesday, February the eighth. And let's hope we get a good turn out."

The weather remained bitterly cold for the remainder of the week with temperatures dropping below freezing by night and struggling to reach more than three or four degrees Celsius by day.

Before long, everyone was complaining about the cold. But it didn't last; on Saturday the temperature rose, the heavens opened and the South West had a very wet day.

On Sunday morning, Elizabeth put down the phone inside the kitchen of Chy-an-Gwyns and glared at the rain streaming down the widow. "Oh, Greg, why is the weather so miserable here? Rain is just so boring and tedious. It's not fair, especially when Wills tells me it's snowing in London."

Greg, sitting at the table checking emails on his laptop, laughed.

"Come on, Liz, you know very well why the weather is usually wet here when elsewhere has snow."

"Well, yes, I know, but it still seems unfair. Wills said they've had an inch or so already and there are families out on the Green building snowmen."

Greg looked over the top of his reading glasses at his wife. "I should have thought the presence of snow would have alarmed you rather than evoked jealousy. After all, it might be awkward for Wills and Lydia to get to the hospital if the baby decides to put in an appearance today."

Elizabeth shook her head. "I don't think there's much chance of that happening. Wills said Lydia's feeling fine. Besides the baby's only two days late at present and that's commonplace for the first. I daresay she'll go another week yet. If you remember neither of our two were on time."

"Are you coming to the meeting next Wednesday?" Tally asked her cousin, Jess, from behind the bar of the Jolly Sailor where she worked on Saturday nights.

Nodding, Jess handed a pint to her husband, Clive, who was chatting to her brother, Ollie. "Yes, Mum reminds me about it every time I see her. I do think it's a really good idea though, doing something for the Diamond Jubilee, that is. I know Granddad feels very strongly about it too, but the poor soul is much too old and frail to do anything much to help. I believe it was during the early days of the Queen's reign that he first discovered Trengillion, or something like that."

On Monday February the sixth, Ned Stanley put his bookmark inside the *Da Vinci Code*, poured himself a glass of Merlot, switched on the television and sat down by the fire eager to see Andrew Marr's *The Diamond Queen.* He watched the television with the volume turned higher than usual, for he was determined not to miss a single word. He was enthralled; the programme brought back many memories and left him feeling nostalgic and also a little melancholy.

Ned switched off the television during the News which followed. Trouble in Syria and all the rest: it seemed he had heard it all before. Instead he let his thoughts drift back to February sixty years earlier. Following an illness in 1952, as a young twenty five year old school teacher he had left London behind to recoup his strength in the then unfamiliar county of Cornwall.

Ned grinned. Everything had been so different back then. There was full employment. Farmers were able to make a decent living and fishermen too. As for television, well, very few people owned one and those that did were content with viewing a nine inch screen in black and white with just one channel on air for a few hours each day. Now there were hundreds of channels to choose from, twenty four hours a day.

Ned refilled his empty glass and resumed his thoughts.

Back in 1952 not every household had a telephone, hence red phone boxes were ubiquitous. Now everyone it seemed, young and old, had mobile phones, some of which were so clever they had access to the Internet and doubled up as cameras, computers and God only knows what else. Messages could be sent by the push of a button to arrive at their destinations almost instantly. And online everything it seemed was available by the click of a mouse.

Ned shook his head. It was too much for his old brain to comprehend. Technology, as his mother used to say, didn't exist back in their day. No, back then everything was so much simpler. People paid for their purchases with pounds, shillings and pence and the only credit was hire purchase. Goods were made in Great Britain. Sheffield made cutlery, Northamptonshire shoes, Nottingham lace, and Leicestershire lingerie. In Wales and up North they produced coal, Lancashire produced textiles and Staffordshire pottery. Domestic fridges and freezers were only for the rich. Food was stored in pantries and shopping done on a daily basis. Milk was delivered to the doorstep by the milkman before most people had risen from their beds. Bread was delivered by the baker. Meat came from the butchers. Fruit and vegetables from the greengrocer. The ironmonger sold DIY materials. The fishmonger sold fish. Ladies' clothes were bought from dress shops and menswear from gents' outfitters. Supermarkets, in their infancy, were small and sold nothing but food, in tins, packets and bottles; most main meals were just meat and two veg. Ned laughed. Now exotic dishes were readily available in gigantic supermarkets using recipes from all over the world, and all were ready to be heated by the microwave in minutes. He thought of the postman; back then he came twice a day. He thought of shoes; when they were worn down they were taken to the cobblers, and clothes, whatever their condition, were never thrown away.

"Make do and mend," chuckled Ned, wistfully.

Without doubt, life since 1952 had moved on at an alarming pace. Flights to foreign shores had long since replaced camping holidays to seaside resorts in the British Isles. And buses, once a popular mode of transport, now carried only a few passengers on crowded roads, for most families owned at least one car.

Images of the Old School House as it had been when he and Stella had first moved there in 1953 flashed across Ned's mind. They had been lucky. The School House had a bathroom whereas many homes in Trengillion and throughout the country still had outside toilets.

Ned sipped his wine. Wine was a rare thing back then too. Men drank weak beer. Every village had a thriving pub and towns boasted several. Pub food was a pasty, a porkpie, or a withered ham sandwich.

Ned sighed. Sadly, then, as now, the country was in a poor way financially. Austerity was widespread. Britain was still recovering from five years of war and some things were still rationed.

Trengillion of course was much different too. It was before the Penwynton Estate had been built. Penwynton Hotel was then a private dwelling and still owned by Charles, the last of the powerful Penwynton family.

Ned sighed, wistfully. Back then everyone knew everyone else and the Old Police House, currently the home of dentist, Ian Ainsworth, his wife, Janet and their family, had actually housed a real village bobby and his family.

The church was well attended and its vicar had resided in the Old Vicarage where now his daughter, Anne, lived with her husband, John, and son, Ollie.

Ned looked up at the mantelpiece where a picture of Stella took pride of place and thought of all the wonderful people he had first met in those long distant, halcyon days; all were now gone, bar one: Gertie Collins, then Gertie Penrose. She was the only person with whom he could reminisce over days long gone by.

Ned leaned forward and gazed into the fire. "To think it's sixty years since I first set foot in Trengillion. Sixty years! Ridiculous! It's such a very long time." Unsteadily he raised his glass. "Here's to you Trengillion. Here's to you and all your inhabitants, past, present and even future. Thank you for the life you've bestowed upon me. Thank you for welcoming me with open arms. I've enjoyed every one of my sixty years. My sixty glorious years."

Chapter Three

Much to the delight of Linda Stevens, the Jolly Sailor was extremely busy on Wednesday evening. Tally who was in for the meeting, helped out on the bar as people arrived, for Justin and Morgana were struggling to serve the ever-growing crowd promptly.

At half past seven, noting the door was no longer opening and closing, Linda suggested they begin the meeting. First, she suggested, they elect a committee. Nominations for a chairperson were requested but none was forthcoming. Anne, keen to get things moving, suggested Linda herself take the role. A collective sea of nodding heads endorsed Anne's recommendation. Tally seconded the motion and Linda was unanimously elected chairperson.

In due course, Janet Ainsworth was elected as secretary and Jamie Stevens, who had worked in a bank prior to running the Penwynton Hotel along with his wife Linda, was elected as treasurer. Volunteers for committee members were a little more forthcoming. They were:- Gregory Castor-Hunt, Elizabeth Castor-Hunt, Anne Collins, Trevor Moore, Matthew Williams, Morgana Thornton, Clive Lewis, Ian Ainsworth, Nick Roberts, Jill Roberts, Ollie Collins, Candy Bingham, Susan Penhaligon and Wayne Tilley.

After two hours of intense debate, committee members, along with villagers also present, had decided how they wanted to celebrate the Queen's Diamond Jubilee. A street party was to begin proceedings, but in a field rather than the street. And to negate the risk of bad weather, a large marquee would be hired. Tea would be followed by entertainment from local talent and possibly one or two well-known minor celebrities if resources would stretch to the cost. Stallholders would also be invited to sell their wares throughout the day and charged a nominal fee of five pounds for the privilege of doing so.

After much debate it was agreed the venue would be the back gardens of the Penwynton Hotel, rather than the village recreation ground. That way the Hotel's facilities would be accessible and a good power supply would obviate the necessity of a generator as would be the case if the venue were the recreation field.

Fund raising was considered to be the most pressing item of debate. Jamie and Linda Stevens donated five hundred pounds to kick off the procedure and Justin matched it pound for pound.

During the evening of Thursday, February ninth, as Elizabeth sat watching the *Ten o' Clock News*, the telephone rang. She leapt up to answer it. Wills was on the other end of the line. "Hello, Mum. It's snowing again."

Elizabeth laughed. "Hmm, I saw you were in for another sprinkling when I saw the forecast. But I thought you were ringing to impart the much awaited news rather than keep me up to date with your weather."

"Oh, so you're not jealous of our snow then?"

"No. It's been beautiful here today. How's Lydia?"

Wills laughed. "She's putting on her coat because we're off to the hospital."

"What!" Elizabeth squealed. "You mean, baby's on the way?"

"Yes, at long last. I wasn't going to tell you, but Lydia said if you rang here and there was no answer you'd probably panic."

"Only if I got no response on your mobile either. But if it's snowing, will you be able to get to the hospital alright?"

"The roads are fine, Mum, don't worry. It's not settling because of the traffic, and the paths are okay because they still have grit on them from the weekend."

"How exciting. You will keep us informed of events, won't you?"

"Of course, but I think it's unlikely there will be much happening tonight, so I suggest you try and get some sleep and I'll ring around seven in the morning to give you the latest details."

"Sleep! That's a tall order, but you're quite right of course. I'll do my best."

"Good. Anyway, Lydia's waiting so I must go. I'll speak to you in the morning."

"I look forward to it. Good luck and tell Lydia we send our fondest love and very, very, best wishes."

"I shall. Bye, Mum."

"Bye, Wills."

In London, the following afternoon, snow which had settled on the dark, bare branches of trees overnight, was blown from its resting place by a gentle breeze, giving the illusion that fresh snowflakes were falling. And as the flakes fell from the trees onto the melting snow below, baby Edward came into the world weighing eight pounds seven ounces. He had only a small amount of hair, but what little there was, was as dark as ebony. His eyes were hazel brown and his quiet, pitiful cry, brought tears to the eyes of his proud mother.

"He's perfect, isn't he, Wills? Perfect in every way," she said, stroking the baby's small, soft head. "I love him to bits, already."

Wills sat on the side of the bed with his arm around the shoulders of his tired wife, overcome with emotion and the sudden realisation of responsibility for the welfare of someone so small. "For once in my life, Lyddy, I'm lost for words," he said, tightening the grip of Lydia's shoulder, "And I can see now why Mum always got over excited when she talked of the births of Tally and me. There really is no other experience like it."

"Have you rung your mum yet?"

"No. I rang *your* mum and said you'd ring her as soon as you were able, but I wanted to get myself more composed before I rang mine, you can't imagine how wound up she is at present."

Lydia laughed. "I can and I love her because of it. Now off you go and put her out of her misery. It's time she knew she has a beautiful, healthy grandson."

After Wills had called, Elizabeth immediately rang Greg at work, and then her sister, Anne, to relay the good news. She thought about ringing the mobile of her daughter Tally, but decided against it as Tally should be on the road driving home from school. Instead she sent a brief text message. Happy that the immediate family members had been informed, she put on her coat and walked down to the village, her destination Rose Cottage.

Inside the cottage, Elizabeth found her father reading the last chapter of the *Da Vinci Code.* He put the book down on his lap as she entered the room, very much aware she had good news to impart.

"I take it you're a grandmother," he smiled, before she had time to speak.

"Yes, and you are a great grandfather, again, Dad."

"Don't remind me," grinned Ned, "great indeed! But what a shame the young fellow won't have a great grandmother too. She would have been so thrilled, would your mother."

"But at least she was able to enjoy being a great grandma for a few years," said Elizabeth, removing her coat. "She adored little Florence, didn't she."

Ned nodded. "And Flo adored her."

Elizabeth knelt on the floor by her father's feet and took his hands in hers. "Would you like to know your great grandson's name, Dad?"

Ned laughed. "Not if it's one of those ridiculous, weird names youngsters seem to be lumbered with these days."

Elizabeth shook her head. "No, it's not. In fact quite the contrary. Wills and Lydia have named him Edward. Edward Stanley Castor-Hunt. And he is to be known as Ned."

"Oh, no, Liz. I hope Wills didn't insist. It's too one-sided. What about Lydia's side of the family?"

"It was Lydia's idea. Wills said he'd like to have Stanley as a middle name since it was my maiden name, but Lydia went one step further and said he must have Edward as his first name. She's very fond of you, Dad. Isn't that sweet?"

Monday, February the thirteenth saw the beginning of the school's half term holiday and because she also had the week off work, Tally opted to help Justin and Morgana in the Jolly Sailor so that their full time barmaid could go away to Spain for the week with her husband and children.

The following day was St Valentine's Day, and Tally was much surprised to find amongst the post a card with her name neatly written in capital letters on the pink envelope. Puzzled, she opened it but try as she might, she had not the slightest idea who might have sent it. Nor did she know whether or not the sentiments expressed in the flowery verse were serious or just teasing. She decided on the latter, for she was not aware of anyone interested in her as a potential partner, and she had not been romantically linked since Keith, her erstwhile boyfriend from whom she had parted company the previous summer. Tally laughed. On reflection, it was most likely a silly prank by some of her pupils. Nevertheless, she still put the card on the sitting room mantelpiece and fantasised that she had a secret admirer.

Later in the morning, Tally left Chy-an-Gwyns, and walked into the village to Number Three Coronation Terrace to visit her cousin Jess. While she was gone, an Interflora van called at Chy-an-Gwyns with a dozen sweetly scented red roses. It was Tally's mother, Elizabeth, who took the flowers from the delivery man, and for a whole minute, before she had a chance to read the label, believed they were a gift for her from Greg, her husband of thirty four years. Elizabeth laughed, disappointed yet at the same time relieved. After all, she and Greg had mutually agreed to curtail the buying of cards and gifts for St. Valentine's Day once they had achieved the ten year milestone of marriage.

Elizabeth took the flowers into the kitchen and placed them in a bucket of water, and then because she was impatient to know from whom they had been sent, she dispatched Tally a text relaying the exciting occurrence. Tally was dumbfounded. Jess, on hearing the news, was thrilled and both young women, eager to establish the identity of the mysterious admirer, went through the names of all unattached males with whom they were acquainted. Their enthusiastic efforts, however, were fruitless, for after a considerable length of time and countless suggestions, they were none the wiser.

"The only thing I am confident about is that my original thoughts when I had just the card, were wrong. I mean to say, there's no way the kids at school would be responsible for all this. A card maybe, but they'd never waste their precious pocket money on flowers, especially roses."

Jess giggled and bit her bottom lip. "Are you working at the Jolly Sailor tonight?"

"Yes, why?"

"I think it might be worth popping down for a drink then. After all, if someone has gone to all this trouble then surely they'll want to see you tonight. I'll give Mum a ring and see if she'll baby sit."

"But Tuesday night is usually fairly quiet with just a few regulars in. I know it'll be a bit busier tonight because it's St Valentine's Day, but even so, the extras will all be couples, so I can't believe whoever sent the flowers will be in. It's a real mystery."

Jess' eyes widened. "I suppose we ought to take into consideration the fact that your admirer might already be married."

The colour drained from Tally's face. "Don't say that, Jess. It'd be too embarrassing, because when all's said and done, I know the wives of most of our regulars."

"But he doesn't necessarily have to be a local, inasmuch as someone living in the village. He might be an occasional visitor or perhaps even a colleague of yours at the school."

"In which case, he'll not be in the pub tonight because his presence would be too obvious."

"Perhaps that's what he wants. After all, there's not much point anyone sending flowers if they're not going to chase it up."

Tally, deep in thought, didn't reply.

"On the other hand," giggled Jess, impishly, "your admirer may not even be a man."

On Wednesday, Jim Haynes, encouraged by the mild, dry weather tinged with occasional sunshine, cycled up to his allotment and spent the morning cleaning out his greenhouse and polytunnel. Once done he pulled up old cabbage stumps and a few yellowing weeds. He did not dig over the earth, however. He deemed it too early, and he never sowed seeds into the soil before April.

As Jim cycled home past the driveway which led to the Old Vicarage, Jess, having been to visit her mother, emerged through the gates. Jim stopped and put his foot to the ground as Jess flagged him down.

"I'm glad I've seen you, Jim. I was going to ring you anyway. The thing is, I've decided to put fajitas on the menu this summer, which means I'll need tons of peppers."

Jim laughed. "Just as well, I'm experimenting with three new varieties this year then, as well as my old reliable favourites that is. I'm growing different varieties of tomatoes too, including White Cherry and Brown Berry, which, would you believe, are white and brown."

"Really!" said Jess, "White and brown tomatoes. How fascinating. They'll look really pretty in salads. I know you can get yellow ones because they've been around for years. I hope they're a success, Jim, because the kids will love them."

"Ah, just remembered, I'm growing lemon cucumbers too. If the pictures are accurate they'll look a bit like melons."

Jess giggled. "Lemon cucumbers! Whatever will they think of next?"

"Actually, they're nothing new, they've been around since Victorian times when they were hugely popular. Anyway, I've deviated a bit, haven't I? You said you're going to do fajitas this summer. Sounds great. I'll have to pop in for a meal when you open because I've actually never eaten them before."

"Really! In that case you must come to dinner on Saturday night. I'm giving a little party to try out some new dishes which I'm hoping to put on the menu this year, including fajitas. I've already tried them out on Clive and he loved them."

"That's really kind of you, Jess, but I don't want to intrude."

"Don't be daft, Jim. You should be amongst my guests, after all you do supply the Pickled Egg's veg. Anyway, you'll know everyone because it's mostly family, plus Janet and Ian, and the Moores."

"Well, if you're sure I'd love to join you. I've not seen your mum for a while and we always liked to have a chat about gardening. I think she's nearly as fanatical as me."

On Saturday evening, Jess and Clive welcomed their guests at Number Three Coronation Terrace to sample Jess's latest concoctions. Jim, feeling peckish, was one of the first to arrive. A close second was Tally.

"How's school?" Jim asked, as she poured a glass of wine and took a seat by his side.

She half turned up her nose. "So, so. You know, good days and bad."

"Hmm, so you chose the wrong profession."

Tally laughed. "Well, I didn't really choose it at all, it chose me."

Jim raised his eyebrows. "I'm confused."

"Because I really didn't know what I wanted to do with my life I went for the easy option. Mum was a teacher once upon a time and of course so were Grandma and Granddad and so I thought it might be in my blood."

"And now you're not so sure."

"Hmm, something like that. Don't get me wrong, Jim, I love the school, my fellow teachers and most of the pupils, but I really don't think it's quite me. I'm too flighty. I'm inconsistent and I find it hard to be on my best behaviour all the time."

Jim threw back his head and laughed. "In other words, you lack authority because you're more like the children than the children."

"Yes, something like that. And at the end of the day, teaching's a serious business and I just don't think I'm serious enough."

Jim patted her hand. "You should have a pub, Tally. You're very much at home behind the bar of the Jolly Sailor. A pub would suit you down to the ground."

She nodded. "You may well be right. The trouble is I have very little savings, and pubs, in spite of the economy, still cost a pretty penny. What's more, I'm not sure I'd want a pub anywhere other than Trengillion."

"Hmm, I can see your dilemma. There's something about Trengillion, isn't there? I'm not a native, of course, but I wouldn't want to live anywhere else."

"Precisely, so it looks as though I'll have to stick to teaching."

The weather was glorious on Sunday and so many people were out and about, washing their cars, tidying their gardens and walking down the lanes and along the coastal paths. Inside Ebenezer House, Jim Haynes, inspired by his first taste of fajitas, sowed the three new varieties of pepper seeds he had acquired, in propagators which he placed on sunny window sills to speed up their germination. When finished, he switched on his laptop and looked at polytunnels; after all, if he was growing a lot more peppers than usual he would need more space. When he found one of a suitable size, he ordered it and then went up to the allotments to clear a space ready for its assembly.

Ned, who spent much of his time indoors, felt the beautiful day drawing him out to soak up the sunshine. Saddened that he was too frail to take a long, brisk walk, he put on his jacket and ventured slowly into the garden, where snowdrops, grouped in large clusters, formed white mats beneath the old apple tree. Ned felt sad. Stella had always been so excited by the first snowdrop to bloom.

He wandered round to the front of the garden, where daffodils in bud towered over purple crocuses along the edge of the path. Stopping beside a camellia to admire its large pink blooms, he was startled by a sudden voice seeming to come from nowhere.

"Oh, no. I'm ever so sorry," said the voice, "I didn't mean to alarm you. Are you alright?"

Ned looked up. Peeping over the fence, surrounded by the yellow flowers of a forsythia, a pretty woman was smiling,

Ned grinned. "Yes, I'm fine. My hearing's not what it was. I didn't hear your footsteps."

"Well, you probably wouldn't have anyway because I've got my old slippers on. May I come round and introduce myself? It's not very comfortable squeezed between these plants. The forsythia's fine but the rose by my legs is really quite prickly."

Ned nodded. "Yes, please, do come round."

He watched as she disappeared from view. He heard the gate of Ivy Cottage open and then close. Almost immediately the gate of Rose Cottage opened and the slight figure of his new neighbour tripped merrily up the path. As soon as she reached him she held out her hand.

"My name is Jill Roberts. I live next door, but then I expect you've already worked that one out."

Ned laughed. "Yes, and I'm Edward Stanley, but everyone calls me Ned." He sighed. "At least everyone used to. These days I usually answer to Dad or Granddad. Most of my contemporaries have gone you see, my wife included, and because I used to be headmaster of the school here, most of the younger generation call me Mr Stanley."

"Oh, I'm sorry. About your wife, that is. Had you been married long?"

"Fifty eight years."

Jill gasped. "Crikey, that is a long time. And when did you lose her?"

Ned felt a lump I his throat. "Last November and I miss her ever so much. It's horrible living alone but I mustn't grumble. My family are very good to me and call in frequently."

Jill smiled. "Do your family live locally?"

"Yes. I have two daughters, both are married and both living in the village. I also have four grandchildren and three of them live in the village too."

Jill noticed he was shivering. "I think you ought to get back indoors. It's quite chilly standing around in spite of the sunshine."

"Yes, you're quite right. I don't suppose you'd like to join me for a coffee, would you? I'd appreciate the company and I'd like to hear all about you."

Jill stepped forward and took his arm. "Of course. Coffee would be lovely."

Ned made the coffee. Jill helped without undermining his capabilities. They then sat in the living room and talked of their lives.

As Jill finished telling of her husband's career in the police force she pointed in the direction of the house next door. "So, out of curiosity, who lives on the other side of you?"

"Ah, that's Valley View and the home of Maurice Lamont. He's the chef at the inn and seems to be a pleasant fellow. He's been next door for a fair few years now."

"Oh yes, I know who you mean. I saw him in the pub the other day and I've seen him walk by our house on several occasions too, no doubt on his way to work." She took a sip of coffee. "So, does he live there alone? From the outside it looks to be quite a big house."

"It is a fair size and yes he does live alone. He used to rent it from a chap in Falmouth but a few years back he was able to buy it because it was in need of modernisation. The owner decided to sell it, you see, rather than go through the hassle of having builders in and so Maurice bought it for a very favourable price."

"Hmm, lucky Maurice."

Jill watched as Ned picked up a small packet and from it and take out two tablets. "So, without sounding too nosy, what are they for?"

Ned moaned. "Not really sure. Medicine's never been my thing, you see. But I had a heart attack the day after losing Stella, so I assume they're something to do with that."

"Oh dear, how horrid for you. But I remember reading last month that the loss of a loved one through bereavement increases the risk of heart attack twenty one fold."

Ned nodded. "But apparently the risk drops to a mere six times after six days."

"Poor you. Thank goodness you have family nearby, and now Nick and I are next door you must not hesitate to ask for our help too, should you need it."

"Thank you."

As Ned popped the tablets into his mouth Jill's mobile phone rang. She grinned when she saw who was calling.

"I expect you're wondering where on earth I've gone," she giggled, the phone at her ear.

Ned couldn't hear the caller's response.

"Come round, love. You really must meet our neighbour and I'm sure he'd like to meet you too."

"Sorry," said Jill, dropping the phone in her pocket, "needless to say that was my other half. He's been looking for me everywhere. I only popped out to cut some daffodils, you see. There are loads of them blooming in the front garden."

"And you haven't picked one," said Ned, remembering she had come round empty handed.

She grinned. "That's because I heard you cough and being nosy I wanted to see what you were like."

A knock on the front door caused Ned to jump.

"That'll be Nick," said Jill, springing to her feet.

"You might have trouble opening the front door," said Ned, "God only knows when it was last used."

"In that case I'll go out and call him round the back."

Ned watched her disappear into the kitchen and call her husband's name. He gave a contented nod, confident his new neighbours were worthy occupants for Ivy Cottage, just as those who had come and gone before.

Chapter Four

On the twenty-ninth of February, the Jubilee Committee held their second meeting, this time in the Penwynton Hotel. The purpose was to allocate duties to various members and discuss fund raising options. After much debate members decided to arrange a sponsored walk over the cliffs to Polquillick and then back to Trengillion by way of the lanes; the time proposed was sometime during the Easter holiday and the exact date was to be decided at a future meeting. It was also agreed to distribute flyers throughout the village requesting saleable items which could be sold by members on a rota at various car boot sales in the area.

Linda was able to report that she had been in contact with her cousin Danny in London, a former member of sixties' pop group Gooseberry Pie and that he had agreed to bring along a relatively new, but popular band he was managing to perform at the Jubilee celebrations.

"That's excellent news, Linda, well done," said Trevor Moore, "one more well-known act from up country should round off the lineup nicely along with the local acts we've hired."

"Does anyone have any suggestions?" Linda asked.

"How about Polly Jolly?" said Jill Roberts.

"You mean Polly Jolly the comedienne?" frowned Matthew Williams, "surely we couldn't afford her fees."

Jill smiled, sweetly. "Actually I think we could. Polly was a neighbour of ours in Bristol a few years back, wasn't she, Nick? It was before she was famous but we've always kept in touch, you know, Christmas cards and suchlike. I'm sure she'd do it providing she wasn't already booked elsewhere."

"Wow, that'd be great," said Jamie Stevens, "she's hilarious and pretty gorgeous too. She gets my vote."

Linda's eyebrows rose over the top of her reading glasses. "Okay. Is everyone in agreement then?"

All nodded. It was therefore settled that Jill would contact her erstwhile neighbour as soon as possible.

After the meeting, several Committee members, including Ollie and Clive, called in at the Jolly Sailor to mull over details of forthcoming events and to tell Justin and Morgana of the latest developments. Tally, who had the evening off work, was already there with her cousin, Jess. After buying drinks, Ollie and Jess' husband Clive, joined Tally and Jess where to their amusement they found Tally, who, none the wiser as to the sender of her Valentine card and flowers, was lamenting the non-event that was her love life.

"It's leap year day today and so if I'd have found out who sent the flowers and card I could have proposed to him tonight," she laughed.

"Assuming he was free to marry," said Jess.

Tally groaned. "Perhaps it's just as well I never found out."

Ollie glanced around the public bar. "Is there no-one here tonight that takes your fancy, Talls? After all leap year only comes round every four years so it seems a shame to waste the opportunity."

"Ha ha, it looks very much to me like you're the only unattached bloke here tonight, so I'm out of luck."

"Anyway, it's time you had a steady girlfriend," said Jess, nudging her brother's arm, "Florence would like a cousin before she's too old to appreciate it."

Tally nodded. "I agree. There's something pretty special about cousins but they have to be in the same age group."

"Then it's too late," grinned Ollie, "Florence is already ten."

Jess shook her head. "Actually she's seven. Fine uncle you are."

Ollie ignored the reprimand. "Anyway, female companionship would interfere with my social life. The sport side of it anyway."

"Humph, you and your damn sport."

"I expect you're looking forward to the Olympic Games," said Clive, "I know I am."

Ollie nodded. "Absolutely, especially with them being in London."

Clive opened a bag of peanuts and offered them around the table. "Will you be applying for tickets to be there in person?"

Ollie shook his head. "No, because I don't want to take the time off work. Besides, I like so many different sports, I'd never be able to decide what to go for. So I shall do like most other folk and watch it on the telly."

"You're not a great one for sport are you, Tally?" Jess asked.

Tally shook her head. "Not really, although I do like to watch tennis and I don't mind a bit of swimming."

Jess tipped a few peanuts into the palm of her hand. "Same here. Swimming that is. I don't have time for tennis as I'm always too busy in the café when Wimbledon's on, and so I'm completely out of touch with who's who now."

The weather in March, as during the previous year, was beautiful. Dry, warm, often sunny and with light-to-moderate easterly winds, Trengillion's inhabitants welcomed the spring-like weather. Several gardeners dug over their vegetable patches and some even risked sowing seeds. Meanwhile, up country, the South East and parts of the Midlands were told a hosepipe ban would come into force on April the first, and in Aboyne, Scotland, the temperature broke all previous records for March when it reached just under twenty four degrees' Celsius. But the good weather did not last. As March made way for April a cold front moved in, and snow and strong north easterly winds swept across the country.

One evening, Jim Haynes, having spent much of the week outdoors, suddenly felt compelled to check his emails. To his utter amazement he found his name had been selected in the random draw for two tickets to attend the Queen's Diamond Jubilee concert at Buckingham Palace. Thinking he must have misunderstood its contents he read the email a second time. Jim was dumbfounded; he had submitted his application in early February believing his efforts would be futile and therefore had not given the prospect of winning a second thought.

In a daze, Jim reached for the kettle and made a mug of coffee. As he sat down to drink it, it occurred to him that he was now faced with an awkward dilemma. Who on earth was he to take with him? He couldn't pass the tickets to someone else because the terms and conditions clearly stated that the name to whom the tickets were allocated must be one of the two people in attendance. Jim scratched his head. Unable to come up with a solution he decided to pop along to the Jolly Sailor hoping a pint of beer might stimulate his thoughts.

Jim found the Jolly Sailor quiet when he arrived. A couple of strangers were in the corner eating scampi and chips, and on a stool at the bar, Trish, female half of the Tilley twins, sat brushing salt from her fingers having just eaten crisps. Jim asked for a pint and likewise sat on a stool at the bar. Trish looked him up and down as he took a five pound note from the pocket of his jeans.

"A penny for your thoughts," Morgana said, as she handed Jim his drink. "You look as though you have all the cares of the world on your shoulders."

"Oh dear, do I? Well actually I have. The thing is, Morgana, I've found myself with a bit of a problem. Well, it's not really a problem, it's more of a predicament. You see, I entered my name into the draw to win two tickets for the concert at Buckingham Palace for the Queen's Diamond Jubilee, knowing I wouldn't win but to my utter amazement, I have. The thing is, I've no idea who to take with me."

Trish's eyebrows rose dramatically.

"Two tickets, lucky old you," laughed Morgana "I should think just about everyone in Trengillion would like to be your escort."

"Do you think so?"

"Absolutely. I reckon you'll have to put names in a hat."

Jim slapped his thigh and grinned from ear to ear. "Yes, that's a brilliant idea. We'll have a Jubilee draw. Anyone will be able to enter for say a pound and the proceeds will go to the Jubilee Committee for celebrations here and whoever wins I shall take with me."

Morgana bit her bottom lip. "Might be a bit risky, don't you think? I mean, you and the winner might not get along too well."

Jim shook his head. "I get along with pretty much everyone here and we'd only be away for the one day anyway."

When Justin entered the bar Morgana told him of the plan.

He nodded his approval. "Excellent idea, Jim. A prize like that will certainly create a bit of excitement and I think to make the trip even better, we'll book and pay for a hotel room too. Do you agree, Morgana?"

"Absolutely, because you, Jim, and whoever wins won't want to drive home straight after the concert as it would be quite late by the time you got out of London."

"That's very generous of you," said Jim, "but please make sure you book a twin room. I'm more than happy to spend time away with most people here, but sharing a bed is a different ball game, especially if the winner's a bloke."

Trish raised her glass of vodka and Coke and laughed lasciviously. "Put me down for a tenner's worth, please."

Chapter Five

"Typical," growled Justin, as he watched the weekend's weather forecast during breakfast. "All that warm, sunny weather in March and now it's turning cold and wet for Easter. I don't expect we'll get half the visitors we might have had if the sun hadn't done a runner."

Morgana smiled. "I expect those already booked will still make the effort, and if the weather's poor some of them will pop in for a drink and something to eat. Rain often works in our favour."

"I know, but what rotten bad luck. Because it's not just the visitors who'll lose out, I was hoping to get in a game of golf sometime this weekend with Ian. That's why I've got so many staff coming in."

Morgana lovingly rubbed the back of his hand. "I guessed there was an ulterior motive for the doldrums, and the staff too for that matter. Never mind, I'm sure there will be plenty of opportunity for you and your precious golf before the summer madness begins, and if it's quiet and we've got too many staff in, you and I can always go shopping. I'd quite like a new dress for the Jubilee do and it'd be nice if you were able to go with me to cast your opinion."

The weather was cool and sunny on Good Friday. Saturday and Sunday were much the same and so Justin and Ian were able to enjoy a day of golf on the Saturday, thus saving Justin from a fate worse than death: dress shopping. But on Easter Monday, as forecast, the weather deteriorated, and the heavens opened.

At Number Four Coronation Terrace, Trish Tilley sat by the living room window watching the rain as it ran down the side of the road and splashed into an overflowing drain.

"A penny for your thoughts," said Wayne, as he entered the room with a mug of coffee for his sister.

Trish reached out and took the mug. "Thank you. Actually, I wasn't really thinking of anything at all. I was just watching, you know, absentminded like. It's rather fascinating the way water flows. Well, it doesn't just flow, it splashes and swirls and then goes into the drain with a gurgle. It's quite mesmerising, come and see."

Wayne did as he was asked and then rested his hand affectionately on his sister's shoulder. "Hmm, I can see what you mean, but I think maybe you ought to get out more. Perhaps you ought to get a proper job to give yourself an interest in life."

Trish turned and looked at her brother. "Cheeky. Remember, when Mum and Dad died we both agreed that we'd do just what we wanted in life and not be beholden to others. I don't want a proper job, Wayne. I'm quite happy watching rain water gush down the road and flogging my jewellery, when the weather's good, that is, just as you're happy with your art work. Mum and Dad worked all their lives doing jobs they disliked and I'm sure that's what put them both into early graves."

Wayne sighed. "Yes, you're quite right, Trish. Mum should have done something in the art line because she was so clever with her hands, and a paint brush too. Poor Mum, she was wasted in that sodding factory." He sat down beside his sister and placed his coffee mug on the window sill. "You're right about our lifestyle too. We've a lot to be thankful for and we wouldn't have the choice about whether or not to do proper jobs if we'd not had the money from the sale of their house to buy this one outright."

Trish squeezed the hand of her brother. "I think they'd be pleased to see that we're independent and standing on our own two feet. It may not be conventional, but at least we're paying our way, and I like to think, giving people who buy our wares something to cherish as well. Your paintings especially must be of great worth to those sensible enough to buy them. But going back to what you said earlier about me needing to get out more. It really isn't necessary, Wayne. I'm quite happy with my lot in life and I'm quite content living with you. But I must admit, it would be nice to have a fella in my life from time to time, and if I'm honest, I really think you ought to have the occasional girlfriend too."

Wayne wrinkled his nose. "Not sure about that. I mean, yes, it might be nice to have a girlfriend, but, well, I don't think it's ever likely to happen. I don't think girls are too keen on blokes with ginger hair, and I'm not exactly scintillating company."

"Then dye it like I do. Really Wayne, you are a Muppet, nobody should live with a hair colour they dislike in this day and age."

"Hmm, maybe I will."

Trish sprang to her feet. "There's no maybe about it. I shall get you some hair dye next time I'm in Helston buying some for myself."

"What! Oh, come on, Trish, don't let's rush into things."

"I'm not rushing, but since you're reluctant I'll give you breathing space and a little challenge. That being, if you've not got yourself a girlfriend by the end of August, then I shall dye your hair with a colour of my choice."

Wayne gulped. "Right, okay, you're on. But to be fair this has to work both ways."

Trish frowned. "Meaning?"

"Meaning, that if you've not got yourself a fella by the end of August then I'm going to cut your hair because I think you'd look a lot more attractive with it shorter."

Trish winced. "Oh…okay, but let's make it easier for ourselves. I suggest it should still count if either of us were to have had a fling with someone anytime during the summer months even if it's over by the end of August. I mean, it wouldn't be fair if you or I met someone and then suddenly got dumped on the last but one day of August, would it?"

Wayne nodded slowly. "Hmm…yes…but it must be a relationship which lasts at least a month. No one night stands and all that."

Trish's shoulders slumped. "What! No, a month's far too long. How about we make it a week."

Wayne shook his head. "Three weeks."

"Still too long. A fortnight."

Wayne nodded. "Okay, a fortnight it is."

Grinning, brother and sister shook hands to cement the agreement.

Saturday April the fourteenth dawned dry but dull; ideal conditions for those taking part in the sponsored walk to Polquillick in aid of Jubilee funds. Eighty three people were due to take part, and if all monies due were successfully collected the event could expect to raise seven hundred and ten pounds.

Walkers met, as arranged, from eleven o' clock onwards outside the Jolly Sailor, where they registered their arrival with secretary,

Janet Ainsworth, and then set off along the lane leading to the bottom of the cliff path. From there they were to walk the coastal path to Polquillick and return home along the lanes; a round trip of ten miles.

The first group to leave were youngsters, teenagers, who didn't want to get stuck behind dawdling, older inhabitants of the village. Next were, Tally Castor-Hunt, Ollie Collins, Denzil Penhaligon, Lucy Ainsworth and Rebecca Williams. After which followed other groups, small and large. And finally, tagging well behind, were, sisters, Elizabeth Castor-Hunt and Anne Collins and their friends, Susan Penhaligon and Valerie Moore. These women, three of whom had been friends for as long as they could remember, ambled along with no intention of trying to break any records.

"I can't remember the last time I went on a sponsored walk," said Susan, teetering over uneven stones as they wound along the cliff path, "in fact I don't think I've ever done one before."

"We have," said Elizabeth, "it was donkey's years ago though, when we were kids. I think it was to raise money for the church or it might have been the school, I can't remember."

Anne nodded. "You had chicken pox, Sue, that's why you don't remember, because you didn't go."

Susan laughed. "Ah, yes, I remember now. I was really ill, wasn't I? Delirious in fact. I suppose that's why it's a bit of a blur. I wonder how much was raised back then."

"Forty one pounds, eleven shillings and sixpence" said Anne, with confidence. "I know that because I mentioned it to Dad the other day. It was Mum's job to collect the money, you see."

"Fancy Dad remembering that but then he always did have a good head for figures, didn't he?" said Elizabeth." When we were young he was always telling us how much things cost when he were a lad."

"Was forty one pounds and whatever you said much money back then?" Valerie asked.

"Yes, but it doesn't sound much, does it? It was before decimalisation, of course, and a pint of beer would have cost about one shilling back then."

Susan groaned. "Five pence for a pint of beer; that makes me feel really old. Surely we can't have been around that long."

Elizabeth stopped to catch her breath, "It was in 1965, so we've actually been around a lot longer."

Valerie laughed. "1965. That was the year I was born."

The other three women groaned. "Oh, to have been born that recent," said Susan, wistfully, "we were all born in the fifties, weren't we girls? And that sounds so ancient now. I'm dreading being sixty, it sounds so matronly." She groaned. "I mean, well, fancy being old enough to go the Over Sixties' Club."

The women simultaneously paused, and then without consulting each other, sat as if by telepathy, to rest on a patch of grass.

"I wonder what it was like here before we were born," Anne mused. "It's silly, but because old films and photos back then are in black and white, I image Trengillion being in black and white too, but in reality it must have been very much as it is today."

"Colour wise, yes," said Elizabeth, "but nearly everything else will have changed."

"Except the coastline," said Susan, waving her hand across the face of the horizon, "that never changes, not noticeably anyway, just a bit of erosion here and there. The boats are bigger though, and made of fibreglass nowadays instead of wood."

Anne nodded. "It's funny to think the houses on Penwynton Estate didn't even exist back then, but they didn't, because I well remember when they started to build the first one; now there are dozens."

Elizabeth smiled. "And the Penwynton Hotel was still a house when we were kids too. Do you remember it after the last of the Penwyntons died? The poor house stood empty and forlorn and the grounds were all wild and overgrown. It was really spooky."

Susan sighed. "I remember it well. We had a den in Bluebell Woods. Oh, happy days! Being young was such a doddle, wasn't it? Nothing to worry about and all the time in the world to enjoy whatever life threw at us."

Anne's brow wrinkled as she counted on her fingers. "Do you realise the pub's name has changed five times in our lifetime."

"Five," said Susan, attempting to recall, "I can only think of four."

"It's definitely five," said Anne. "It was The Ringing Bells Inn to start with, when it was owned by Mr Newton who married Dorothy

Treloar. And after them came that weird bloke, you know, Wild West Withers: we were friends with his dishy sons Roger and Colin. They moved over Falmouth way after they left here."

Susan nodded. "I'm with you so far, and he, Mr Withers, changed its name to the Sheriff's Badge."

"That's right, and then after that poor chap, the student working at the Hotel, got shot in the woods, he decided he didn't like guns anymore and so changed it to the Badger because everyone called it the Badge anyway."

Susan laughed. "That's the one I'd forgotten, the Badger, how ridiculous, no wonder the next people changed it to The Fox and Hounds."

"The Godsons," said Elizabeth, joining in, "Gerald and Cassie Godson, they were a really nice couple, and kept horses in the old stables."

"And it's been the Jolly Sailor now for ages, ever since Justin arrived and that must be at least ten years. In fact it's thirteen because he came in 1999 and was here for the eclipse. Gosh, what a lot of water has gone under the bridge since then."

"1999, that's when Trevor and I first moved here, but by the sound of it we dipped out by not being here earlier. What fun you must have had when you were young."

"But we are still young," said Susan, jumping to her feet, "young at heart anyway."

Valerie smiled. "Well, you know what I meant, that being Trengillion sounded like the perfect place to grow up."

Anne nodded as she too stood up. "It was and still is in my opinion."

"It's home," said Elizabeth, "and I know I've said it before, but I wouldn't want to live anywhere else in the world but here."

"Hear, hear," said Susan.

When the children returned to school after the Easter break they spent a lesson learning about the ship *Titanic* and the centenary of its sinking which had occurred the previous day, April the fifteenth. Florence, who had heard many tales of the sea from her late great grandfather, Percy Collins, left school much disturbed by the consequences of the ill-fated ship's voyage. When she reached home, escorted to the gate by her best friend and her best friend's mother, she found her great grandmother, Gertie Collins, in the kitchen eating fruit cake, having popped in from next door for a chat with her granddaughter, Florence's mum, Jess.

"Why the glum face?" chuckled Gertie, as Florence dropped her school bag on the table, without the usual smile.

Florence's mouth promptly turned upside-down. "Miss told us about a big boat today. It hit an ice burger and sank and lots of people were drowned. But it wasn't a fishing boat like Great Granddad Percy had. It was much, much bigger and had big black flannels and it was taking people to America. The ladies all had long dresses on and big hats cos it was a hundred years ago."

Jess smiled as she helped Florence take off her jacket. "That was the *Titanic*, Flo, and its sinking must have been terribly sad, just as when ships are lost at sea during war."

Gertie nodded. "And the poor ill-fated *Titanic* sank a hundred years ago yesterday. There's been much mention of it lately. It was on its maiden voyage, you see, and was full of people from all walks of life, rich and poor, not to mention all the unfortunate staff." She sighed. "And the Captain, he died too. What a brave man! He went down with the ship, as did the band who kept on playing 'til the bitter end. It was a dreadful. God rest the souls of them as perished. It should never have happened though, Florence. The designers claimed the ship was unsinkable, you see, and so they didn't provide enough lifeboats." She tutted loudly. "What a silly mistake."

Florence tilted her head to one side and looked earnestly at her great grandmother. "I suppose you remember it, don't you, Granny Gert? Because you must have been a little girl back then, just like me."

Gertie gulped, and lay down her slice of cake, unsure whether to laugh or cry.

The weather for the rest of April continued to be unsettled with frequent heavy showers and strong to gale force winds. But, ironically, in spite of the wet, the West Country was declared a drought zone. For although there was no threat of a water shortage or a hosepipe ban because there was sufficient water in the reservoirs, it appeared that in places streams and rivers were running very low, hence there was a threat to wild life and fish in particular.

Everyone was fed up with the weather. Boxes of bric-a-brac, clothing, books and toys, collected together by the Jubilee Committee for selling at car boot sales, did not leave the spare room at the Penwynton Hotel where they were stored. Gardens on the allotments remained un-dug, leaving weeds to flourish. Washing was difficult to dry. Working outdoors was frequently impossible. Grass grew but it was often too wet to cut it. But the nation still retained its sense of humour by referring to the weather conditions as the wettest drought.

Sunday, April the twenty-ninth was the first wedding anniversary of the Duke and Duchess of Cambridge, but unlike their wedding day the weather was very wet and very windy. Inside the Jolly Sailor, dozens of people eager to escape from and forget about the rain, congregated for Sunday lunch and the opportunity to warm themselves by the pub's welcoming open fire. To Justin's delight, once the roast lunches were eaten and after the plates had been cleared away, no-one had the motivation to return home. The cosy atmosphere was beguiling, the mood jovial and the slightly intoxicated chat quickly passed away the time.

Meanwhile the wind screeched through the village, bending spring flowers, tearing new growth from shrubs and ripping apple blossom buds from branches. Rain water splashed and flowed down the roads, gathering debris and carrying it towards gurgling, brimful drains.

Wayne Tilley, having spent the morning in front of canvas and easel, washed his hands, donned his raincoat, and headed for the Jolly Sailor where his sister Trish had gone two hours beforehand. He was feeling in need of refreshment and relaxation, for painting had strained his eyes and his head ached from concentration.

Outside his home in Coronation Terrace he soon became aware of police presence and for an obvious reason; the old sycamore tree which grew in front of the village hall, had fallen, not on the building, but across the road causing a part blockage. He conveyed the news to the gathering as soon as he reached the pub.

"Oh no, poor tree," said Valerie Moore, hearing Wayne's words as he stood at the bar ordering a pint of real ale. "It must be the unluckiest tree ever. Remember how it got badly singed when the village hall caught fire, I thought it was gone for good back then."

Her husband, Trevor nodded. "I suppose if it's blown right over it'll have to be cut right down now."

Valerie sighed. "In which case it really is doomed."

Jim Haynes shook his head. "If it's cut down it'll soon send up new shoots and grow again. Sycamores are as tough as old boots."

"Actually there won't be any need to cut it down," said newly arrived, Larry Bingham, who had actually witnessed the tree fall and called the police. "It's come right up, roots and all. In fact it's ripped up a considerable area in front of the hall and damaged the wall. I'm afraid it's gone for good this time."

Ollie Collins groaned. "I hope it doesn't mean we're in for another spell of bad luck. I mean, if you remember the last time we thought it was a goner everything went haywire, because not only did the village hall burn down, but we had that freak storm, Robbie Macdonald had a couple of unexplainable accidents, the mini bus carrying the old folks back from an outing toppled off the road, and that poor kid drowned."

"Ugh, don't," said Jess, "I've gone all goose pimply."

The rain continued for the rest of the day, hence many stayed at the pub until darkness fell, and after Justin rang last orders, they staggered home very much the worse for wear.

Chapter Six

May began with a day of much welcome sunshine. This prompted Linda to ring around as soon as she rose at six thirty, asking for volunteers to take the ever increasing accumulation of donations to the weekly car boot sale at Rosudgeon, near Penzance. Several people expressed keenness to go but because of work and commitments only two were free so to do, Elizabeth Castor-Hunt and Susan Penhaligon.

It was a beautiful day to be out and about and Elizabeth and Susan were delighted to see there were plenty of other sellers' cars lined up when they arrived just before eight o' clock: all determined to enjoy the weather and hoping it would last for several hours.

They were allocated a pitch at the end of a row, next to a couple selling fruit and vegetables. As they opened their boot to unpack their wares and lay them out on an old wallpaper pasting table loaned by Janet Ainsworth, they were amazed to find themselves beset by a small group of people, pushing and shoving around the boot of Susan's car, turning things over and pulling items from cardboard boxes, all desperate it seemed to get a bargain.

"Gordon Bennett," hissed Susan, grabbing a coffee pot before it toppled onto the grass, "they're worse than kids in a sweet shop."

Elizabeth smothered a smile as she placed a box of old records on the grass. "I expect they're all hoping to find that certain something which might be worth a fortune. You know what I mean, such things often crop up on the *Antiques Roadshow*, bought for fifty pence, but worth several thousand."

Susan looked down at the ornate vase in her hands. "Ming, by any chance?"

Elizabeth giggled. "Trago Mills. It was mine. I bought it a few years ago because I thought it'd be a perfect match with our dining room curtains, but it wasn't quite the right shade and actually clashed, that's why I've finally got round to disposing of it."

Susan lay the vase on the table. "Well, I'm sure it'll soon be snapped up because it's really pretty." It was. Susan found a five pound note thrust into her hand before she had time to unpack anything else.

By lunch time the field was packed full of bargain hunters walking, often three or four abreast, between rows of parked cars, while others, weary after browsing, sat outside catering vans, eating chips and burgers, pasties and ice cream. Elizabeth and Susan, both eager to have a look around, took it in turns to wander through the rows, seeking things which might come in useful. In time, both had bought nearly as much as they had sold.

When other booters began to pack up their unsold goods, Susan and Elizabeth, both tired from standing in the sun, decided to do likewise.

"Oh well, that's a few more pounds for the Jubilee fund," said Elizabeth, "but I should like to have taken more."

"I don't know, sixty three pounds isn't bad. I think it's going to take a long time to get shot of all this stuff though. It doesn't actually look any less than when we arrived."

"No, it doesn't. I'm glad I don't have to do this all the time. I think the novelty would soon wear off, especially if the weather was poor."

Before they had finished the people in the van beside them closed the vehicle's doors and drove off.

"They've left something behind," said Elizabeth, going to see what was in the box. She laughed. "Yuck, just some rotten tomatoes and pears."

"Which reminds me, who's going to look after Jim's veg and so forth when he goes gallivanting off to the big city?" asked Susan, carefully wrapping a glass decanter.

"Anne," Elizabeth promptly replied, "that is unless her name comes out of the hat in which case I shall volunteer."

Susan nodded. "I'd love to go with Jim, but at the same time whoever wins will miss the activities here. And then there's all the hassle of travel. It's a fair old way to go just for one concert."

"Yes, but it's not just any old concert, is it? It'd be a once in a lifetime experience and don't forget there's the picnic as well."

"Hmm, I suppose so, although I'm not too keen on the concert's line up. Having said that it'd be nice to see Paul McCartney, if only for old time's sake. We were, after all, big Beatle fans once upon a time, weren't we?"

Elizabeth grinned. "We were big fans of Gooseberry Pie too, so I reckon, as it's unlikely either of us will win the London trip ticket, we'll have to make do with Danny's new band."

On the evening of Bank Holiday Monday, May the seventh, the Jolly Sailor was extremely busy with optimists all hopeful of winning the chance to accompany Jim Haynes to London for the concert in front of Buckingham Palace. Drinks flowed, the chat was lively and as the appointed hour approached, many, feeling lucky, bought more tickets to enhance their chances, and others, happy to sit and soak up the cheerful atmosphere, enjoyed the chance to chat with neighbours and friends whom they seldom saw.

"It was nice today not to have the News dominated by voting results, wasn't it?" Ian Ainsworth chuckled, as he stood by the bar chatting with Larry Bingham. "I mean to say, our own nation's council elections have been enough, but to have the French and Greek elections foisted on us too, well, it's all been a bit much of late."

Larry nodded. "And we didn't even go to the Polls for the council in Cornwall. Still, it'll be our turn next year."

Ian stepped aside to let someone pass by. "Mind you, I must admit I was glad to see young Boris keep his job as London Mayor. The Olympics wouldn't be the same if old Ken had got back in. Not that I have anything against Ken, but he just isn't Boris, is he? Although to be fair, I must confess he has made me smile on occasions. But Boris, well, the man makes me laugh, and he's not the buffoon the media like to make him out to be."

"I take it you're referring to his comments at the end of the Beijing Games, something about wiff waff coming home. Very amusing, I must confess. I agree with you regarding Livingstone too, he always struck me as a decent enough bloke."

"Yes, and tonight I suppose we should be focusing on this summer's big do. I mean here in the village of course, not London."

Larry drained the glass of his third pint. "That reminds me. Candy tells me you've got the lovely Polly Jolly doing a stint at our Jubilee do. That's a feather in the Committee's cap, I must say."

"No credit to me, I'm sorry to say," said Ian. "It was Jill and Nick Roberts' doing. Apparently, they used to be neighbours of hers, before she got famous, that is. I must admit I was surprised she agreed, and I believe she's going to stay here at the pub."

"So Candy said. It'll be interesting to see if she's as attractive in the flesh as she is on the telly."

"Probably not. I daresay she'll be all wigs and make-up when on TV. I think it's a shame women feel they have to be caked in make-up and false this and false that to be attractive, and as for this air brushing nonsense in magazines, I think it's a travesty because I'm sure it has a detrimental effect on my giddy girls."

Laughing, Larry stood his glass on the bar and asked for a refill. "Another for you, Ian?"

"I wouldn't say no," the dentist said, draining his glass, "but better make it a half."

"Got work tomorrow, I suppose."

"No, we never open when Flora Day falls on a week day. Most of us still go in though and watch the activities from the waiting room. Good view up there."

Larry took a ten pound note from his wallet. "I'm taking the day off too, and I thought I'd pop in for a while since it looks like it might be fine. I haven't been for years and I must admit, I'm a bit of a sucker when it comes to brass bands."

Ian nodded. "Me too but I must admit it drives me mad when the damn tune gets stuck in my head for days on end."

Before the draw took place, Linda Sevens, Chairperson of the Jubilee Committee, announced that a total of four hundred and sixteen pounds had been raised through pursuit of the highly acclaimed prize.

A round of applause was the spontaneous response and Jim felt several hands heartily slap his back, while others eagerly shook his hands. Jim acknowledged their appreciation with a slight nod of the head; he felt proud but at the same time he was a little apprehensive and as he glanced around the bar and saw the faces of enthusiastic ticket holders, all eager to see their names drawn from the hat, he rapidly felt unnerved. Suddenly the notion of taking unknown company by way of a random draw didn't seem such a good idea.

His hands turned clammy; his stomach churned, and when Justin reached for the bucket held by Janet Ainsworth where last minute names had finally been added, he felt light-headed.

"Right, is everyone ready?" Justin shouted, shaking the bucket.

The crowd cried 'yes' in unison.

Trish Tilley flicked back her long, lank, hair, crossed her chubby legs and lowered the scooped neck of her figure hugging jumper to reveal a glimpse of her ample cleavage. When she looked Jim's way and winked, what little colour there was left in his face drained away. Feeling like a lamb facing slaughter, Jim began to pray.

"Good," said Justin. "Now, all we need is someone to draw out the name of the lucky winner. Any volunteers? I suppose it ought to be someone who hasn't bought a ticket or even Jim."

Jim shook his head. He didn't want to be responsible for what could well be a self-imposed disaster.

"Better be me then," said Linda, stepping forward, "as much as I'd like to go, it wouldn't be practical to leave Jamie with the Hotel during such a busy time of the year."

Justin laughed. "Same goes for Morgana and me. Let Linda through, please, folks."

Linda reached the bar and looked back at the hopeful crowd. Suddenly, she wished she had not volunteered. To disappoint so many eager faces seemed a poisoned chalice. She looked at Jim standing close by, beads of perspiration hung on his white brow and he looked on the verge of passing out. Shuddering she turned to face Justin who was vigorously giving the bucket a final shake.

"Here goes," she said, raising her arm to reach inside the bucket, "good luck, everyone."

"God help me," whispered Jim, closing his eyes, not wanting to see or hear the winning name.

Linda handed the folded piece of paper to Justin. Not a sound could be heard as Justin slowly unfolded the paper. His lips twitched and then broke into a broad smile. He looked through the crowd searching for the face of the winner. "I'm extremely delighted to announce that the winner is none other than our very own, Tally Castor-Hunt. Congratulations, sweetheart."

Tally was stunned. She felt faint as those standing nearby patted her back and expressed their good wishes. "Wow, I don't quite know what to say. I've never won anything before in my life." She looked at Jim. "I hope you don't mind it being me, Jim."

Jim felt his face flush as the anxiety vanished in a whoosh. "Of course I don't mind," he grinned, fighting back tears of relief, "I just hope you'll not find my company too boring."

Tally laughed. "Boring. Don't be silly, Jim. I'm sure we'll have a brilliant time. Anyway, I think you're a star for giving all of us the chance to share your good fortune."

Jim grinned and glanced to where Trish Tilley sat, but already she had turned away and was ordering another vodka and Coke, and chatting to Maurice the chef, who had just finished work in the kitchen.

Flora Day dawned dull and overcast, but before the first dance began the sun peeped through the clouds heralding a bright, sunny day. Many people from far and wide poured into Helston to join in with the festivities, and those who stayed at home were able to enjoy the good weather in their own environments.

Inside the newly erected polytunnel on his allotment, Jim potted out pepper plants into compost-enhanced soil and staked them with rigid garden canes. He sang as he worked, his thoughts not on the task in hand, but drifting instead towards the two days he would have with Tally for company in London. Jim was without question, elated, overjoyed. He was not a religious man, but he thanked God for his good fortune.

Chapter Seven

Sitting beside the living room window of Rose Cottage, Ned sipped coffee and watched the deep purple blooms on the lilac tree swaying above the old wooden garden gate in the gentle south westerly breeze. He sighed. Stella loved the delicate perfume of those flowers and had always kept a bottle of lilac cologne in the bathroom for everyday use.

He looked at his watch; the time was a quarter past eleven and so there was still plenty of time before he needed to think about lunch. He finished his coffee and returned the mug to the kitchen. The weather was fine; he would cut a few of the sweet scented stems and take them to the churchyard.

The best lilac blooms, Ned found, were higher than he had anticipated and consequently were out of his reach, but not one to be outdone, he returned indoors to fetch his walking stick. Once back in the garden, he stood beneath the lilac tree and pulled down the branches bearing the freshest blooms with his stick. After successfully snipping off the fragrant flower heads with secateurs, he laid them in a heap on the lawn until he was satisfied a large enough quantity was cut to make a worthy bunch. Job complete, he returned the walking stick to the kitchen and locked the back door.

Walking steadily along the pavement clutching the flowers, Ned grinned with self-satisfaction. He felt cutting the lilac had been a great achievement and proved he was not as senile and inept as some might think. Not, he conceded, that anyone had ever accused him of ineptitude, but it was glaringly obvious that both Elizabeth and Anne didn't trust him to do menial tasks such as filling the coal scuttle, cooking, paying bills and putting washing in the machine. Ned grinned. Perhaps it was payback time, for he well remembered being accused of fussing over his mother, Molly, when first she was widowed. Ned sighed. Yes, in retrospect, he had fussed, and she had not even had a heart attack.

By the church lichgate Ned paused to catch his breath. His legs felt a little unsteady and he knew he would be severely castigated if either of his daughters should discover he had been out without his walking stick. But if the truth be known, Ned hated the damn thing; it made him feel old, and a chap, even at the age of eighty five, still had his pride.

Once Ned felt his breathing was steady and his heart rate had slowed, he composed himself and walked beneath the lichgate and onto the gravel path, tightly clutching the gift for his dear, late wife. As he neared the most recent graves he became aware of someone, a woman, sitting on the bench his mother had bought and dedicated to the memory of her husband, Major Benjamin Smith. When he got a little closer, the woman waved, rose and stepped forward to greet him. It was his new neighbour, Jill Roberts.

"Ned," she said, as they met, "I thought it was you but couldn't be too sure until you were a bit closer. Oh, what a charming bouquet. Lilacs are lovely flowers, such a delightful rich perfume. We had a huge lilac bush growing back in Bristol which always had loads of flowers but the scent was miserable in comparison with these."

Ned grinned as they continued to walk along the path. "Must be a different variety then, but it'd be a real coincidence if they were the same. According to my daughter, Anne, there are over a thousand different varieties of lilac, in fact there are thousands of different varieties of most things."

"What! Good grief, I'd never have guessed there were so many. I take it your Anne is a keen gardener."

Ned nodded. "She is," he said, with pride, "and her head is full of facts, figures and unpronounceable Latin names."

Jill smiled. "I sometimes watch *Gardeners' World*, but frequently curse, because whenever something spectacular takes my eye it invariably has an unmemorable name and is instantly forgotten."

"I suppose it's the way we're wired. Anne relishes long names and the more complicated the better."

"So where does your Anne live? She's obviously in the village because she's on the Jubilee Committee."

"Yes, she lives at the Old Vicarage. She's done wonders with the gardens there. They were in a pretty bad way when she and John, her husband, moved in and so was the house; it had been empty and neglected for years, you see."

When they reached the bench, Ned sat down. "I'd better sit before I fall. What a curse old age is."

"I think you're marvellous," said Jill, taking the flowers while he lowered himself down onto the bench, "you may not be very robust but there's nothing at all wrong with your mind."

He patted her hand with affection. "Thank you, I do my best to keep my wits about me."

While Ned rested, Jill, after offering, put fresh water in the urn on Stella's grave and then carefully arranged the lilac blooms to Ned's satisfaction. Job accomplished, she sat back down beside Ned.

"Thank you," he said, "your kindness has saved me having to bend; not my favourite task because regrettably I'm not as flexible as I used to be. I was lucky to find you here."

"I came here on a whim. I think there's something fascinating about graveyards, especially the old forgotten parts. I often used to wander around the one near us in Bristol: the setting was so tranquil."

Ned took a deep breath and sighed. "I know just what you mean, Jill, and it seems very sad to me that in future years Trengillion's inhabitants will walk around this churchyard, as you have just done and I too have done on many occasions, and yet they'll know nothing about my dear departed contemporaries. What they were like, I mean. Just as you and I can't see or feel the passions, the delights and enthusiasm of generations gone before us. Trengillion's future residents, will, as do we, just see rows and rows of stones engraved with names and countless dates, both of which tell very little. For unless the interred happens to be the vicar or squire, there's not even any indication as to what part they have played in village life or of what they have died. Yet the place will look much the same in years to come. The Virginia creeper on the tower will be green in the summer, turn red in the autumn and then the leaves will fall and it'll be bare until late spring. The daffodils, crocus and primroses will bloom each year along the path, and notices will be pinned to the lichgate telling of church news. The sun will shine and the rain will fall, the wind will blow and snow will occasionally cover the old gravel path, but they who rest in the boundaries of these old stone walls will all be forgotten. It's very sad."

"But if they're empathetic, Ned, future generations will sense the affinity you describe," said Jill, touched by his words. She linked her arm through his. "I suppose you knew many who lie here beneath the earth."

He nodded. "Yes, there's not one person who's been buried here in recent years that I've not known. It was different when I first came here, of course, because I didn't know many people then, but that was sixty years ago."

"Really! So you're not Cornish then."

Ned grinned. "No, I'm not Cornish and neither was Stella. We met when she came to teach English at our school in London. Sounds soppy I know, but it was love at first sight."

Jill smiled. "No, it doesn't sound soppy, and if your daughters are anything like their mother then she must have been very lovely."

"She was lovely. Anne is very much like her, both in looks and manner, she has her artistic talents too. Elizabeth, on the other hand is more like my mother."

"And did your mother live in London too?"

"No, she lived in Clacton before coming down here. She and my father had divorced, not the done-thing back then, but that's another story and one which I've never been fond of telling. It all worked out well in the end though and both my parents remarried."

Jill smirked. "Would it shock you to know that both Nick and I have been married before?"

Ned shook his head. "No, very little shocks me these days. Well, that's not quite true. Lots of things shock me, but not things like divorce," he laughed, "and living-in-sin, as we used to call it back in my day."

In the back gardens of the Old Vicarage, amongst the faded flowers of tulips and daffodils, Anne Collins planted out snapdragons, godetia and cosmos that she had raised from seed. When the task was finished, she fetched hanging baskets from the greenhouse which she had planted up earlier in the month, each one crammed with trailing royal blue lobelia, red pelargoniums, and white petunias, carefully selected patriotic colours to commemorate the Diamond Jubilee. The hanging baskets, six in total, she hung on the brackets around the back of the house where they would get the most sun and were protected from the cold winds. Pleased they looked good, she then wandered into the orchard to inspect the fruit trees, keen to see if much blossom was left intact. To her dismay most of it had been blown off in recent gales. She sighed, it looked as though it was to be a poor year for fruit.

After checking the washing to see if it was drying, she filled a bucket with hot soapy water and scrubbed the patio slabs with a hard bristled broom before rinsing it down with the garden hose. When it was nearly dry, she fetched the garden table and chairs from the back of the garage and placed them on the patio. She nodded with satisfaction, all was ready now for summer.

Before she returned indoors she pulled several stalks of rhubarb from the clump in the vegetable garden. Ollie and John were both very fond of rhubarb crumble and so she would make one for dinner to follow the lasagne she had already made. For she knew both would be hungry; they were putting a new roof on a large house in Polquillick, hence there was much fetching and carrying to be done.

When the crumble was made, Anne went upstairs to get the book she was currently reading from the bedroom. She took it into the kitchen and dropped it onto the table. She was beginning to feel weary and in need of a rest. It was after all, her day off from working on the reception desk at the Penwynton Hotel and she felt she had earned a break. After making a sandwich for her lunch, she made a cup of tea and took both into the conservatory to make the most of the sun.

When the sandwich was eaten she laid down the plate and opened up her book, but her concentration was not focused on the written word; her mind wandered towards the long bank holiday weekend in early June, the Jubilee celebrations, and especially Danny Jarrams. She smiled thoughtfully, recollecting Danny's dashing good looks in his younger days when he was the bass guitarist with sixties pop group, Gooseberry Pie. Without doubt he was the heartthrob of many and she, in later years, had been fortunate enough to meet him when it was discovered he was related to the people who had bought Penwynton House to convert into a five star hotel. Anne smiled. Time had not done Danny any great favour. He, like so many pop stars from the sixties, had aged considerably; his face was wrinkled, his slim physique had been replaced by a barrel like shape and his hair was as white as snow. Anne laughed. But his smile was ever ready, his sense of humour unchanged and when all was said and done, he was still fantastic company and she would always have a soft spot for him.

On Thursday evening, Oliver Collins, known to all as Ollie, threw his sports bag onto the passenger seat of his black Golf GTi and then climbed into the driving seat. After changing the disc in his CD player to something by which to relax, he started up the engine and reversed from the spot where he was parked. He yawned: it had been a long day. Building was hard work, especially when climbing up and down scaffolding was involved, and the fifty lengths in the pool had drained him of his last bit of energy. But it was worth it. He loved swimming, loved exercise and keeping fit. Building therefore was the perfect job and he had no desire ever to do anything else. Besides, he and his cousin, Denzil Penhaligon, both worked alongside their fathers in the family business. Their fathers were brothers-in-law and husbands of Susan Penhaligon and Anne Collins. Ollie laughed. No wonder some folks got baffled by the relationship, it did sound rather confusing.

The car left Helston and headed out on the A3083 towards Trengillion on the Lizard peninsular. The weather was looking good, the sky was clear and if it kept fine and there was not much wind, then Ollie planned to go out in his kayak at the weekend, most likely on Saturday afternoon. He might even take his rod and do a bit of fishing.

As he passed RNAS Culdrose, he glanced towards the high perimeter fence. The Olympic flame was due to arrive at the naval base the following day. Ollie was truly thrilled by the knowledge that the Games were to be held in London; it filled him with pride and he was eagerly looking forward to August.

Chapter Eight

It was dull and overcast on the evening of May the eighteenth when the golden plane from Athens touched down on the runway of RNAS Culdrose in Helston. On board was the Olympic flame accompanied by HRH Princess Anne, Lord (Sebastian) Coe, London Mayor: Boris Johnson and Footballer: David Beckham. Many of Trengillion's inhabitants, even those with little or no interest in the Games, watched events unfurl on their television sets, proud that such a monumental happening was taking place on their doorstep

The following morning dawned bright and clear and over the cliff tops at Lands End hundreds of spectators awaited the arrival of a Search and Rescue helicopter from RNAS Culdrose to deliver the Olympic flame to waiting officials. The event was televised live from Britain's notorious landmark and the glorious morning showed Cornwall at its very best.

Ben Ainslie, who had grown up and learned to sail in Cornwall, was the first of eight thousand torch bearers chosen to carry the flame on its seventy-day relay to all corners of the United Kingdom, before it reached its final destination, London, for the 2012 Olympic Games.

On the first day the flame and its entourage wound their way through Cornish towns and villages. Thousands of people, from all walks of life, lined the streets beneath black and yellow bunting. They clapped and cheered; they waved Union flags and patriotic banners as the torch passed by. The atmosphere was celebratory and the spectators were proud to have witnessed the historic moment.

"Did you go into Helston to see the torch thingy this morning?" said Elizabeth Castor-Hunt to Susan Penhaligon, who sat with her feet resting on a stool in the Jolly Sailor that evening.

Susan nodded. "Yes, and so did the world and his wife. I've never seen the place so busy for anything other than Flora Day. Did you go in?"

Elizabeth giggled. "Yes, but our original intention was to go right down to Lands End because we wanted to see Ben Ainslie, but regrettably we didn't get up in time and so watched that bit on TV instead. We still got to Helston though, and I agree, the crowds were fantastic. I'm so glad we went. I mean, it was a once in a lifetime experience, wasn't it? And I thought it was wonderful."

"Absolutely. I might even watch the Games as well," laughed Susan. "The torch has kindled a liking in me for sport."

Elizabeth scowled. "Well, I wouldn't quite go that far. Although for much of the time I'll have little choice other than to watch it. Greg's fanatical about sport, you see, especially track events. If I have to watch, I prefer things like swimming and diving. I quite like the dressage too."

"Not hockey then?"

Elizabeth laughed, spilling a little of her wine on the surface of the polished table top. "Yuck. Do you remember hockey in our schooldays, Sue? Dreadful, wasn't it? At least it was at Grammar School. I hated every minute of it."

"It was just as bad at Secondary Modern," said Susan, "and netball; that was pretty dire too. Mind you, the unflattering gym-knicks didn't exactly help."

"Ghastly, weren't they?" Elizabeth smiled wistfully, "I liked games best when we had torrential rain and so did a bit of old time dancing in the school hall instead."

"Or watched tennis during Wimbledon fortnight because Miss was keen to see a particular match. In fact, thinking about it, the only sport I ever really liked at school was rounders. Do you remember that, Liz? At junior school, I mean, when your dad was headmaster and we used to play it in the playground with Mrs Reynolds."

"Yes, I remember. I really liked Mrs Reynolds. It's sad to think she's gone now as are much of that generation."

"Hmm, in fact I think there's only your dad and my mum left now, and when they're gone, daft as it might seem, we'll be the old timers."

On Sunday morning, inside Number Four, Coronation Terrace, Trish Tilley, rose at four thirty, dressed and then went down to the kitchen where she made coffee and pushed two extra thick slices of white bread into the toaster. When the bread was sufficiently browned, she spread it with butter and a generous layer of ginger marmalade, she then sat at the kitchen table and turned on the radio to establish whether or not the day was likely to stay fine. To her relief, it was.

When toast was eaten and coffee drunk, Trish placed the dirty plate and mug on the draining board, hoping, in her absence, Wayne would wash them. For sometimes he did and sometimes he didn't: it all depended what frame of mind he was in. If he woke artistically focused, then washing up was not a chore his creative side could possibly endure; on the other hand, if he was feeling imaginatively bereft, then he would do the dishes in order to pass the time.

From the refrigerator, Trish took sandwiches made the night before and dropped them into a carrier bag, along with two packets of crisps. From the coat pegs in the hallway she then lifted her jacket, picked up her handbag and left quietly by the front door.

Outside, day was just breaking and the sun was rising steadily above the houses on the opposite side of the road. Trish unlocked her badly parked van, climbed into the driving seat and set off for Hayle on the north coast of Cornwall, where she went every dry Sunday morning for the car boot sale.

Four hours after the departure of his twin sister, Wayne rose from his untidy bed, slipped on his check dressing gown and went downstairs. In the kitchen he fried four rashers of bacon and three eggs in the non-stick pan and warmed the contents of a can of baked beans in the microwave. He ate all while watching the *Andrew Marr Show* on the television. Eventually bored by politics, he switched it off, and when his plate was empty, he crossed to the sink and proceeded to wash the dishes for, Wayne Tilley was in anything but an artistic frame of mind for two reasons. Firstly he had drunk too much real ale the previous night in the Jolly Sailor, and secondly, he was still incensed by the ridiculous comments of a bespectacled, overpowering, female holiday maker, who, on hearing he was an artist, had foisted on him her ludicrous, warped belief on the subject of modern art. Hence, not only did Wayne wash the dishes but he dried them too, and put them back in the cupboard.

After washing up, Wayne switched on his laptop and read the latest news. Because he was still in an argumentative frame of mind, he left derogatory comments after each article he considered invited conflict.

Wayne was sitting at the kitchen table typing a particularly frenzied rant when his sister returned from the car boot sale. She looked somewhat glum.

"I take it you've not had a good day," he said, as she dropped her handbag on the table and threw her jacket on the back of the chair.

Trish wrinkled her nose. "Hmm…so so. Things started off alright, in fact I took forty quid in the first hour, but it went downhill after that. Something smells good, have you been cooking bacon?"

"Yes, would you like a coffee?"

Trish sat down. "Yes, please. I'm feeling pretty knackered. I'm hungry too. I might pop down to the pub for a roast."

Wayne stood up and reached for the kettle. "If you do, I think I'll join you. I need to eat to get rid of this damn hangover."

Trish grinned. "I guessed you'd had too much when I heard you come in last night. You made a right racket."

Wayne took two mugs from the cupboard. "Sorry, Sis. I won't make any excuses because I don't even remember coming in. In fact, the only thing about last night I do recall, is arguing with some goddamn awful woman about modern art."

Trish groaned. "I'm glad I wasn't there then: you can get quite obnoxious on that subject."

"Not as obnoxious as that silly cow," said Wayne, sitting, "she really put my back up."

"Everyone's entitled to their own opinions, Wayne. You shouldn't take everything to heart so much."

"Maybe not. Anyway, were any of the Jubilee Committee lot at the car boot sale?"

Trish took a quick swig of coffee. "Yes, Janet and Ian Ainsworth."

"That's good. I'd volunteer to go but it'd mean not drinking on Saturday night and that'd suck."

"You could always go to Rosudgeon with me one Wednesday. In fact if we took everything in my van there would only be one entrance fee to pay and so that would save the Committee a few bob."

Wayne nodded. "I might do that. Anyway, how much did you take in the end?"

"Dunno. I've not totted it up yet."

She put down her empty mug on the table, opened up her bag and pulled out a small tin. "Here, you count it. I started off with a twenty pound float. I'm going to have a quick shower."

The Jolly Sailor, as always, was busy on Sunday lunchtime. For many felt it cost no more to eat at the pub than it would to cook a roast at home. That was the excuse made by most women anyway, and the men folk, glad of the chance of a pint and thrilled there would be no washing up, felt there were no grounds for argument.

Trish and Wayne grabbed seats in the public bar after a family put on their coats and left. Wayne then went to the bar and ordered two roasts, one large the other regular. When he returned to the table with two pints, Trish looked a million miles away.

"Penny for your thoughts," said Wayne, leaning back on the plush upholstery.

Trish sighed. "I was just daydreaming and imagining Tally Castor-Hunt was ill and in her place Jim begged me to go to London with him for the concert."

Wayne laughed. "Bit far-fetched, Trish. I mean, if she were ill, and I think that very unlikely as she looks a picture of good health, then I expect they'd put the names in the hat again."

Trish scowled. "Killjoy."

"Anyway, if you're thinking of Jim as a potential boyfriend to avoid me cutting your boring hair, I suggest you think again. Jim looks to me like a crusty old bachelor whose only interest is growing things, and you, dear Trish, most certainly don't have green fingers. Why, you even managed to kill off the aspidistra I gave you as a joke, and that's pretty bad considering its common name is the Cast Iron plant."

"Yeah, well, I reckon there was something wrong with it. Anyway, I'm not looking for a husband, am I? So it doesn't matter if he is a crusty old bachelor. God forbid! I'm not in the least bit interested in marriage."

Wayne was laughing when Janet and Ian Ainsworth walked into the bar. "I'll be back in a mo," he said, "I just want to go and ask the Ainsworths how they did at the car boot this morning."

"Okay."

Peering over the top of her pint glass, Trish cast her eyes around the bar to see if there were any newcomers who might be of interest, especially unattached males. She sighed deeply. As usual there were none.

'Oh, dear Lord,' she thought, 'please bring me a fella. He doesn't have to be drop dead gorgeous, but it'd be nice if he was, and he doesn't have to be rich, but it'd be brilliant if he had a bob or two. He doesn't even need to be single, but I suppose it'd be better if he didn't have a wife. Having said that, he doesn't necessarily have to be here to stay, a fleeting holiday maker would be nice, as long as he's here for at least a fortnight. I just want to feel desirable, be needed, and I don't want my sodding hair cut.'

The door of the pub opened and in walked a tall handsome stranger with a haversack on his back. He had longish blond, straw-like, wavy hair which brushed against the collar of his gaudy, short sleeved shirt. His Bermuda shorts were white and showed off the deep tan of his long legs. Before he spoke he smiled, emphasising the cornflower blue of his bright eyes. Trish, momentarily stunned, nearly fell from her seat.

"G'day sport," said the stranger to the landlord, as he approached the bar.

Justin frowned, puzzled, miffed, and then a broad grin spread across his face. "No, I don't believe it. Swampy. Bruce Swampy Marsh. Well I never." He abandoned his position behind the bar and rushed out to greet the new arrival, heartily shaking his hands and slapping his back.

"Swampy, what are you doing here? I mean, how long are you here for? Christ man, I'd hardly have recognised you."

Swampy grinned. "I'm back over here for a month. I arrived last week but needless to say I went to see the family first. But now I'm looking up old chums."

"That's brilliant, but how did you know where to find me?"

"I went to your folk's place on the off chance they were still there. They told me you'd taken a pub in Cornwall and gave me the address."

"And have you driven down or did you come by train?"

"I've driven. Mum's loaned me her car because she doesn't use it a great deal, and now Dad's retired she can always borrow his anyway."

Justin, aware the bar was silent as everyone sat puzzled, trying to establish the identity of Bruce Swampy, rested both hands on the new arrival's shoulders. "Folks, this is my very good friend, Bruce Marsh, better known to me as Swampy. I've not seen hide nor hair of the bugger for fourteen years, not since we retired from the Navy together and he emigrated to Australia."

Trish felt faint. She couldn't believe her luck. She didn't realise a prayer could be answered so quickly and considered perhaps it might be far more worthwhile her attending church on Sunday morning rather than messing around at car boot sales.

Justin introduced Swampy to Morgana, his wife.

"Pleased to meet you, sweetheart. I hope you've managed to tame the old devil."

Morgana's eyebrows rose. "Hmm, not sure about that. And how about you, Bru…er...Swampy, do you have a wife?"

He laughed. "Not on your Nelly, sweetheart. Too much fun to be had being a single bloke, and the Sheilas down under, I know, aren't the marrying kind, anyway. So, what's a fella have to do to get a drink around here?"

"Lager?" Justin asked.

"Yep, and one for yourself and the good lady too."

"No, these are on me," said Justin, indicating to Morgana to pour the drinks. "So, Swampy, what are you doing these days? Still in engineering?"

"No, gave that up a year or two back. I'm a landscape artist now and I love it."

"An artist!" exclaimed Justin, somewhat taken back, "but I didn't even know you could paint."

"Well, it was something that never really cropped up in the Navy, but it was a real passion of mine back when I was a kid. And when I was a spotty youth I even contemplated going to art collage. So you see, when faced with the beautiful scenery of Oz, well, it sorta kindled an old flame. I've gotta a little studio out the back of my place and my work can be bought at all sorts of commercial outlets. To be honest, I'm doing alright, in fact far better than I'd be if I'd stuck with engineering."

Trish listened, open mouthed, in disbelief. Swampy was into her brother's favourite subject, art. And landscape art at that. He was handsome, single, here for more than a fortnight, not interested in marriage, and quite well off. She grinned from ear to ear. It looked as though the new arrival was being offered to her on a plate. Her hair was safe.

Chapter Nine

The weather turned cooler towards the end of May and many feared the Jubilee weekend would be wet, cold and miserable. However, the prospect of rain didn't dampen the spirits of all; a huge marquee was on order along with waterproof gazebos for the stall holders as a safeguard against the weather, and as the vast majority of Committee members were pessimists anyway, they half expected rain.

On Thursday the thirty first of May, as the big weekend drew nearer, an unusual happening occurred in Trengillion. At lunchtime, as the church clock struck the midday hour, a colourful gypsy-style caravan was spotted travelling through the village at a steady pace beneath overcast, dull grey skies. It passed the village hall where workmen busily rolled fresh tarmac over the area where the sycamore tree once stood. It passed villagers, drawn by the spectacle, watching from behind net curtains, over garden walls, through hedges, and on the footpaths, all fascinated as it slowly drifted through the village, pulled, not as one might expect, by a horse, but by an old, black Zephyr Six car.

To the surprise of Morgana, hanging new curtains in one of the guest rooms, it pulled up outside the Jolly Sailor, and from the car stepped a bizarre couple wearing clothes more suited to the late nineteen sixties than the beginning of the twenty first century. Morgana was intrigued. She hurriedly finished fastening the second curtain to the track, jumped down from the chair on which she stood, and rushed downstairs to see who the strange visitors might be. In the bar she found them paying for drinks. He had a pint of Guinness and she had a half of sweet cider. Morgana smiled politely as Justin introduced her.

"Sweetheart, do come and meet Windflower and Sandy, they're currently touring Britain and decided to come here when they saw an advert in the paper for our Jubilee celebrations. Windflower reads the Tarot cards, you see, and thought her services might be a useful attraction."

"Really," Morgana grinned, standing by Justin's side, "how fascinating. I'm sure your skill will be greatly appreciated. Astrology and astronomy are both of great interest to me and so I may well learn something from you."

Windflower nodded, causing a strand of her long jet black hair to slip from its clip and part cover her tanned, weather beaten skin. "I look forward to reading the cards for you," she said, in an accent sounding a cross between South African and American.

Morgana turned to Sandy. "And how about you, do you have any revealing talents?"

He laughed. "Unfortunately, not any more. I used to be a trapeze artist in the circus, but needless to say those days are now but a distant memory."

"How sad," sympathised Morgana, trying hard to imagine Sandy as a younger man, but still with a straggly walrus moustache and long, unkempt hair tied back in a ponytail, dangling, as he niftily swung high in a circus tent.

He seemed to read the expression on her face. "It was a fair while ago and it all came to an end after I had a nasty fall. I've done other acts with the circus since then, knife throwing, juggling, even working with the elephants, but nothing compares to the swings."

"I'm impressed," said Morgana, "not that I've ever been a fan of the circus. I always found the clowns irritating, even as a child. Slapstick was never my thing."

"I'm inclined to agree with you there," said Windflower, lifting her glass of cider from the bar, "but to be fair, some of the clowns we've come across have been smashing and frequently deep thinkers too."

Justin frowned. "I'm confused by the Tarot Cards. How do they fit into a circus act?"

Windflower giggled, almost childlike. "They don't, or rather didn't. I was a tightrope walker in my early circus days. Reading the Cards is something I've taken up since we left."

"Phew, rather you than me," said Morgana, "I couldn't walk a tightrope if it was only a few inches from the ground. I hate the way it wobbles. The mere thought of it makes me feel light headed."

"Hmm, not the thing to do if you suffer from vertigo," said Sandy, "but then neither are the swings."

"No, I suppose not."

Justin grinned as Morgana, who was obviously feeling giddy, leaned against the bar. He turned to the former performers. "And so did you two meet in the circus?"

Sandy and Windflower began to answer together. Windflower gave way to her husband. "Yes, it was a fair few years ago now. We both left shortly after we got married, didn't we, sweetheart? It's a great life for a while but eventually the travelling and continuous upheaval starts to get tedious and you long to sleep beneath a proper roof within the security of solid walls."

"And to put down roots," said Windflower.

Morgana was about to ask for how long they had been married, but quickly decided it would be impertinent as they could well be very sensitive about their ages. Instead she said, "How long are you intending to stay in Trengillion?"

"Just for the Bank Holiday weekend," said Sandy, "In fact the reason for our calling in here, apart from light refreshment, that is, was to ask whereabouts there might be somewhere we could stay."

"A caravan site," added Windflower, hastily, "preferably not too commercialised, "as you can see we're somewhat old fashioned and take delight in peace and quiet."

"Then your best bet would be Home Farm," said Justin, "a working farm run by David and Judith Pascoe. It's a lovely spot away from it all down a leafy lane in a valley."

"Sounds right up our street," said Sandy, finishing off his Guinness. "How do we get there?"

Justin drew a rough map on the back of an old beer mat. The visitors thanked him for his help, shook hands and vowed to visit the pub again as they left.

"They seemed a nice couple," said Justin, putting the empty glasses on the draining board.

"Hmm, yes, but I wouldn't be at all surprised if the reason they want a quiet spot, is so that they can smoke the old wacky baccy."

Justin laughed.

"Anyway," continued Morgana, hearing the engine of the old car start up, "thank goodness they have a caravan. I wouldn't be too keen on having them stay here."

Justin washed the glasses and reached for a cloth to dry them. "That's rather cynical of you, Morgana. I liked them, and you should never judge a book by its cover."

Morgana raised her eyebrows. "Want a bet on that?"

Justin watched the vintage car and gaudy caravan pull away from the spot outside the window. "Well, no, I don't think I do."

Windflower and Sandy found Home Farm with ease and after consulting other campers on the field they walked along a well-worn track to the farmhouse to book their stay on the site for the duration of the long bank holiday weekend. Once done, they chose a secluded spot for their caravan, tucked in a corner well away from the other campers and sheltered from the south westerly winds by a tall, wild hedge. After they had made themselves at home, they decided to take a stroll to get familiar with their new surroundings.

Windflower was delighted with the walk; they followed the narrow lane down which they had recently driven, leading back towards the village. The hedgerows were a blaze of colour; red campion, bright yellow buttercups and the odd late bluebell, all mingled together with an abundance of white, lacy cow parsley. And in a shady spot, beneath overhanging trees, Windflower found sweetly scented violets growing in clusters alongside the last of the spring primroses.

"I wish we lived in the country," she said, linking arms with Sandy, "it's so much more interesting than the town, even on a day like today when the sun isn't shining. There's more scope to bring out the romantic in me. I think, deep down I'm a country girl at heart."

Sandy laughed. "That's as maybe, but there's not much work to be had in the country, love, especially in off the beaten track locations like this. In fact, I should think there's not much going on at all, besides a bit of farming and looking after holiday makers, and even that's only for a few months of the year."

Windflower shook her head. "No, there'll be more than that. Shops for instance, and schools and hospitals. And then there will be traditional things like fishing and mining."

"Mining! Come on love, you really are living in the past. I doubt very much there's any mining done in Cornwall now, and I should think fishing isn't what it used to be. Too many foreign imports and all that."

Windflower was not convinced. "I should still like to live down here. I could read the Cards to bring in a bit of cash and I'd be able to get a job in a shop or a hotel maybe because there must be jobs in tourism."

Sandy stopped walking and looked at his wife. "And what would I do, and where would we live? I don't have any worthwhile qualifications, that's why I only work three days a week now, and I should imagine houses cost an arm and a leg down here, both to rent and to buy."

"I suppose you're right," she grudgingly agreed.

They continued walking.

"Of course, I'm right, and for that reason we must enjoy ourselves while we're here. I'm sure you'll agree that we ought to go to that nice pub again tonight. The landlord and his lady seemed nice enough, so I reckon they'd be only too pleased if you did a bit of Card reading and entertained their regulars."

On Friday there was a definite party atmosphere in the village. Working people, delighted with the prospect of an extra-long weekend, eagerly looked forward to relaxing before the jollifications on Monday. Meanwhile, stay-at-home villagers were out and about during the day, draping bunting between lamp posts and telegraph poles interspersed with hanging baskets of flowering bedding plants in red, white and blue. And in nearly every garden, strings of plastic Union flags, portraying pictures of the Queen, flapped in the breeze from window sills, porch rooves, garden gates and cast iron railings.

Later, locals and holiday makers alike made their way to the Jolly Sailor; for news telling of Windflower's reading of the Tarot cards the previous evening had travelled fast and many, particularly the ladies, were keen to hear what the future might hold for them.

Most people were thrilled with the answers and advice foretold by the Cards regarding good health, sustaining or attaining stable relationships and maintaining or achieving satisfactory standards of living. The subject of the Cards fascinated the inexperienced and the beauty of the Card's illustrations delighted the artistic and creative. However, for one person the reading of the Tarot Cards left an unsavoury taste in the mouth. Ollie Collins. For him the Death card turned, and he instantly sensed doom, despite Windflower assuring him the Card did not predict, as one might think, his imminent demise.

"My dear Ollie, the emphasis with this card is on endings and new beginnings," said Windflower, sympathetically, "and not necessarily on death by means of bereavement. It can mean the cutting away of deadwood and disposing of unnecessary things in your life to make way for new developments. You should not fear the worst."

But Ollie was not convinced. From the moment that hateful card had turned his future seemed ominous and dark and he foresaw bleak days, weeks, months and years looming ahead.

Saturday dawned bright and sunny, but according to the weather forecast it was not set to last. Not that anyone was surprised, it was after all a Bank Holiday weekend.

Danny Jarrams, one time bass guitarist with sixties band Gooseberry Pie, was due to arrive at the Penwynton Hotel around lunchtime along with a new band he was managing called The Discordant Dukes. Linda, not sure the name conjured up a sound worth hearing, had during a number of phone conversations, tried to persuade her cousin to change it, but Danny insisted the band was doing *great* on the London scene and the folk in Trengillion would go crazy too when they heard them. Linda wasn't sure the inhabitants of Trengillion were ready to go crazy, but she knew there was no point in arguing: after all The Discordant Dukes had agreed to forgo a fee and had opted for full board and lodging at the Hotel for a week instead, and Danny had emphasised on several occasions the fact that the lads were very patriotic. Nevertheless, she was a little apprehensive and prayed they would not be uncouth in any way and offend the other guests.

Linda was in the conservatory watering tubs of tropical plants when she heard of their arrival from Anne who rang her mobile. Linda's apprehension intensified, convinced Anne's voice subtly masked the desire to giggle. Nervously she returned the watering can to a cupboard hidden behind a weeping fig and went to welcome her cousin and his musical associates. But nothing could have prepared her for the sight which greeted her eyes.

There were four Discordant Dukes. Danny introduced them one by one. The lead singer was Duke Red. He was tall, had bright, pillar box red, spiky hair; wore red jeans and a matching T shirt. The drummer was Duke Blue. His long, thick curly hair was the same shade of royal blue as his shorts and check shirt. The guitarist was Duke White. Beneath his peaked white cap, a snow white pony tail dangled down the back of the plain white shirt he wore tucked neatly inside his belted, pressed, white cotton trousers. The saxophonist was Duke Black. His short, jet black hair was matched by a trimmed pointed beard and a Salvador Dali moustache. He wore a black leather jacket and black denim jeans. Linda's heart sank. And then she laughed. "Well," she said, much cheered, "at least I won't have any trouble remembering which one of you is which."

Inside the Jolly Sailor, Justin and Morgana made last minute preparations for the arrival of Polly Jolly, the comedienne, who was also booked to entertain the party goers at the Jubilee celebrations. For Polly, when offered the choice of free accommodation at the Hotel or the village pub, chose the latter because she preferred the intimacy of smaller establishments; she also rather liked the pub's name. Justin and Morgana were thrilled, because unlike Linda and Jamie and their guests, The Discordant Dukes, both knew of Polly Jolly having seen her on the television on numerous occasions. Meanwhile, to familiarise themselves further with her line of humour, Justin borrowed a couple of DVDs from Wayne Tilley, who claimed to be her number one fan.

Swampy, who since his surprise appearance had enjoyed the comfort of one of the guest rooms inside the Jolly Sailor, gathered together his few belongings before the arrival of the celebrity guest and dropped them onto the floor of Justin and Morgana's living room where he was to sleep on the sofa for the duration of the long weekend. He then went down to the beach to enjoy the smidgen of sunshine he'd noticed from the window before it disappeared altogether.

Swampy found the beach was quiet as is often the case on Saturdays during the holiday season due to it being change-over day. But Swampy wasn't too concerned over the lack of people; he was feeling somewhat tired, for over the last week he had spent much of his time with a drop-dead gorgeous blonde staying with her family at the Hotel. However, she was gone now and he was glad of a little time to rest and recharge his batteries ready for the Jubilee weekend.

The tide was low and so he walked down the beach and climbed the sides of the Island. When he reached the top he sat and looked out to sea. Cornwall was great. He just wished it and the rest of the British Isles were a little warmer. Looking back on his childhood he felt sure the sun had shone on a more frequent basis and recalled his mother often referring to June as Flaming June. He laughed: perhaps in retrospect she had been cursing the weather.

Polly Jolly wasn't due to arrive much before tea time. Nevertheless, on the off chance she should arrive early, many locals made a bee-line for the Jolly Sailor at lunchtime, all eager to be the first to spot the much vaunted celebrity. Consequently, the pub kitchen was very busy and much to the astonishment of chef, Maurice Lamont, every other diner ordered an omelette which according to a celebrity magazine was Polly Jolly's favourite lunch; as a result, when the lunch time session finished only one egg remained on the usually near-full tray.

"I suppose I ought to ring Judith and ask her to drop some more up, but it seems a liberty at such short notice and I know she and David are pretty busy at present with extra campers here for the Jubilee," said Maurice, scratching his chin.

Tally, working because Morgana had gone to Rebecca's salon to have her hair done, agreed. "I suppose I could always pop down to Home Farm and collect some," she said, loading empty plates she had cleared from the bar into the dishwasher. "It'd be a nice walk and I've nothing else planned."

"Would you?" said Maurice, reaching for the phone, "You're a star. I'll just ring the farm to make sure they have plenty of eggs and put them in the picture."

Tally decided to go straight to Home Farm after finishing work but first sent her mother a text telling of her excursion in order to diminish any apprehension which might arise should she not get home at the usual time. Tally actually thought it was an unnecessary action, after all she was in her early thirties, but she was aware that for as long as she remained under her parents' roof, they, and especially her mother, would regard her as a juvenile, unlike her slightly older brother Wills, who, just because he was married, had a baby and lived up-country, was considered grown up and worldly.

With a cardboard box containing a tray of eggs tucked safely beneath her right arm, Tally left the farm house and took a short cut across the field where the campers had pitched their tents and parked their caravans. When she saw the old gypsy-style caravan in the corner which belonged to Windflower and Sandy, she paused. The previous evening she had been working while Windflower had read the Tarot cards for a considerable number of people, hence Tally, who in her younger days had been much influenced by astrology, had missed the opportunity to have her fortune told. Feeling the desire to know whether the Cards might be able to give her an insight regarding her future and especially teaching, she wandered over to the Gypsy-style caravan and knocked on the door on the off chance that Windflower could spare her a little time. No-one answered, yet a window was open and Tally was convinced she'd heard voices as she had approached. She knocked again. Still no response. Disappointed and confused, she gave up and headed home to Chy-an-Gwyns after dropping off the eggs at the Jolly Sailor en route.

Later in the afternoon, Gertie Collins looked from the living room window of Rose Cottage while visiting Ned and sighed. "Oh dear, it looks like the rain isn't far off." She drummed her fingers on the window sill and shook her head. "I can't believe we're in for a miserable wet weekend. It's so unfair, especially when you think of all the hard work and preparation the youngsters have put into it all."

Ned smiled. "That's life, Gert. But it's not so much Trengillion's celebrations I feel sorry for as those scheduled in London and the South East. It looks like they'll be getting a proper soaking. At least the heaviest of the rain down here will have long passed over by Monday and so for our festivities the weather should be reasonably dry. Although I must admit, the evening's not looking too good."

Gertie turned and sat down on the settee beside Ned. "I know, but everyone had such high hopes. Susan tells me there will be a full moon on Monday night and it'll be wasted if the damn cloud's thick."

Ned laughed. "Why does it matter? Or were you thinking of taking a stroll through the Hotel gardens in the moonlight with a dashing young fellow, Gert? Tally tells me one of Justin's old friends has turned up from Australia and by all accounts he's very attractive."

Gertie hit Ned with a lightweight feather cushion. "Cheeky! Are you saying I'm too old for such romantic flights of fancy?"

Ned shook his head. "No, Gert. I'd never say such a thing. Anyway, we'll still all have a good time, you wait and see. As long as the rain holds off everything will be fine. And even if it doesn't, there will be the marquee to shelter in."

Gertie smiled. "Ever the optimist, eh, Ned?"

Ned nodded. "It's the only way, Gert. I learned that from Stella. I used to let the weather get me down but not anymore. No-one can do anything about it, not even the Queen herself, although I'm sure she would if she could. It's a case of making the best of a situation, something we British are really good at."

Chapter Ten

Polly Jolly arrived at the Jolly Sailor just after three in the afternoon as the first raindrops began to fall. With her was a friend who she introduced as Abigail Armstrong. The Thorntons were surprised. They knew Polly was not coming alone, but had expected her companion to be a male partner, despite the fact she'd asked for a twin room.

After being introduced, Abigail did most of the talking; she appeared to be very organised, efficient and charming; she was also bossy. The reason became apparent when she informed them she was Polly's agent. Morgana was not entirely convinced that the relationship was simply professional but Justin appeared not to care.

"She's here," he said, after they'd left Polly and Abigail upstairs to settle in their room, "and whether or not she and Abigail are agent and client or romantically linked really doesn't matter."

"Maybe not, but there's something about Abigail I don't like. She gives me the creeps. On the other hand, Polly is lovely."

Justin nodded. "Yes, she is and I'm sure Abigail will be too once she lets her hair down and we get to know her."

The forecast rain was little more than drizzle hence the Jolly Sailor was even busier on Saturday evening than it had been at lunch time. News of Polly Jolly's safe arrival travelled fast, and that, along with the long weekend and Windflower's Tarot Card reading, meant there was reason to be out for almost everyone.

Polly Jolly, dressed in jeans and turquoise tunic top, sat with Abigail and her band of admirers in the corner of the public bar, telling funny stories and listening to her fans chatter. While in the snug, Windflower amazed soothsaying enthusiasts with her skills and efficiency. Ollie, after his disconcerting Card reading the previous evening, joined the Polly Jolly camp followers, wishing to distance himself as far as possible from the menacing Cards. Swampy on the other hand, was much taken with Windflower; there was something about her that enthralled him. Without question she was enigmatic but perhaps it was her strange attire that fascinated him. The long kaftan which brushed against her sandalled feet; the black crocheted shawl draped around her shoulders or the yellow scarf part covering her jet black hair; or maybe it was her hands part-hidden in black fingerless lace gloves which niftily and skillfully turned the Cards. Whichever it was, Swampy was beguiled and he watched her for most of the evening, much to the dismay of Trish Tilley who had been trying to catch his attention ever since she'd realised the dumb blonde he'd been hanging around with the previous week appeared to have gone home.

After closing time, as Tally collected empty glasses, she mentioned her visit to Home Farm and the failure of Windflower and Sandy to answer their caravan door even though she was convinced, having heard voices, that they were both in.

"Windflower was probably out," giggled Valerie Moore, draining her wine glass and slipping on her jacket, "and if so Randy Sandy most likely had another woman in there."

Tally was surprised. "You've got to be pulling my leg."

Valerie shook her head. "No, seriously, I'm not. I was watching him tonight while Windflower was reading the Tarot cards, he slipped away on several occasions and was flirting with every female present under the age of fifty. You must have noticed. I saw him pinch Trish's bum but he seemed particularly smitten with Abigail. I watched them after he accosted her coming back from the loo, he could barely keep his hands off her."

"Abigail, but surely she's gay." said Tally.

Ollie laughed and shook his head. "No, she's not. And contrary to gossip doing the rounds tonight, neither is Polly Jolly."

Jess, poked her brother's arm. "Hey, you're blushing, Ollie. I saw you having a quiet tête-à-tête with Polly after her fans had dispersed. Very cosy, I reckon she's got the hots for you."

Ollie did not respond but his facial expression confirmed the possibility expressed by his sister.

"So, if Sandy did have a woman in the caravan, who do you think it was?" Tally asked, trying to recollect whether or not either of the voices she had heard were familiar. "I mean to say, they've only been here for a couple of days."

Valerie shrugged her shoulders. “God knows, but whoever it was must be pretty hard up. I mean, have you seen the size of his beer gut and all that straggly, coarse, tangled hair? Ugh, I think he’s repulsive and he reeks of smoke.”

“It was probably a holiday maker anyway,” said Jess, casually, “his conquest, that is. On the other hand, Tally, Sandy may have been home with Windflower and they didn’t answer because they didn’t have their teeth in or something like that.”

“Like it,” laughed Clive, slapping his thigh, “and Windflower probably didn’t have time to put her witch’s wig on.”

“Or her thick layers of make-up,” said Jess.”

“Hey, I like Windflower,” piped up Swampy, “she’s real cool and fascinating to watch.”

Trevor Moore nodded. “I agree, and I think you lot are being a bit harsh. Poor old Windflower. You shouldn’t knock her for trying to make the best of her looks.”

“Humph, mutton dressed as lamb,” said Valerie, disparagingly.

“I can’t agree with you there, Val,” said Jess, “I mean surely the stuff they both wear is real old hat. Nobody under the age of forty would be seen dead wearing kaftans these days, not unless it was for fancy dress.”

“I suppose you’re right, but I was referring more to the over use of make-up. It’s not seemly for an older women to be plastered like she is, and by doing so can only mean she’s trying to look younger.”

“I expect it’s because she has gypsy blood,” said Tally, placing empty glasses on the bar, “that’s if she is a real gypsy.”

“They were both in a circus according to Justin,” said Swampy, “not that that means they don’t have gypsy blood. Not much to choose between the two if you ask me.”

“I’m more miffed by her accent,” said Clive, “I mean, where the hell is she supposed to be from?”

“I think you’re all missing the point,” said Ollie, “Windflower and Sandy are both show biz types albeit on an amateur level. What you see is no doubt not the real them at all. It’s all an act, and I bet in reality they live in a cosy semi in Tunbridge Wells where she’s a solicitor and he’s a bank manager.”

“Why Tunbridge Wells?”

“Dunno, it’s the first place that came into my head.”

Jess nudged her brother's arm. "I bet that's where Polly Jolly lives and you said it without thinking."

"Actually," said Ollie, "Polly lives in Acton. Got a nice town house there which she bought earlier this year. She was telling me about the work she's had done on account of the fact I'm a builder and understand things like that."

"How romantic," giggled Tally.

"Polly has gorgeous hair," said Rebecca Williams, "its condition is fantastic."

"Unlike Windflower," said Clive, "as I said earlier I reckon it's a wig."

Rebecca nodded. "I think it is too. I saw her outside the post office this morning and noticed it had a very artificial shine to it, a bit like nylon, but you'd probably not notice so much indoors."

"Told you so," laughed Clive, "and Rebecca should know."

Rebecca Williams was the wife of local fisherman, Matthew, and ran a hairdressing salon at her home in Fuchsia Cottage, part inherited from Matthew's parents, Betty and Peter. Betty had also been a hairdresser and had opened the Fuchsia Cottage salon when her children, Matthew and Jane were small. On Betty's retirement Rebecca took over the salon, but it was not until Betty died, two years after her husband, that Matthew and Rebecca finally moved into Fuchsia Cottage after Matthew's sister, Jane, sold her share in the house to her brother.

Rebecca tutted. "Don't be too quick to judge Windflower. The reason she wears a wig might be for medical reasons. You know, she might have lost her hair through alopecia or even worse be undergoing chemotherapy. Neither of which is a laughing matter."

"No, surely not," said Tally, shocked, "she looks too well."

"Does she though?" said Valerie, beginning to feel guilty, "All the make-up she wears might be to hide something or other. You know, a pallid or blotchy complexion."

"And she is very skinny," said Clive, "well, too skinny for my liking anyway, and too old of course."

"I think we must all be a little kinder to her from now on," said Jess, suddenly feeling uncomfortable, "not that we've been unkind anyway, other than making nasty comments in here tonight, that is. And when all is said and done, she's ever so nice and very friendly."

Valerie nodded. "I agree, but I still think old Sandy is a randy sod."

On Sunday morning, beneath leaden grey skies and a freshening wind, the marquee was delivered to the Penwynton Hotel and erected on the lawns by the firm from whom it had been hired. When the job was finished, Committee members walked around inside the huge construction, their faces beaming with delight and satisfaction.

"Well, it's an absolute beauty," said Linda, looking out of a large picture window, "I never dreamt it would be this big, or this light and airy."

"It won't look anything like as big when we've got the stage up," said Ian, "I'm glad we went for the smallest available, stage that is, not marquee."

Danny Jarrams peeped round the flap of the open doorway and asked if he might take a look inside.

"Of course," said Linda, stepping aside, "and we hope it meets with your approval.

Danny walked around looking from floor to roof top. He nodded. "It's great, cousin, better than I'd imagined. The Dukes will fit in here fine if the weather's crap tomorrow. And that dolly, Polly Jolly is really petite so she'll have no problems either."

"Dolly, Polly Jolly," repeated Anne, with an amused frown, "I see your sense of humour hasn't matured, Danny."

Danny pulled a childlike face. "Which reminds me. I keep meaning to ask, what are the local kids like? The ones playing here tomorrow, I mean, before the Dukes."

"They're good," said Justin, enthusiastically, "we've had them playing at the Jolly Sailor a couple of times and they've gone down really well."

"Hmm. What sort of stuff do they play?"

"All sorts," said Ian, whose younger son was one of the band members, "old and new. In fact they've put their heads together and written a few tunes, including one especially for the Jubilee which will be heard for the very first time tomorrow."

"But surely you must have heard it," said Linda.

Ian shook his head. "No, they hired a hall in Helston for rehearsals so that no-one in Trengillion would hear it before the big day."

"Wow," said Danny, "they sound switched on, it looks like the Dukes are gonna have some serious competition. I better make sure they're in top form tomorrow."

After coffee, served by Linda in the Hotel lounge, Committee members drifted back towards the village. For some their destination was the Jolly Sailor and Sunday lunch, others went home to watch the broadcast of the Royal Pageant cruising down the River Thames.

Tally worked during Sunday lunchtime so that she could soak up some of the ever increasing party atmosphere prior to her trip to London with Jim. Repeatedly she was asked if she was excited. The answer was yes. She was also apprehensive, but she kept that feeling to herself. For although she had known Jim for many years, she had to admit she didn't really know him at all. He was just one of the locals and she knew next to nothing about him. This, however, did not deter Tally in any way. She had an outgoing personality and prided herself on getting along with pretty well everyone. Besides, her Auntie Anne thought the world of him, and her cousin, Jess, repeatedly sang his praises and extolled his talents where horticultural skills were concerned. Tally laughed. She had little or no interest in gardening and so she was a trifle anxious about finding a subject which might unite them during the long drive to London.

When Tally finished work at three o'clock, Justin insisted she have a drink with Morgana and himself as she would not be around to toast the Queen along with everyone else on Monday. Tally agreed and sat on a bar stool watching Justin pour red wine in the largest stemmed glass he could find.

"I'm surprised Jim hasn't been in today," said Morgana, elbows on the bar, "he usually comes in on Sunday lunchtime."

Tally smiled. "He rang me last night and said he was spending the day on the allotment making sure everything's okay. He then intends to relax and have an early night. I, of course must do likewise, especially as I'm driving."

"I take it you're going in your car then."

"Yes, Jim's not sure his old van would make the journey, but he's agreed to drive if I get tired. But I don't expect I shall. I like driving and relish the chance to travel some distance."

Morgana nodded. "I see, and is anyone looking after Jim's allotment while he's away?"

"Auntie Anne," said Tally, taking a sip of wine, "she's going to make sure the stuff in polytunnels is alright. It's unlikely anything will want watering outside if there is rain forecast."

"Which sadly there is," sighed Morgana.

Justin nodded. "Damn shame about the weather. I watched a few minutes of the Thames Pageant when I went to our quarters a while back. It's drizzling in London, but it doesn't seem to have dampened spirits or affected the turn out."

"Like the Coronation," said Tally, "Grandma and Granddad Stanley lived in London back then, you see. It was just before they got married and they always emphasised the spirit of the British is second to none, and when all's said and done, what harm can a few drops of rain do?"

Inside the Old Vicarage, Anne and John Collins played host to their respective, widowed parents, Ned Stanley and Gertie Collins, having invited them round to watch the Thames Diamond Jubilee Pageant on their new forty two inch, flat screen television set, bought specially for the weekend's events.

Over one thousand boats participated in the flotilla which sailed down the Thames from Battersea to Tower Bridge, led by a belfry boat and followed by small paddle boats manned by people from all walks of life.

The weather in the City was fine with a hint of sunshine and a fresh wind blew as the Queen, the Duke of Edinburgh, Prince Charles, the Duchess of Cornwall, the Duke and Duchess of Cambridge and Prince Harry, joined the flotilla on board the royal barge, *Spirit of Chartwell*, at Cadogan Pier.

Spirit of Chartwell, beautifully decorated with over ten thousand flowers, was followed by pleasure boats, working boats and Dunkirk little ships, making up the largest flotilla ever amassed on the Thames. And on the banks of the river, millions of people, some ten deep in places, waited to see the flotilla on its seven mile run.

"Doesn't the Queen look lovely," said Gertie, "she's just so graceful, so elegant. Not like me, I'd look like a carthorse beside her."

John laughed. "Is the Queen older than you, Mum, or younger."

"Older by a few years, not quite sure how many."

"She's the same age as me," said Ned, with a little pride, "we were both born in 1926. Her Majesty in April and me in August."

"Well, in that case she really is amazing, and I think her outfit is gorgeous. Having said that Camilla looks lovely too and so does young Catherine."

"I think the Duke's remarkable as well," said Ned, "he's been by the Queen's side all these years, and apart from the odd verbal gaff his behaviour has been impeccable."

John, Anne, Gertie and Ned continued to watch as the pageant continued on its journey down the river, all pleased that the weather seemed to be keeping fine. But eventually, as the first boats approached Tower Bridge, to the dismay of all, the heavens opened.

"Are you both warm enough?" Anne asked Gertie and Ned.

"I'm fine," said Ned.

"Me too," said Gertie.

"What made you suddenly ask that?" said John.

Anne shivered. "The weather on the television. As soon as I see rain I feel chilly: it's psychological, I suppose. Anyway, if you're all okay, I'll make do with a thicker cardigan and then I'll make a cup of tea if you'd all like one, and I'll bring in a few slices of chocolate cake as well."

Everyone nodded as Anne rose to her feet. "Good, I'll be back shortly."

At six o'clock, the London Philharmonic Orchestra and Royal College of Music Chamber Choir, performed the 'National Anthem', 'Land of Hope and Glory', and 'Rule Britannia' from the last boat in the flotilla. The orchestra played below decks in the dry, but the young choir who stood on top of the boat, sang in the rain.

Gertie shuddered. "Now seeing them *is* making me feel cold. Poor things. Why didn't anyone have a rainy day plan? Look, they're soaked to the skin. They'll catch their death of cold."

John grinned. "That's such an old wives tale, Mum. You can't catch a cold simply by getting wet. Colds are caused by a virus."

"Humph, well that's as maybe, but it can't do anyone any good getting soaked to the skin like that."

"John's right of course," said Ned, "but resistance to a virus may well be lowered if a person gets wet and is shivering for any length of time."

Anne jumped up and switched on an electric fire which she placed near to John's mother. "Talk of wet, cold and people shivering is making me feel cold again."

John placed his hand on Anne's forehead. "Sounds like you're sickening for something. I hope you'll be alright for tomorrow."

"Yes, I'll be fine when the choir finishes and I can imagine them going off for nice hot showers and baths."

Their eyes returned to the television screen where the orchestra continued to play and the young choir continued to sing, as fireworks sparked, flashed and boomed from Tower Bridge. It was a truly spectacular display in the finale of the grandest event staged on the Thames for three hundred and fifty years.

And the Queen, in spite of her age, stood, as did the Duke of Edinburgh, throughout the entire pageant.

Chapter Eleven

On Sunday evening, the Jolly Sailor was much quieter than on the previous two nights due, Justin assumed, to the fact that the following day would not only be eventful but quite hectic for organisers, stall holders and parents with young children. Windflower did not appear as she needed plenty of sleep before a busy day reading the Cards, so said her husband, Sandy, who popped in for a couple of pints while his wife rested.

Polly Jolly, however, was present. She wanted to make the most of her brief visit to Cornwall, therefore she and Abigail were the main focus of attention for those who did venture out. Ollie was delighted for two reasons; one, he was very much taken with Polly, and two, Windflower's absence meant he was not constantly reminded of the wretched Death card which he considered, despite Windflower's protestations, was in danger of dominating and manipulating his life.

By ten twenty the inn was very quiet; the public bar was nearly empty and the only people in the snug bar were Ollie, Polly, Abigail and Sandy.

Morgana smiled as Justin prepared to ring last orders. "Shame to break up the cosy party in the snug. Ollie looks more relaxed than I've ever seen him. What a pity Polly will be gone soon as I think she and Ollie make a lovely couple."

Justin laughed as he rang the bell. "Ollie and Polly. Their rhyming names certainly do have a charm, but don't you think Polly is a bit too old for Ollie?"

Morgana shook her head. "Ollie is in his early thirties and Polly her early forties, ten years is neither here nor there. Besides, Polly looks years younger than she is."

Wayne, with his elbows on the bar, heard what was said. "Why is it I always dip out as far as talent is concerned? I mean, I've been potty about P.J. for as long as I can remember but I don't think she even knows I exist. And it's the same with all women. I sometimes wonder if I'm invisible."

Morgana sighed, sympathetically. "Perhaps you ought to exert yourself a bit more. You know, join in with more conversations."

Wayne shook his head. "The trouble is I'm shy and I never have much to say until I've had a drink. Then I have another problem; I get argumentative, especially about art." He sighed deeply. "What's more, I don't think P.J. is much interested in art and that's about the only subject I know much about. That and photography."

"You're on the Jubilee Committee," said Justin, pouring a couple of large brandies for two holiday makers, "and from what I've been told you've made a valiant contribution."

Wayne nodded. "Thanks Justin, I do my best, but I think both me and Trish are destined to spend the rest of our lives stuck with each other's company because her love life is as lacklustre as mine."

Justin grinned. "I wouldn't be too sure about that, Wayne. Trish was with Swampy earlier this evening and they seemed to be getting along rather well. In fact they took a taxi into Helston a while back because they both fancied a few drinks in town and then an Indian."

Wayne raised his eyebrows and his look suddenly turned to one of alarm. "Really! No! How much longer is Swampy here for?"

Justin was puzzled by the question. "How long is he here for? Only a couple more days. He said he'd like to stay for the Jubilee do and then he'll have to be off on Tuesday because he's flying back to Oz on Wednesday."

Wayne fanned his face with his hand. "Phew, that's a relief."

"A relief," repeated Justin, "what do you mean?"

Wayne grinned. "Can't tell you right now. But ask me again the last day of August and I'll tell you then."

On Monday, Tally switched off her alarm clock as its shrill bells rang through the stillness of the early morning. She fell back on the pillow and groaned. Getting up was never a task Tally found easy, not even when it was for something special.

As her eyes slowly began to close again, her mobile phone rang. Tally reached out and looked at the screen. The caller was Jim.

"Hi, Jim," she said, desperately attempting to stifle a yawn.

"Hi, Tally, glad to hear you're awake. I thought you might not be up yet."

"Cheeky! I've been up for ages," Tally lied, "is everything alright?"

"Yep, I've just made my second coffee and I need to throw a few things together then I'll be ready. How about you?"

"Same here, except my bag's already packed. I did it yesterday when I got home from work."

"Brilliant. Hope you've got something warm to wear, it could well be chilly later."

"Hmm, I have. A nice thick jumper as well as a coat."

"Good. I'll see you at half six then."

"Yes, I'll be there. Bye, Jim."

"Bye, Tally."

Tally laid her phone down beside the alarm clock as it began its second bout of ringing. Quickly she turned it off and pushed back the duvet.

Through a chink in the curtains, sunlight cast a thin, bright streak across the carpeted floor. Delighted to realise it was not raining, she stepped out of bed, crossed the room and threw back the curtains. The morning was clear and bright and the flat calm sea sparkled in the golden sunlight. Tally sighed. She was looking forward to her London trip but at the same time regretted she would miss the festivities in Trengillion, especially if the day was likely to be fine.

Unable to face breakfast, Tally made a mug of coffee and switched on the television to the News channel. The weather forecast was on and she was relieved to see that London was likely to stay fine for the day.

When her mug was empty she went back upstairs to the bathroom and took a shower. She then dressed in casual clothes: jeans, striped top and flat shoes suitable for driving. As she checked the contents of her handbag were in order, Elizabeth walked into the kitchen.

"Everything ready?" she asked.

Tally nodded. "Yes, and Jim's up because he rang me a short while back."

"Good, I shall think of you both this evening, when you'll be in the Mall and we'll be watching Danny's Dukes or whatever they're called."

"The Discordant Dukes," said Tally, "and I'm sure they'll be very good."

Elizabeth smiled. "They will be if they're anything like Gooseberry Pie used to be. But I was only a kid back in their day and we were more taken by the band's good looks than their music."

Tally picked up her overnight bag and put it on her shoulder. "Much like today then. I hope you've remembered to set 'record' for the concert."

"Of course. Your dad did it yesterday. We'd like to see it anyway, as we'll not be back from our own do 'til long after the Concert's finished."

"Good, well, I'll be off, then. I hope everything goes to plan in Trengillion today and that the weather stays fine."

"I'm sure it will. Now please drive carefully, love; remember you're not used to motorways." Elizabeth gave her daughter a hug. "I'm sure you'll have a wonderful time. I must admit I quite envy you both."

Tally laughed. "And in a way I quite envy you."

Elizabeth picked up Tally's car keys and pushed them into her daughter's hand. "Off you go or you'll be late and please convey our regards to Jim."

Tally kissed her mother's cheek. "Will do. Bye Mum."

"Bye love."

Jim was waiting by the gate of Ebenezer House, a rucksack on his back and sunglasses hiding his brown eyes. Like Tally he was dressed casually, in jeans, short sleeved shirt and trainers. As he sat beside her and removed the glasses it struck Tally, for the very first time, just how good looking he was.

"Did you have breakfast?" he asked, as Tally released the hand brake.

"No, I didn't fancy anything at this ungodly hour. How about you?"

Jim shook his head. "I felt the same. I thought we might stop somewhere en route if we're making good time. Exeter maybe."

"Sounds good to me."

In the grounds behind the Penwynton Hotel, Jamie Stevens walked around the huge white marquee to check that all was well. The early morning air smelled sweet, fortuitously refreshed by the previous day's rain, and the only sounds to break the silence were birds singing in the trees and the gentle rustling of bunting, fluttering in the light south westerly breeze. He looked to the sky; large patches of blue stretched between the sparse clouds. He sighed and said a silent prayer. Was it too much to ask that the day stay fine?

There was a buzz of excitement in the Hotel dining room when the four Dukes came in for breakfast dressed in their usual individual colours. Guests old and newly-arrived, had heard that they were band members and due to play later in the evening and many felt privileged to be in close proximity to the stars of the show, although some, and in particular male guests, would have preferred to have had Polly Jolly in their midst.

By mid-morning, inside half of Trengillion's kitchens, women were baking quiches, pasties, pies, cakes, scones, buns and tarts for the tea party, while others buttered rolls and bread for sandwiches and made individual jellies, trifles and blancmanges.

Inside the Jolly Sailor, Maurice made canapés, chilli sausage rolls, smoked salmon and chive vol au vents and spicy cheese muffins. He was filling the vol au vents when Swampy walked into the kitchen.

"Wow, Mo, something smells good."

Maurice grinned as Swampy filled the kettle. "Make mine a coffee, milk and two sugars."

Swampy nodded. "Are you going to this jamboree today?"

"Yep," said Maurice, "we're closing the place after lunch so I get the rest of the day off. Should be a good do especially as they're having a beer tent up at the Hotel. Needless to say, that should keep me amused. How about you?"

"Yeah, I thought I'd give it a go and that's why I've stayed on. I'm off, back up-country tomorrow, you see, and then I fly home to Oz on Wednesday. I reckon I'd better make the most of my last day because I don't expect I'll be back for another year or two." He poured boiling water into two mugs. "I'm gonna kind of miss this place, I can see why Just likes it so much and the natives seem really friendly."

"Yeah, and I heard you took Trish out last night for a curry."

Swampy laughed. "That's right, I did. She's alright and a good laugh but I'm mighty glad I'm off tomorrow because I've a feeling she's the sort that once she gets her talons into a fella, she'll not let go without a fight."

Maurice looked surprised. "You must have misread her body language. She's always given me the impression she has no desire whatsoever to get married and all that."

"Really! That's odd, because she seemed really fed up when I told her today would be my last full day here."

Chapter Twelve

Early on Monday morning, Ollie was out in the back garden of the Old Vicarage digging up the root of a dead tree for his mother, when he received a call from Polly Jolly. She said she was up and about and was going to relax on the beach for an hour or two before lunch if he'd like to join her. Ollie thought for a moment; he could always finish off the tree the following morning before work or even leave it until the weekend. After all two hours with Polly was too good an opportunity to miss and he was confident his mother would understand. Without further deliberation, he downed tools and dashed into the house to wash and change.

Ollie found Polly on the beach, but to his dismay saw Abigail was there also and she evinced no sign of leaving. To make matters worse, a constant stream of fans persistently stopped by to exchange words, tell of their admiration and to ask for autographs.

"Is it like this wherever you go?" Ollie asked, drawing a stick man in the sand with a small piece of driftwood. "It'd drive me nuts."

Polly smiled. "Pretty much, but there are times when I'm not recognised, especially if no-one knows I'm in the area. But of course when, like here, it's common knowledge I'm due to perform tonight, then I find fans are usually on the lookout. Isn't that so, Abby?"

Abigail nodded. "That's why I'm usually reluctant to leave Polly on her own, you never know what weirdoes are lurking out there."

Ollie scowled. "Christ, Poll, it sounds to me like you need a bodyguard as well as an agent."

She laughed. "I don't think my popularity or celebrity status quite run to that."

Ollie's face suddenly clouded over. "I had Windflower read the Tarot cards for me on Friday night and the sodding Death card turned up. It's made me a bit paranoid and it's a horrible feeling."

"I heard about that," said Abigail, "Sandy told me. He said it had upset you, but I wouldn't give it another thought if I were you. I reckon they talk a load of tosh."

"What, just Tarot Cards readers or soothsayers in general?"

"All of them. Fortune tellers, mediums, card readers, gypsies who sell lucky charms; they all talk crap."

"Hey," said Polly, patting Abigail's arm, "it's not all crap. What about the lucky scarf you bought for me? I wouldn't dream of going on stage without it."

"Lucky scarf?" said Ollie, nonplussed.

"Yes, Abby bought me a scarf some time back, it's white and covered with beautiful red poppies. It's really pretty. She said it'd bring me luck and it has, my popularity has increased dramatically since I've been wearing it, hasn't it, Abby? You must have seen it Ollie, that's if you've ever watched me on the telly."

Ollie grinned. "I have watched you on several occasions but I can't say that I remember a scarf, Poll. I'm a bloke after all, and we're not supposed to notice things like clothes, hairstyles and fashion."

Abigail giggled. "You're the type then that dreads being asked 'does my bum look big in this?'"

Ollie nodded. "You've got it in one and before you ask, no, neither of you have big bums."

Abigail pointed to a thatched cottage at the top of the beach. "I see that cottage is for sale. Any idea what they're after?"

"Cove Cottage. It's three hundred and fifty thousand."

"What! That's ridiculous. It looks tiny."

"Hmm, it certainly isn't very big but it does have a fantastic sea view. It used to belong to my Auntie Liz and Uncle Greg and they sold it quite a while back to Iris Delaney, the actress. That's probably why it's so expensive, because it was her rural retreat."

"That's interesting," said Polly, "I wonder why she's selling it."

"Because she practically lives in the States now so hardly ever gets the chance to come down here," said Ollie. "I think the novelty of a Cornish cottage began to wear off after a while too. I mean, lots of people got to know the place as hers and so as soon as she put in an appearance there were groups of fans waiting outside, whereas when she first bought it no-one really knew it was hers and she could just be herself."

"Perhaps you ought to buy it," said Abigail, nudging Polly's arm. "It could be your rural retreat."

"It's certainly tempting, but by the time the estate agents open up again on Wednesday, after the holiday, we'll be hundreds of miles away."

"You could always check it out on the Internet," said Ollie, hopefully, "it'd be really great if you could escape down here from time to time, we'd all be pleased to see you."

Abigail laughed. "And especially you."

Ollie grinned. "Yes, and especially me."

Following their last meeting on the eve of the big weekend, the Jubilee Committee unanimously agreed to offer Sandy and Windflower a pitch in the Hotel gardens, free of charge, because they felt Windflower's Tarot card reading was a crowd puller and they were keen for the day to have as many attractions as possible to ensure the continued enjoyment of those attending. Therefore, shortly after breakfast, Sandy and Windflower's Zephyr Six towed their caravan along the narrow lane which led to Home Farm, and through the village to the lawns behind the Penwynton Hotel. Several Committee members were already there laying out tables for stall holders. To the delight of Sandy and Windflower, they were allocated a prime pitch between the huge marquee and the beer tent.

"Looks like you're lucky with the weather," said Sandy, as he unhitched the caravan from the tow bar on the old Zephyr Six, "so you might not need that marquee."

Jamie looked up at the blue sky. "Well, actually we'd planned to have a marquee all along. In fact, I think having it might even have influenced the weather to be fine. You know what I mean. If we'd not booked it, then it'd be wet, but now that we have, the rain will most likely give us a miss."

Windflower laughed, as she hooked the caravan door open to let in the sunshine. "I'm sure there will be plenty of folks glad to sit inside it anyway. After all it's still none too warm in spite of the sun and if the wind gets up it might well be quite chilly."

Jamie nodded. "And we might still serve tea in there, just to be on the safe side. We'll see. Not sure about the entertainment though, because unfortunately there is rain forecast for later tonight. The local band and even Polly might be okay but I reckon it'll be raining by the time we're ready for the Discordant Dukes."

Sandy whistled. "Oh dear, that could be catastrophic with all the electrical gear."

Jamie sighed. "Precisely, so the problem is, where do we erect the stage? We can't move it half way through the entertainment."

"Where is it at the moment?" Windflower asked.

Jamie pointed towards the marquee. "In there, lying around in pieces. I really think the Committee will have to have a quick meeting, not that anyone will know exactly when the rain's likely to start. Unless your Cards can help, Windflower. Can you tell us what time to expect the rain?"

"If I could help you, I would," Windflower giggled, "but I'm afraid forecasting the weather is way out of my range."

While Sandy drove the Zephyr away to the Hotel's car park, Windflower took a walk through the gardens; when she reached the pond she was enthralled.

Alongside its curved edge, a slate path wound and twisted beside a hedge of fuchsia bushes dripping with purple and red flowers. A small wall, just the right height for sitting on, ran alongside the path and at either end, stood pergolas, each entwined with climbing roses, honeysuckle and clematis which almost hid the rustic wooden frame.

Beneath one of the pergolas, Windflower briefly sat on a sturdy bench to take in the delicate scent of the flowers and admire the mass of colourful blooms. She then rose, sat at the side of the pond and watched as the mist-like sprays from two fountains rose into the air and gently splashed down into the water where goldfish darted beneath and between the lily pads and yellow flowers of a water lily.

She stood. Beyond the pond lay a wild flower meadow. Windflower walked towards it and stood at the top of four newly constructed steps cut into a steep bank which led into the field. She watched, mesmerised, as the flowers swayed in the light breeze like colours in an ever changing kaleidoscope. With a deep sigh, she turned and walked back towards the intense activity and preparations for the forthcoming day, wishing with all her heart that she and Sandy could move to an area such as Trengillion.

Among the stallholders setting up their wares was Trish Tilley, who when she arrived was delighted to find she had been allocated a pitch next to the beer tent and opposite Windflower's caravan. She was ecstatic. The chance to sell her jewellery, enjoy a pint of vodka and Coke, and watch the crowds sauntering around in the welcome sunshine, greatly appealed. Furthermore, with any luck, ladies queuing to have the Tarot cards read, might well peruse her stall and buy a few trinkets.

Wearing flip-flops, unflattering white leggings and a loose, sparkly, pink top which barely covered her large rear end, she unpacked her wares and laid them out artistically on a royal blue velvet table cloth. Nearby, Sandy was talking to Greg Castor-Hunt: he caught Trish's eye and winked. Trish raised her eyebrows: she had heard on the grapevine that Sandy was a bit of a ladies' man. She grinned; perhaps her luck was in. On the other hand she mustn't be too rash, Swampy would be coming to the Jubilee do later and he had been great fun the previous night. Trish groaned. What did it matter anyway? Swampy and Sandy were both due to leave Trengillion the following day and so once they were no longer on the scene it would be back to the drawing board: a fling with either could not prevent the unwelcome haircut. As she hung bracelets on the arms of a stainless steel tree, she began to wish she had never made the silly agreement with Wayne.

Inside the beer tent, Justin set up pumps, fixed optics to a makeshift wall and stacked crates of bottles ready for the beginning of the Jubilee Jamboree. Meanwhile, Morgana and Maurice remained in the Jolly Sailor on the off chance a few locals might want to pop in for lunch. The pub was then to close for the rest of the day, Maurice was to have the evening off, and Justin and Morgana were to run the beer tent, all profits from which would go to Jubilee funds.

Other stalls in the process of being set up were run by various local organisations: the church, the school, the WI, the drama group, the Over Sixties' Club and the playgroup. Car booters also had pitches and came from far and wide, and in order to dispose of left over items donated for the fund raising car boot sales, various Committee members had agreed to take it in turns to sell the remaining bric-a-brac.

Chapter Thirteen

Tally and Jim's drive to London passed quickly, and despite Tally thinking she and Jim might have very little in common, thus limiting subjects for conversation, it was quite the opposite. Both talked of their early lives, families and friends, but the common ground was Trengillion and its inhabitants, the Jolly Sailor and Wimbledon tennis; they even had similar tastes in music.

On arriving in London, Tally drove to the home of her brother, Wills and his wife, Lydia and there she and Jim also changed into outfits more suited to a royal occasion. Leaving behind the car they then went by Underground to their hotel, for even though they realised they were too early to book in, as rooms were not available until after two o'clock, they hoped they might be able to leave their luggage. To their delight, however, the charming young man on reception, who was the son of the proprietor, realising the reason for their London visit, allowed them to their room early as it had already been cleaned and was ready for their occupation.

Tally and Jim expressed their gratitude and ran up the stairs eager to leave their belongings and make headway to the Palace. The room was small but more than adequate for their needs. Had Tally known she was to accompany Jim they could have stayed with Wills and Lydia for the one night, but since Justin had already booked and paid for the hotel room it had seemed silly not to use it, after all, it was part of the prize.

After a quick cup of coffee, Tally and Jim took the Underground to Green Park where they joined the long queue stretching back down the Mall. In all there were twelve thousand concert guests. Ten thousand had won tickets in the ballot and two thousand were specially invited charity workers associated with the Royal Family.

On entering the Palace gardens, guests were presented with individual picnic baskets each one packed with gastronomic goodies, and a plastic poncho for protection should the weather happen to be wet. The weather, however, was fine; the sun shone and beneath blue skies, guests sat on the extensive lawns, chatting, drinking, eating;

enjoying the momentous occasion and entertained by comforting classical music performed by the Royal Academy of Music's Australian String Quartet who played on the banks of the Palace's tranquil lake.

Tally was awestruck when she opened up her picnic hamper; inside was a lavish five-course menu created by famous chef, Heston Blumenthal. Its contents included chilled soup, smoked Scottish salmon, Diamond Jubilee Chicken, strawberry crumble crunch, chocolate cupcakes decorated with gold crowns, lemon and caraway cupcakes, and a cheeseboard which included West Country farmhouse cheddar and Red Leicester, with Prince Charles' oat biscuits and Harvest Chutney.

"It looks much too good to eat," said Tally, excitedly turning over the contents, "I wish I could keep it all for ever as a memento, but I can't because I'm actually hungry."

Jim, who had his hamper opened on his out-stretched legs, responded with a mouthful of smoked salmon. "It's far too good to keep and leave to rot for the sake of a souvenir. The salmon is delicious, but I can't pretend I'm too keen on the idea of cupcakes because I don't really have a sweet tooth."

Tally's eyes lit up. "In which case I'll swap my salmon for your cupcakes, because although I like salmon I don't actually like it when it's been smoked. Everything else has my seal of approval though."

"Deal," smiled Jim, as they exchanged delicacies, "but don't blame me if you feel sick later after all the sweet stuff."

"I won't, because I'm not going to eat all the cake now. I'm going to save some for Mum, she's very fond of cake and I want her to see something of our lovely gifts. Having said that, if I get peckish she might have to make do with a picture instead. In fact I shall take a picture of the whole hamper right now while the sun's shining so everyone back home will be able to see our goodies."

Using her mobile phone, Tally took several pictures of the hamper, of Jim, the crowds, the Quartet, and the Princesses Beatrice and Eugenie whom she could see mingling with nearby guests.

"I wonder how things are going back home," said Tally, feeling sorry for everyone who was not sitting in the Palace gardens, as she dropped her phone back inside her bag and sipped her complimentary champagne, "I hope the weather is as good as it is here."

"Should be," said Jim, dipping an oat biscuit into his jar of chutney, "I watched the forecast before we left this morning and it'll be fine there until evening, and then regrettably, it'll rain. Here, on the other hand it should stay fine all day and night."

"I saw the forecast too. Lucky us, and I mean that with all my heart. It seems weird, don't you think, that we were still in Cornwall this morning? It seems like we've been here for absolutely ages."

Jim pulled a face. "I hope that doesn't mean you think the time's dragging because of the boring company."

Tally laughed. "Most certainly not. To be perfectly honest I'm thoroughly enjoying myself and I can't think of anyone else I'd rather be here with."

Jim raised his eyebrows. "Wow, now, that's what I call a compliment."

Before the tea party in the marquee, the Committee, having finally decided to risk having the entertainment outside, quickly assembled the stage and lighting behind the Penwynton Hotel on an open grassed space slightly sheltered by trees. Inside the Hotel, Linda, concerned some people might find sitting for long in the early evening a little on the chilly side, especially the not so young, looked out old blankets not used since the Hotel had switched to duvets thirty years earlier.

"Are you sure they're alright, Linda?" Jamie asked, as large heavy duty plastic bags accumulated in the hallway. "I mean they're not full of moths or anything like that."

Linda smiled. "No Jamie, they're fine. I know they're ancient but they've been stored and sealed in these bags since they were last used and laundered."

She lifted a large pale yellow blanket from a bag and shook it to prove her point.

Jamie nodded. "Okay, they're fine, and it's just as well you've found them because I'm sure the temperature will drop considerably once the sun makes its exit. Anyway, the stage is nearly up now, so our fate regarding the weather is in the lap of the gods. I'm pretty confident we'll get away with it though. It certainly doesn't look or feel a bit like rain at present."

The weather in Cornwall remained beautiful with warm sunshine throughout the afternoon and just enough wind to keep the flags and bunting flapping. Meanwhile, music from loud speakers, selected to represent the past six decades, drifted around the enthusiastic gathering; several were even enticed to dance.

After the tea party which finished at four o' clock, everyone, except for the organisers who had much clearing up to do, returned outside. Children leapt, jumped and screamed on the bouncy castle, played on bales of straw, had their faces painted, scrounged money from their parents for the lucky dip and watched a puppet show.

Adults, frequented the beer tent, browsed the stalls and purchased plants, clothes, bric-a-brac, vegetable produce, homemade cakes and Trish's jewellery, while the curious queued outside the old gypsy caravan to wait their turn for Windflower to read the Tarot cards.

Meanwhile, darting amongst the crowds, Jess' husband Clive, keen to capture the day's events on film, mingled with a camera around his neck, taking pictures of everyone and everything, determined that the Diamond Jubilee celebrations should be preserved for future generations. And on padded garden chairs, those who preferred a more sedate lifestyle, sat happily in the sunshine making the most of the good weather, the holiday and the opportunity to do nothing without need of an excuse.

"Have you had the Cards read by that extraordinary looking young woman in the gypsy caravan, Gert?" asked Ned, as she pulled up a chair by his side. "I hear she's very good."

Gertie grinned. "Not yet, I might do later. Having said that, this morning our John was telling me that Ollie got the Death card when he had the Cards read in the pub the other night and it's fair put the wind up him. Apparently it doesn't actually mean death though, not in the dying sense anyway, it means ending things and new beginnings, whatever that might imply. Anyway, are you going to have a go?"

"I think it's a bit late in life for me to look into the future. Not only that, I really think it's best not to know. Not that I believe in such tripe and neither should poor Ollie."

"Oh, I don't think you'd be saying that if your mother was still around."

"I should and I frequently did," said Ned, peering sternly over the rim of his glasses. "Mum knew very well I didn't believe in all her jiggery-pokery." He then laughed. "Although I have to admit some of her predictions, premonitions and far-fetched theories were rather amusing."

"And if I remember correctly some were rather accurate."

Ned sighed. "Yes, I suppose they were. Poor old Mum, I admit I was unkind to her at times, but she was a good sort and without doubt had a wacky sense of humour."

"And a wacky sense of dress," said Gertie, smiling wistfully. "Those were the days, eh Ned. When your mum was around, I mean. Things were so much simpler then, and life went by at a much slower pace. I'm sure we all laughed more too, and the News wasn't anything like as gloomy as it is nowadays. Not that it's been depressing this weekend, thanks to the Jubilee. It's not just the News though, it's everything. I mean, take adverts on the telly for instance, they're so damn complex and I haven't got the foggiest idea what half of them are trying to get me to buy. Not like the days when they advertised Pepsodent. Everyone knew that was toothpaste, even the dimwits. And as for this www. business, that goes straight over my thick head."

Ned laughed. "World Wide Web, Gert. That's what it stands for, and to a point I think the Internet and all the gubbins that go with it must be rather useful. But I agree with you; life was much better when things were less complicated and I'm sure we had more fun because of it."

Gertie patted Ned's hand. "You know, sometimes I think the youngsters today don't even realise that we were young once. And I have to admit it's pretty hard to believe it myself when I look in the mirror. But we were young, weren't we, Ned? And we had dreams, hopes and aspirations, just like they do today."

"You're getting philosophical, Gert."

"Am I? Well, that must be a first."

"Don't belittle yourself, Gert. You're no mug."

She laughed.

"Anyway," said Ned, watching as the local band set up amplification on the stage, "are you looking forward to seeing the pop groups?"

She chuckled. "I think you'll find today they call them bands, and yes, to tell you the truth, I am looking forward to them. Percy always said the music of today was rubbish compared with what we had in our day and I daresay a lot of it is. But I still like to have a jig around and get my old feet tapping and as my hearing's not what it was, I doubt it'll be too loud."

"Hmm, I think tolerance of youth regarding music must be a female thing then, because your sentiments are much like Stella's were, and mine much like Percy's. Having said that, I'm all for anyone having a go, and Danny was a gifted bass guitarist back in his day, so perhaps this young group of his will be talented and do him proud."

Gertie nodded. "I'm looking forward to hearing Polly Jolly too. I know she can be a bit crude at times but then most comics are these days, aren't they? Not that I mind too much, because I've never actually been what you might call refined."

Ned took her hand and squeezed it tightly. "You've always been politeness personified to me, Gert. And I'll knock the stuffing out of anyone who says anything to the contrary."

Gertie threw back her head and laughed. It was good to hear him being frivolous. "Fancy an ice cream, Ned? I could eat one and if I leave it too long they'll most likely be sold out."

Ned rose. "I'll get one for you, Gert. I couldn't eat one myself. Still full from tea, but I'll get you one."

"No, you won't," said Gertie, indicating he was to sit back down, "you're to rest, doctor's orders, and it's a fair old stroll to the ice cream stall."

Ned grinned. He knew it was no use arguing. "Alright, you win. But at least let me pay for it."

Chapter Fourteen

When the last of the plants, flowers and vegetables on the produce stall Anne and Susan had run for the Church funds, were finally sold, the ladies cleared away the rubbish into black plastic bags and tossed them into large wheelie bins secreted in the Hotel's walled vegetable garden. They then dismantled the trestle table, placed it in an outhouse near to the old stable block, now converted into accommodation for seasonal hotel staff, and then went to the beer tent for a much deserved drink. For as Committee members they had contributed much to the celebratory event and both were delighted by the way the day had so far gone.

In the tent they me Jill Roberts and Elizabeth, likewise taking their first alcoholic beverage since clearing away the leftovers and debris from the tea party.

"Cheers," said Elizabeth, raising a glass to her sister and friends, once all had a drink in hand, "let's hope the evening is as successful as the day has been so far."

Four glasses chinked and four voices shouted, "Cheers," after which they went outside and sat on a picnic bench in the sunshine.

"I'm surprised and delighted by the number of strangers here," said Elizabeth, "I expected most people to be local."

Susan nodded. "I thought the same and I'm so glad the Committee decided to open up the event and advertise. The modest entry fee charged for non-locals must have helped the funds loads."

"It has," said Anne, "I was talking to Jamie about it yesterday. Tickets have sold well this last couple of days. Having said that, you'll find some of the strangers here are actually Hotel guests who of course didn't have to pay. The group over by the stage certainly are, and so are the young couple looking at Trish's jewellery."

"You mean Trish's trash," laughed Susan, "I bought some earrings from her at the car boot sale in Rosudgeon a few weeks back and they fell to bits the first time I wore them."

"Did they?" said Anne, touching a row of delicate silver stars dangling from a chain around her neck, "I bought this necklace from her last year and it's been marvellous. I've worn it lots too and it looks as good now as the day I bought it."

"Really," said Susan, clearly surprised, "Do you mind me asking how much you paid for it?"

Anne shook her head. "Of course not, it was fourteen ninety nine and worth every penny."

"Ah, perhaps that explains it then, my earrings were only ninety nine pence and so not the bargain I thought."

"Just goes to show," said Elizabeth, foraging in her handbag for a tissue, "you get what you pay for."

"Changing the subject, does anyone know who that bloke is over there?" asked Jill, subtly pointing towards a tall, shaven headed man wearing a long black raincoat and sunglasses, "he looks shifty and appears to be all on his own."

"I spotted him earlier," said Anne, glancing towards the person in question. "He was watching Abigail Armstrong while she was talking to the chaps who were setting up the stage."

"Was he? Well whoever he is," said Susan, wrinkling her nose, "he's obviously a pessimist."

Anne frowned. "Whatever makes you say that?"

"The coat. He's dressed for rain."

"Ah, but he's also wearing sunglasses," smiled Jill, "so he can't be that much of a pessimist."

"Hmm, you're right," said Susan with a scowl, "then he must be a spy."

"A spy," Jill roared.

"Yes," said Susan, tilting back her head and draining her glass. "He'll be a spy: probably Russian."

Elizabeth giggled and brushed a stray strand of hair from her face. "Right, Sue, so why would a Russian spy be here in Trengillion?"

"I don't know, but we'd better keep an eye on him because I reckon before long someone will pass him confidential information: Government secrets or something like that."

The stranger, as though he knew his character was being scrutinised, disappeared into the beer tent. Seeing him go, Elizabeth picked up Susan's empty glass and sniffed it. "The wine you're drinking must be stronger than it says on the bottle, Sue. Either that or your glass has been laced with loopy juice."

Susan stood up. "Well, whatever it is, I think it's going down rather well. Is anyone else ready for another? My round."

Three empty glasses were rapidly placed on the table in front of her.

In the beer tent, Wayne Tilley was keeping a watchful eye out for his idol, Polly Jolly. He knew she was around somewhere because her agent, Abigail Armstrong, was talking to Sandy, who was at the makeshift bar buying his wife, Windflower, a white wine spritzer. Knowing Polly would most likely join Abigail when she did put in an appearance, Wayne decided to amble casually over in Abigail and Sandy's direction to eavesdrop on their conversation ready to make a contribution to the dialogue should the opportunity arise.

"How much longer is Windflower intending to read the Cards?" Abigail asked Sandy as he dropped change from the drink into the pocket of his jeans.

Sandy shrugged his shoulders. "I don't know, darling. I expect she'll carry on until the queue disappears, she hates letting people down."

Abigail was aghast. "But she'll miss all the entertainment if she doesn't soon call it a day."

"That's what I said, but she won't listen to me and she looks dead beat."

Abigail took the spritzer from Sandy's hand. "Here, let me see if I can make her see sense. I have the knack when it comes to handling entertainers."

To Wayne's dismay Abigail left the tent, glass in hand, and Sandy, after giving him a cursory nod, crossed the tent to where fellow campers from Home Farm were sitting on bales of straw chatting to Morgana.

Feeling dejected, Wayne sat down on an unturned empty crate and surveyed the few people inside the beer tent. Most were strangers in groups, families or couples. He looked to see if there were any unattached females and to his relief saw there were not. Wayne did not oppose the notion of a girlfriend, he just didn't want to be in the situation where he would have to do any wooing. He knew it wasn't his strong point and if he were honest, he would rather have his hair dyed than be faced with chatting up a potential sweetheart, unless of course it was Polly Jolly.

Wayne turned around and looked to the back of the tent. In the corner sat a man, also alone. He was tall, had a shaven head, wore a long black raincoat, and on top of his bald head rested a pair of expensive looking sunglasses. Wayne watched the lone man with interest. He was writing something in a notebook, apparently oblivious of the goings-on around him. Wayne wondered who he was, what he was writing and what he was drinking. Suddenly the man rose, stuffed the notebook into his pocket and asked Justin for a G and T. Wayne grinned, at least one of his three questions was answered. With glass in hand the stranger then went outside. Instinctively Wayne picked up his pint and followed, feeling something was amiss. But the stranger did nothing untoward. He ambled out into the sunshine and sat on a bench where he watched the children's puppet show.

Shortly after six, light clouds began to accumulate in the early evening sky over Trengillion and the sun lost its cheerful brightness. But the wind remained light, leaving it still pleasant enough to sit outside, even for older members of the community who had been issued with the much welcomed blankets.

Trish Tilley, disillusioned by Swampy who seemed more interested in drinking with Maurice the Chef than paying her any attention, wondered what Sandy was doing. She thought it was unlikely he was aiding his wife with her Card reading, therefore it might be worth her while tracking him down. After all, in the Jolly Sailor he had pinched her bottom and earlier he had winked at her so the chemistry between them had to be good. She sighed. She meant no harm and had no desire to wreck his marriage; all she wanted was his company, to hear a few flattering comments and to feel he thought she was worthy of his attention. Optimistically, she packed away the jewellery into three cases hidden beneath the table and removed the velvet cloth on which she had displayed her wares. She then went to her van parked at the front of the Hotel and tossed everything inside. Glad the day's work was done, she wandered back towards the beer tent where she had last seen Sandy. To her dismay he was not there, but rather than waste the visit she bought herself a vodka and Coke and then went back outside to look for him. To her utter disgust she spotted him talking to Abigail outside the gypsy-style caravan. Cursing, she tossed her head, but despite the quick jolt, her lank, listless hair remained unruffled, foiling the dramatic effect intended. Feeling rebuffed she walked to the stage area where rows of seating were rapidly filling.

By half past six, all the stalls were cleared away ready for the evening's entertainment. It began promptly with a performance by the local band, who cleverly sang songs to suit all ages and tastes and expertly finished their act with the song they had written specially for the occasion in honour of the Queen. And because of its catchy, clever refrain, which band members encouraged the audience to sing along with, it was a huge success and won a rapturous round of applause.

After a short break, allowing partygoers time to refill their glasses and stretch their legs, early fifties music played over loud speakers to keep up the celebratory spirit. When all were seated once more, Polly Jolly, wearing her lucky scarf, black skinny jeans and a flowy, chiffon top, took her place on the stage and within minutes had the audience in hysterics. Wayne, who made sure he had a seat on the front row, clapped, whistled and cheered throughout her act, thoroughly beguiled by her every word: his face locked in a constant, lascivious grin.

After Polly finished her performance to a round of euphoric applause and a standing ovation, she was eagerly met by Ollie who handed her a large glass of Chablis. As he took her hand, Abigail appeared from the sidelines and heartily congratulated Polly. She then went into the beer tent to refill her empty pint glass in order to leave the two lovebirds alone.

Polly, feeling warm and clammy after her act, asked Ollie if they might walk through the gardens and find somewhere quiet to sit. They found a bench dwarfed by a magnificent rhododendron laden with deep purple blooms. Polly sat and took in several deep breathes, for although the evening was not hot, nerves and anxiety always raised her temperature and made her legs feel jelly-like, after which it took a while for her to wind down and relax.

On the stage, Morris dancers had now taken up their positions to entertain for a short period, prior to a conjurer and then the highlight of the evening, a performance by The Discordant Dukes.

There seemed little enthusiasm at first for the eight Morris dancers as everyone's ears were still ringing with the catchy song by the local band and the hilarity of Polly Jolly's wit. However, when the Morris men began to dance and the bells on their shins tinkled and rang along with the accompaniment of a tuneful accordion, attention was quickly gained and some of the audience stood and clapped in time to the music. And by the time the dancers had finished jigging, waving their white handkerchiefs and rhythmically clattering their wooden sticks, nearly all onlooker's feet were tapping.

When she entered the beer tent for her refill, Abigail found Windflower and Sandy already there ordering drinks.

Abigail raised her eyebrows. "Did you not see Polly's performance?"

Sandy nodded, as Morgana handed him a bottle of Guinness. "Yes, we stood at the back because all the seats were taken."

"She was very funny," said Windflower, stifling a yawn, "I'm dead chuffed to have seen her perform live, and I shall keep a look out now to see when she's next on the television."

"That's nice, it's always good to get positive feedback. Did she meet with your approval, Sandy?"

He nodded. "Yes, sweetheart, I was very impressed. She's a very talented young lady with a glowing future ahead of her."

Windflower rubbed her eyes.

"Oh dear, you still look awfully tired," Abigail commented, noting dark shadows beneath Windflower's eyes, "I hope you've not over exerted yourself."

Windflower stifled a second yawn. "Yes, I must admit, I am rather tired and I suppose I may have overdone it today. Reading the Cards takes a lot of concentration, and now I've stopped I feel absolutely shattered. I don't think I've ever done so many people in one day."

Sandy stroked her hand. "Why don't you go and get a bit of shuteye, love? Forty winks will do you the power of good and recharge your batteries."

She sighed. “I would, but I don’t want to miss the other band, The Discordant Dukes. Everyone’s talking about them.”

“Take a nap and I’ll wake you. They’re not due on for a while yet.”

“Are you sure?”

Abigail said, “They’re due on at eight. After the Morris dancers and the conjurer there will be a short break during which the Discordant Dukes can set up their gear, and then, I’m told, someone’s going to make a speech before the band.”

Sandy groaned. “I hate speeches. Who’s making it?”

Abigail shook her head. “No idea, one of the Committee, I suppose.”

Windflower paused for thought. “I wonder why Polly Jolly’s act was so early in the evening. I mean, I should have thought someone as famous as she is would be near to, or top of the bill.”

Abigail smiled sweetly. “She was going to be but then asked for an early spot. She suffers badly with nerves, you see, and apart from that I think she was keen to get it over and done with so that she could relax and spend some time with young Ollie.”

Windflower yawned again. “I see.” She drained her glass and laid it down on an upturned beer crate. “Right, I shall be off then, but please don’t forget to wake me, Sandy: half an hour will be enough to refresh me and I daresay I’ll be out like a light the minute my head hits the pillow.”

Sandy leaned forward and kissed her cheek. “Of course not, sweetheart. Sleep tight.”

Chapter Fifteen

In London, Tally and Jim seated high on the stands surrounding the Queen Victoria memorial, soaked up the atmosphere, eagerly anticipating the huge event unfurling before their eyes. Above, the early evening sky was a rich shade of blue; its colour broken only by infrequent wispy, white clouds, chivied along by a gentle breeze.

At half past seven, as the bright golden sun shone through the trees in the Mall casting long shadows over the crowd, the concert began with Robbie Williams singing a lively version of 'Let Me Entertain You', backed by the melodious brass instruments of the Band of the Cold Stream Guard. Next came will.i.am and Jessie J. who were succeeded by boy band JLS. Gary Barlow and Cheryl Cole then sang a duet, and were duly followed by living legend, Sir Cliff Richard.

From her handbag, Tally took out a bag of Everton mints. She prodded Jim's hand and whispered, "Would you like one?"

Jim looked at her quizzically. "Do you ever stop eating, Tally?"

She giggled. "Of course, but I fancied something minty because my mouth feels in need of freshening up after all the delicious flavours we had earlier. Were I at home I would of course have cleaned my teeth."

Jim took a mint. "Good point," he said, and leaned back to enjoy the rest of the Concert's line-up which included, pianist Lang Lang, Alfie Boe, and Jools Holland who sang with Ruby Turner. They were followed by Grace Jones who skilfully sang whilst spinning a hula hoop around her waist. Next to preform were Ed Sheeran, Annie Lennox and Renee Fleming.

As Tom Jones sang two of his greatest hits, Tally dreamily gazed up at the sky. The foliage covering the avenue of trees which ran along either side of the Mall, glowed a beautiful rich green, pleasingly tinged with gold due to the perfect evening sunlight. She nudged Jim's arm. "Look at the trees, Jim, aren't they beautiful? And look at the enormous crowds below, I really can't believe I'm here."

Jim agreed. The area around the stage and the Queen Victoria Memorial was a sea of Union flags and all along the Mall, as far as the eye could see, crowds of enthusiasts, eager to hear and see the Concert, had their vision aided by huge television screens sporadically placed on either side of the wide road amongst the trees.

The Queen, who was not present when the Concert began, subtly arrived mid-way after the performance by Tom Jones. She was escorted to her seat by Prince Charles and his wife, the Duchess of Cornwall. Prince Philip was not with her, for earlier in the day, Buckingham Palace had announced that the Duke was in hospital with a bladder infection and was to remain there for several days.

The Concert continued after the Queen's entrance. Gary Barlow and The Commonwealth Band, with Gareth Malone and the Military Wives' Choir, sang a song specially written by Gary Barlow and Andrew Lloyd Webber for the Diamond Jubilee. Shirley Bassey followed with one of her greatest hits, the theme tune to the James Bond film, 'Diamonds are Forever', and then Kylie Minogue sang a medley of her hits.

After Kylie the spotlight moved away from the stage to a small balcony on the front of Buckingham Palace, where Alfie Boe and Renee Fleming sang 'Somewhere' from *West Side Story.* Tally gasped in awe, moved, mesmerised, as coloured lights flashed across the front of the Palace, projecting quivering flowers onto the building. She clutched Jim's arm. "I've gone all goosepimply, it's just so beautiful, so spine chilling."

Back on stage, Elton John sang 'I'm still standing', 'Your Song' and 'Crocodile Rock'. Next was Rolf Harris and then Stevie Wonder who played the keyboard and sang 'Sir Duke', 'Isn't She Lovely' and 'Superstition'. But for many the most memorable performance of the evening was when Madness sang 'Our House' from the roof of Buckingham Palace, accompanied by videos projecting streets from around the country onto the front of the building. As a tribute to the Queen, the final line of 'Our House' was mischievously changed to our house, in the middle of *one's* street.

Paul McCartney was the last artiste to perform; he sang 'Magical Mystery Tour,' 'Let it Be', 'All my Loving', 'Live and Let Die' and 'Ob-La-Di, Ob-La-Da'.

After the performances of musicians whose repertoires covered the six decades of the Queen's reign, Prince Charles charmed the crowd with a folksy but heartfelt speech, after which he called for three cheers. As the cheers faded away, everyone sang the 'National Anthem', and then the Queen lit the last of four thousand two hundred beacons which stretched across the United Kingdom, the Channel Isles, Isle of Man, the Commonwealth and Overseas United Kingdom territories.

The lighting of the beacon was followed by the grand finale, a colourful firework display outside the Palace, accompanied by patriotic songs.

Tally and Jim sang stridently and cheered loudly and heartily, along with the rest of the seated audience and the crowd gathered along the Mall. It was breath-taking and draining but everyone seemed determined to give it every last bit of energy.

Afterwards, Tally, enthralled by the speech, the fireworks and the atmosphere, raised her phone and took more pictures to capture the moment. As she lowered it she realised the battery was very low.

"Damn," she muttered to Jim, in hushed but angry tones, "I knew I'd forget something. I've not brought my phone charger with me. It's still plugged in the silly socket by my bed. Why on earth didn't I put it in my bag when I unplugged it this morning? What a loser."

Jim laughed. "Oh dear, I expect you'll be lost now then. No texts, no tweets, no Facebook and no calls. Poor you."

Tally scowled. "Hmm, but I suppose I can always borrow yours if I feel I must get in touch with home."

Jim shook his head. "I'm afraid not. I haven't brought it with me."

"What!" Tally's face dropped, "why ever not?"

"I didn't have much credit left and as I'd not got round to topping it up I decided to leave it at home."

"You numpty, do you mean to tell me you're on Pay-as-you-go? That's just so old-hat."

"Yes, I am because I only use my mobile to send texts. I much prefer to use the good old landline for calls, you see."

"Humph. Well, the good old land line's not much good to you when you're three hundred miles away from home, is it?"

Jim gave Tally an unexpected hug. "You look really pretty when you're angry," he laughed, "but if you really feel the need to ring home then we'll find a good, reliable, old-hat phone box. Meanwhile, let's go and find a pub, because I could murder a beer."

On the stage behind the Penwynton Hotel, as the crowds patiently waited, preparations were being finalised for the much talked about performance by the Discordant Dukes. Sandy, realising their appearance was imminent, walked briskly to the gypsy-style caravan where his wife lay sleeping. He attempted to wake her by calling her name but she did not rouse. He shook her gently but her breathing was deep and she did not respond. Feeling it would be cruel to use unnecessary force, he decided to leave her sleeping and to return instead to Abigail waiting outside the beer tent.

The Discordant Dukes did not disappoint the large crowd assembled around the small stage. In spite of the gathering clouds rolling in from the south west, spirits were high and the mood enthusiastic and eager. The Dukes, familiar to all for their resplendent outfits in individual colours, went one step further for the Jubilee performance. Over their shirts they wore pure silk, Union flag waistcoats, delicately smothered in tiny glittering sequins, and on their feet, black Doc Martin boots with the flag patriotically painted on the ample toecaps in florescent paint.

The band skipped through the gathering to a rapturous round of applause, determined to get the crowd on their feet and dancing along with their music. The crowd, a large number of whom had made frequent trips to the beer tent throughout the day, were not disappointed. They clapped, hooted and cheered as the Dukes leapt onto the stage and picked up their instruments. And as the first notes twanged through the cool night air a spontaneous round of rapturous cheers drowned out the first few chords and men, women and children leapt into the aisles ready to dance the night away.

Inside the Penwynton Hotel, Linda listened through the open window to the Dukes' music. She tapped her feet and jigged around, thrilled that her cousin Danny had not let her down. She wished she were out in the garden mingling with the crowds but knew her place was in the Hotel. Someone had to be on duty at all times and she had deemed it unfair to expect any of the staff to forgo the happy event.

Not that there was much to do in the Hotel. Most guests were outside enjoying the entertainment and they had purposely closed the Hotel bar so everyone would patronise the beer tent.

Standing at the back behind the audience watching the Discordant Dukes, Swampy and Maurice the Chef, with lager bottles in hands, stood arms around each other's shoulders, swaying, not so much in time to the music but more as a way of providing mutual support to enable each other to remain standing.

"I'm gonna miss you, buddy," slurred Maurice, taking a swig from the nearly empty bottle, "Not many blokes can drink as much as you and me and remain standing. You're a star."

Swampy attempted to reply but his words were lost in a series of rapid hiccups.

"You need another drink," said Maurice, convinced Swampy's nearly full bottle was empty, "it'll cure the hiccups. Come on, let's go and see Justin and Morgana."

Justin and Morgana were both standing outside the empty beer tent listening to the music when the two new-friends-cum-drinking-partners staggered towards them. Morgana tutted. "I thought we'd got rid of you two for a while."

Maurice held up his bottle. "I need another drink and so does Swampy."

Swampy hiccupped, raised his nearly full bottle upside-down causing the contents to splash over his flushed face.

"Jesus, it's raining," he hiccupped, tugging at Maurice's arm, "we better get inside before we get drenched."

They both lumbered through the tent entrance and fell into a heap on the down trodden grass. Justin, half amused and half cross stepped towards them with every intention of helping both to their feet, but neither was ready to move. They lay, eyes closed, breathing heavily and snoring loudly. Justin carefully separated them and put scrunched up towels beneath their heads, he then went back outside to join Morgana and enjoy the music.

Ollie and Polly, having finished their drinks, left the garden shortly after the Discordant Dukes began to play, not because they disliked their music, but because it made conversation difficult and they wanted to be alone. Besides, they knew it would still be audible anywhere in the Hotel's grounds. Arm in arm they walked down towards the pond and the pergolas, part-built, Ollie told Polly, by his father, John, many years before.

The evening was calm with just enough breeze to cause Polly's lucky scarf to flutter softly around her slender neck. When they reached the grass bank beyond the pond, they stopped and sat down on newly created steps which led into the Hotel's wild flower meadow.

"What a beautiful spot," said Polly, who had not seen the meadow before, "I love wild flowers, they're so much more natural than cultivated ones, less showy, more innocent."

"I suppose that's why you like your lucky scarf."

Polly lifted the end of her scarf and rested it on the back of her hand. "I've always been very fond of poppies, probably because it was my mother's name. I consider Windflower to be a lovely name too. In fact I think flower names ought to be more popular than they are."

"Hmm," grunted Ollie.

Polly let the scarf drop and linked her arm through Ollie's; she rested her head on his shoulder and stroked the sleeve of his shirt. "You seem a little sad, Ollie. I hope you're not still brooding over that silly Tarot reading."

Ollie half smiled. "That, and the fact that you're going tomorrow. The combination of the two isn't exactly a recipe for happiness."

"Nor should either justify the doldrums. Come on, Ollie, there's no reason in the world why we should never see each other again and as for that Death card thing, well, you'll just have to take care, won't you? Anyway, we all have to die someday and Windflower didn't actually give any indication as to when you're likely to pop your clogs. In fact I was told she'd said it more likely meant the end of something, new beginnings and suchlike rather than you waking up dead."

Ollie frowned. "You shouldn't be flippant about death."

"Why not? It's something over which most of us have no control and you, my dear, sweet, Bob the Builder, need to lighten up a bit."

Ollie laughed. "Bob the Builder indeed. Okay, I'll lighten up and change the subject."

"Good."

"So tell me, Ms Jolly, what made you want to be a comedienne?"

Polly smiled, impishly. "With a name like mine what else could I be?"

"You mean to say, Polly Jolly is your real name?"

"Yes, so you see a sense of humour runs in the family."

Ollie laughed. "That's cool - crazy, but cool. I think you must marry me and change it to Polly Collins; that sounds so much better."

"Hmm, I suppose it is a slight improvement. Although, I *was* actually christened Pollyanna, but no-one has ever called me that in my life."

"I see, so tell me, Ms Pollyanna: is making people laugh something you want to do for the rest of my days?"

Polly shook her head. "No, because before long the material will run out and so will my enthusiasm. Besides, I won't need to work for ever. One day I'm in for quite a considerable amount of money, you see. Not that I look forward to that day because it will mean poor, dear Uncle Geoff will be no more."

"Uncle Geoff?" Ollie queried.

"Uncle Geoff is my uncle. Well, I suppose that's pretty obvious. He and my mother were twins and very close. For that reason Uncle Geoff and I have always been close too. Mum died a couple of years back. Poor soul, she was only fifty nine, and because Uncle Geoff never married or had children, he made me his sole heir, and that must have been about twenty years ago. When he made the will, I mean."

"I see," said Ollie, thoughtfully, "I take it he's loaded then."

Polly nodded. "He made his money in property. You know, buying old places, doing them up and selling them for a good profit. He started back in the early sixties when property was relatively cheap, so I'm told. At times he owned whole rows of houses."

"Yes, there was money to be made in that a few years back but you'd be hard pressed to make much dosh now. But your uncle must have had money to buy his first place even if it was cheap."

Polly nodded. "He did. He inherited twelve thousand pounds from his godfather in 1961, so really he couldn't go wrong."

"Blimey! That was a fair bit of money back then. Your poor mum must have felt a bit left out."

Polly laughed. "Well, yes and no. She never was the jealous type, but I think it's because Uncle Geoff felt guilty that he named me as his heir."

"But he can't be that old, can he? If your mother was his twin."

"He's sixty one, but not a well man." Her voice softened, "He has lung cancer, Ollie. He's always been a heavy smoker, you see. Mum tried to get him to give up years ago, but he said if it was the death of him then so be it. He's in a hospice now and spends much of each day watching my DVDs. It makes me feel very humble."

"Yes, I suppose it must. And what about your father? I take it he's still alive?"

Polly smiled. "Very much so, but I don't see a great deal of him now. He has a new lady-love and they plan to marry soon. I'm glad because he was pretty cut up when Mum died." Polly smiled. "It was her dying wish that Dad should marry again, so I know she would approve."

Across the field the mellow sound of a saxophone solo filled the night air. Simultaneously Ollie and Polly felt the first drops of rain.

"Damn, if it's going to start raining I suppose we'd better be making our way back."

Polly shook her head. "Not yet, Ollie, not yet. It's only a few spots, no more than light drizzle and it may even stop."

He felt a lump in his throat as she snuggled up close to him. He hugged her tightly and tucked her lucky scarf cosily around her neck. "Do you have to go tomorrow? Couldn't you stay just one more day?"

Polly looked up and shook her head. "As much as I'd like to stay, I know I can't. I'm due to record a one off show tomorrow night in Manchester, as Abigail keeps reminding me."

"Manchester! Christ, it couldn't be much further away, could it?"

"No, and for that reason we have to make an early start tomorrow. I won't have to drive though; Abigail will do that. She's very good."

"Hmm, I've noticed she watches over you like an old mother hen."

Polly laughed. "She has my best interest at heart and she's an absolute treasure compared with my last agent. I'll tell you about him one day. He was a domineering nightmare and I was glad to be rid of him. Thinking of him gives me the creeps."

Pulling her closer he bent to kiss her, but paused as the sound of approaching footsteps lightly struck the path surrounding the pond.

Ollie sat up straight and looked back towards the Hotel. Someone coughed. "Who's there?" he called out.

The footsteps stopped abruptly. A lone owl hooted from the trees at the foot of the meadow, and the rhythmic thud of a beating drum drifted across the Hotel gardens. But no-one answered.

Inside Rose Cottage, Ned Stanley drained the mug containing the last trickle of his drinking chocolate; he then switched off the television set with the remote control, rose from the settee and took his empty mug into the kitchen. Before locking the porch door, he stepped outside to see if it was yet raining. It was, but thankfully it appeared to be nothing more than light drizzle. Ned stepped back inside the porch, locked the door and the back door also. He then switched off the kitchen light and stifling a yawn, made his way upstairs to bed.

It had been a long but wonderful day. Had he been younger he would have stayed until festivities had ceased, but by eight o'clock he'd admitted defeat, confessing he was feeling tired and a little chilled in spite of the warm blankets. Anne, to whom he was chatting at the time, insisted on getting someone to take him home, for she was concerned he might catch a chill. Linda, who had not been drinking, obliged, while Anne looked after the Hotel. Ned was reluctant to drag Linda away, but knew it was too far for someone as frail as he to walk, and he was comforted by the knowledge she'd still be back in time to hear the much talked about band.

Once back home Ned had switched on the television. He wasn't over keen to see any of the Jubilee Concert at the Palace for he knew he was unlikely to appreciate the music on offer. Nevertheless, he watched part of it simply because it seemed the right thing to do, and there was always the chance he might catch a glimpse of his granddaughter, Tally. However, by nine o' clock, he was finding it difficult to keep his eyes open.

As Ned snuggled down beneath the lightweight feather duvet he heard the bang of the first firework from the Hotel grounds. He would have liked to have seen them, but conceded it didn't really matter; someone was bound to have captured the moment on their mobile phone or iPad, and no doubt young Clive, Jess' husband, was still taking photographs in abundance. Ned sighed as he closed his tired eyes. What a shame Stella had not lived to share the day. She would really have enjoyed the memorable, convivial, festivities, which he felt sure would be a talking point in Trengillion for many, many years to come.

It was drizzling with light rain when Nick and Jill Roberts, mellowed by the music and thrilled with the obvious success of the momentous day, pulled up the hoods on their jackets and wandered away from the main body of the gathering and down towards the pond and the meadow beyond. Behind them the last of the fireworks exploded in the darkening sky, sending glittering, red, purple and blue stars into the night where they sparkled and then faded into obscurity.

Spontaneous applause rounded off the pyrotechnic display, followed by the excited chatter of happy party goers and a raucous, noisy rendition of the 'National Anthem'.

Arm in arm, Nick and Jill approached the paved area around the pond, talking of their love for the village of which until a year ago they had never even heard. Beneath one of the rustic, wooden pergolas bearing heavy fragrant blooms, they briefly stood and breathed in the satisfying pungent scent lingering in the cool night air. By the pond, they paused to watch misty sprays rising from the fountains and to hear the pleasing sound of water as it splashed back into the pond.

In no hurry to return to the gathering around the marquee, they sat down on the surrounding wall looking for fish and admiring the huge yellow water lilies, just visible in the light from a string of dim lanterns. While from the back of the Hotel, the sound of lively voices chatting, equipment being moved and hearty laughter rang out across the Hotel grounds.

After leaving the pond, Jill and Nick agreed they must continue towards the wild flower meadow, a must-see, spectacular sight in June so they had been told, even though they knew with the darkening skies, there would be very little to see. But as they approached the steps both were suddenly aware of the tuneful melody of a mobile phone ringing nearby. Realising they were not alone, they paused to listen for voices but heard nothing until movement in the shadows caused them to stop instantaneously and momentarily freeze. At the foot of the steps, Ollie Collins, unaware of their presence, stood over the motionless body of Polly Jolly. In his hands he held her lucky scarf and lying by his feet was his ringing mobile phone. As the phone stopped ringing, Ollie suddenly bent down, picked it up and then dropped it. He sprang to his feet and breathing heavily looked down at Polly and then to the scarf in his trembling hands. In panic he fell to his knees and let out a mighty roar.

Nick ran to Polly's side. Jill followed close behind. Nick knelt, desperately feeling for a pulse, but he knew, just by looking, that Polly Jolly was dead.

Chapter Sixteen

On Tuesday morning, in the living room of Rose Cottage, Ned Stanley stared blankly at his daughter, Elizabeth, as she knelt before him on the hearth rug having conveyed the distressing news. Once again his world was falling apart.

"But I don't understand, Liz. Why would Ollie do such a thing? It's absurd. There must be some mistake."

Fighting back the tears Elizabeth took hold of her father's hands. "He was found standing over her body, Dad. No-one else was there. The murder weapon was in his hands."

"Murder weapon! But I thought you said she'd been strangled."

Elizabeth bit her bottom lip. Her teeth drew blood. "She had. She'd been strangled by the scarf she always wore. She believed it brought her luck."

Ned leaned back his head. "God forbid. Tell me I'm dreaming, Liz. What you say can't possibly be true."

"I wish it wasn't but I'm afraid it is."

"And what explanation has Ollie given to the police? Surely he hasn't confessed."

Elizabeth shook her head. "No, he hasn't. He says he doesn't know what happened. He appears to have lost his memory."

"Memory loss through trauma," said Ned, "yes, that is a possibility."

Elizabeth's eyes began to water. "Oh, Dad, what can I do? I feel so helpless. So useless, and I never thought I'd see the day when I'd not know what to say to my own sister."

"I don't know," said Ned, releasing his hands from Elizabeth's grasp. "I don't think there is anything you can do, except pray."

He rose and crossed to the window. Outside rain poured down from the heavens and the garden was shrouded with a thick swirling mist. "Does Tally know? He asked.

Elizabeth shook her head. "I don't know. I frequently tried ringing her last night but not once did she answer her phone. And so this morning I went into her room just to make sure she'd not left it behind. Regrettably, I found her phone charger still plugged into the wall, so I can only assume she has her phone but the battery's flat."

"What about Jim. Can't you ring his number?"

Elizabeth again shook her head. "I have tried. I got his number from Jess and I've tried several times, but there's no reply. I've spoken to Wills though, because she left her car at his place. So unless she sees it in a newspaper or hears someone talking about it, I guess she'll not know until poor Wills has to tell her."

"What about the hotel where they're staying."

Elizabeth sighed. "No-one knows which one it is. Justin booked it, but he can't remember its name, and he deleted the confirmation email ages ago after he'd printed off the reservation details and passed them on to Jim. I didn't bother asking Tally where she was staying because it was only for one night and I knew she'd have her mobile anyway. Poor Tally, she'll be devastated when she finds out. She, Jess, Wills and Ollie have always been so very close."

"I know," said Ned, sitting down on the arm of a chair, "I've watched them all grow up over the years. What a dreadful mess." His eyes misted over as he bowed his head. "And I can honestly say now, for the first time since she passed away, that I'm glad your poor mother isn't here. Poor, dear, Stella, I don't think she would have been able to cope with this."

On Tuesday morning, the weather was still fine and dry in London and so Tally and Jim, thoroughly enjoying their short break, decided not to go straight home to Cornwall, but to stay instead and see the Queen arrive back at Buckingham Palace after the thanksgiving service at Saint Paul's Cathedral.

They checked out of their hotel straight after an early breakfast and took the Underground to Green Park where they joined the ever increasing crowd of well-wishers who had already seen the Queen leave for the service. There was, however, quite a long wait until the return of the Royal party, who, along with other dignitaries, were to attend a lunch party at Mansion House after the service. And so with much time to spare, Tally and Jim sat on the grass beneath the trees and ate sandwiches which they had bought at an Underground station on their way to the Mall. And while eating they lapped up the thrilling party atmosphere.

Three hours later, to the peal of ringing bells, cheers and a sea of flags flying, the Queen left Mansion House along with the Duchess of Cornwall and Prince Charles, who took Prince Phillip's place in the Queen's carriage. The Duke and Duchess of Cambridge and Prince Harry followed behind in a second carriage, and as they passed Horse Guards Parade, a sixty gun salute rippled through the air. The lively crowds, energised by the salutation, roared, clapped and cheered.

At half past two, after passing Tally and Jim amongst the crowds along the Mall, the Queen and her close family arrived back at Buckingham Palace. As the gates closed, the road was opened up to allow the jubilant crowds to approach the Palace where they swarmed around the Queen Victoria memorial and pushed towards the gates, all eager to see the Royals and capture their images on phones, cameras and tablets.

No-one's enthusiasm was dampened when the first light drops of rain fell. Nor were spirits suppressed by the crush, noise and slow moving pace. Hence, when the Queen and other members of the Royal family emerged onto the balcony and took their positions for the grand finale, a tremendous roar echoed through the high-spirited crowd.

At half past three, the drone of approaching aircraft rumbled through the clouds. Everyone looked up to see *Lancasters, Hurricanes* and *Spitfires,* majestically plough their way through grey skies and drizzle, followed by the Red Arrows, streaming red, white and blue smoke, over the Palace, whilst the patriotic crowds below, furiously waved their flags.

To the delight of the multitude, the Queen and other members of the Royal family, remained on the balcony for twenty minutes, further igniting the euphoria, jubilation and unrestrained patriotism, as they roared 'Three cheers for Her Majesty' and chanted, 'Long live the Queen'. 'Rule Britannia' followed, and despite the majority seeing nothing of the Buckingham Palace balcony and the rainfall increasing, the crowds, stretching back as far as Admiralty Arch, continued to pour into the Mall, all satisfied just to be there and soak up the thrilling atmosphere.

Once the Royal party had returned indoors, Tally and Jim, caught up in the crowd, drifted into St James' Park to recover.

"I suppose we ought to be getting back," said Tally, reluctantly, "Wills and Lydia must be wondering what's happened to us. We said we'd be back by midday to pick up the car and it's gone four now."

"Nearly half past," said Jim, glancing at his watch, "but I guess they'll put two and two together and realise we've been here. Pity we couldn't ring them though. I don't know which of us is the biggest ass."

Tally laughed. "Me, I guess. After all, I'm never without my phone so I should have been more methodical."

"Hmm, well you can make up for your shortcomings by working out where we can get on the Underground. I'm just following the crowd without thinking."

"We might as well walk along Whitehall and round to Westminster and go from there. But I do wish we could stay just a little bit longer."

"Me too. I suppose we could always pop into a pub for a quick drink just to draw the day out a bit more. I must admit, I'm reluctant to go too. You might not believe this, Tally, but I think these last two days have been some of the happiest of my life."

Tally smiled and linked her arm with his. "Ditto," she said.

Clientèle of the Jolly Sailor had never before sat looking as glum as they did at lunchtime on Tuesday, nor was conversation ever as subdued. Morgana, having attempted to watch a little of the Queen's thanksgiving service on the television, had found her concentration non-existent, her mind continually drifting elsewhere. And Justin couldn't even bear to look at the television, for he knew somewhere in the City was Tally who probably knew nothing of the trouble looming over Trengillion.

In the kitchen, Maurice nursing a very sore head, attempted to prepare lunch for the few people who had appetite to eat. And in Justin and Morgana's living room, Swampy, having just arisen, folded his make-shift bedding and collected together his belongings which he stuffed into his large rucksack. He then went to the kitchen to make a large mug of sweet, black coffee.

Maurice looked up as the kitchen door opened, hoping it was not another order for food. He attempted to smile when he saw Swampy but found using any facial muscles made the headache worse.

"Do I look as bad as you?" Swampy asked, filling the kettle.

Maurice nodded his head. "Probably worse. Make one for me while you're there, and grab me a couple of paracetamol, please. They're in the drawer by the phone."

Swampy took the box of tablets from the drawer, withdrew two for himself and threw the rest to Maurice who failed to catch them. Maurice swore, for the pain intensified dramatically as he bent to pick up the box.

Morgana entered the kitchen to take the meals Maurice had prepared to the waiting customers. She smiled sympathetically at the two hung-over men but did not convey her condolences verbally.

"Will you be alright to drive?" Maurice asked, as Swampy sat on a stool after Morgana's departure. "You look pretty peaky to me."

"I'm not intending to go for a while yet. But I should be alright soon, I think. Justin brought me a coffee this morning while I was still on his settee and he said we stopped drinking shortly after eight. I just wish I could remember. I'm told we both fell asleep on the floor of the beer tent. I mean, how shameful is that?"

Maurice laughed. "I've fallen asleep in far worse places than that, but let's not go down that path."

Swampy groaned. "So, what do you make of last night's tragedy? I can't believe we missed it all. Justin said the police didn't even attempt to question us. They must have thought us a right couple of losers."

"Yep, and so we were. What a mess. Poor Ollie."

"Poor Ollie? But then I don't know the guy. And I'd never even heard of Polly Jolly 'til I got over here."

"I know Ollie quite well and he's alright. He's the quiet, gentle sort. I've never known him lose his temper or fall out with anyone. I've never even seen him legless. And from what I've heard it makes no sense whatsoever because they say he was caught red-handed."

Swampy shook his head. "They say the quiet ones are often the worst, Mo, but let's hope it's all some ghastly cock-up."

Maurice looked up as Morgana entered the kitchen with another order for food. "I'm with you there, mate, but I think it'll take some sort of mastermind to come up with a feasible theory regarding this disaster. And it bothers me that Ollie claiming to have no memory of last night's happening, might be construed by the powers that be, as the oldest trick in the book."

Swampy whistled through his breath. "Jesus! I didn't realise that was the case."

Maurice read the food order and then sighed. "I feel ever so sorry for Tally. She's such a nice kid. And she'll be dreadfully upset."

"Tally," said Swampy, "are she and Ollie friends then?"

Maurice shook his head. "They're closer than that, they're cousins."

Chapter Seventeen

After walking for a while, Tally and Jim found a pub near Trafalgar Square and went inside. It was packed with nowhere to sit and standing conditions were very cramped. But the atmosphere was electric with everyone talking of the weekend's activities and telling of their favourite moments and events.

Jim bought a pint of cider for himself and a small white wine for Tally; she would have liked a large one but knew it would be very foolhardy as she had to drive home. With drinks in hands they drifted into a corner and stood near to a television set hanging from the wall. It was on the BBC News channel and subtitles ran beneath footage of the Queen and other members of the Royal family on the balcony of Buckingham Palace. Tally and Jim watched. It seemed bizarre to think they had just witnessed that very memorable historic event, the recording of which would be viewed for many years to come.

After covering the Jubilee, the screen returned to newsreaders in the studio. Jim turned away and took a sip of his cider. Tally began to turn but then something on the screen caught her eye. She frowned. The image looked surprisingly familiar. She gasped. To her utter amazement the scene on the screen was, without doubt, Trengillion. Mystified, she stared, puzzled by the presence of television crews and the world's media who were standing, of all places, by the gates of her aunt and uncle's house, the Old Vicarage. Intrigued, she eagerly read the subtitles. The colour drained from her face. She reached out, desperately fumbling for Jim's arm. Her eyes transfixed on the screen. Jim read the subtitles. *Cornish builder, Oliver Collins, has been arrested for the brutal murder of much loved comedienne, Polly Jolly*. Before he had time to respond, Tally had fainted and lay in a crumpled heap by his feet.

Inside the Old Vicarage, Anne wept and could not be comforted. John, seated by her side, was dumfounded and still in a state of shock. Outside TV crews and the world's media were gathering by the gates at the top of their driveway; some were even waiting in the recreation field at the back of the house, ready to pounce should Anne or John try and leave the house through the gap in the garden's hedge. In the hallway, the phone was unplugged at the wall, for the only calls Anne and John were prepared to take were via mobiles, the numbers of which were not known outside their circle of family and friends.

Inside her home in Coronation Terrace, Jess, stared at the kitchen wall; her reaction to the arrest of her brother was anger. Anger, because she knew there was no way dear Ollie would take anyone's life, and especially that of someone of whom he was obviously fond, therefore he must have been framed. The question was how, why, and more importantly, by whom?

Jess rose to her feet, dried her red eyes and blew her nose. She then made two phone calls before going into the sitting room where Clive was sitting on the floor trying to explain to Florence why everything was topsy-turvy and Mummy kept crying.

"I'm going to open up the Pickled Egg," Jess announced, head held high.

"What! Are you mad, sweetheart? You'll be torn to shreds by the media."

Jess stood up straight. "Ollie is innocent. He was framed. I shall work, and while I'm working I shall think, and scheme, and work out a way of getting to the bottom of this fiasco."

Clive rose to his feet. "I admire your spirit, Jess, but please don't. The café will be inundated by nosy busybodies. It's foolhardy. You'll not be able to cope."

"I shall because I won't be alone. Janet and Val are going to join me. Between us we'll manage really well. Please don't try and stop me, Clive. I have to go. In a way opening up the café will prove my faith in Ollie. Prove we, as a family, have nothing to hide. Nothing to be ashamed of."

Clive put his arms lovingly around his wife's shoulders. "I respect your loyalty, Jess. I really do. And I understand the reason for your devotion. But the evidence looks pretty cut and dried to me. I mean, how could Ollie have been framed when he was caught red-handed?"

Jess pulled away from Clive and looked at him in astonishment. "I can't believe you just said that. Of course he's innocent. He's as innocent as I am and I shall do everything in my power to prove him so."

Jess stormed from the room without looking back, and when she left the house she slammed the door shut with such force it caused the mirror in the hall to fall and smash into hundreds of tiny fragments.

The gardens at the back of the Penwynton Hotel were cordoned off and several police cars stood on the front driveway. Inside and out police officers took statements from guests while the forensic team searched for evidence.

Linda, still in a state of shock and exhausted after a sleepless night, made coffee and tea to order. She needed to keep herself occupied, needed to drive the previous evening's tragic events from her mind. But it was not possible. The reality returned to her again and again and would not be banished.

As she returned to the kitchen with a tray of empty mugs, Danny appeared, his face pale, his chin stubbly, for he had not shaved. He didn't speak, but as Linda placed the tray on a stainless steel surface, he moved towards her, took her in his arms and hugged her tightly. Neither spoke until Jamie appeared; he had just been interviewed by the police for a second time.

"I can't get Anne's face out of my mind," said Danny, his voice breaking with emotion. "I can see her anguish, her pain, I can still hear her screaming. How cruel that such a wonderful event should end in such mindless, pointless tragedy. It just doesn't make sense."

Jamie patted Danny's back. "I'm as baffled as you, Dan. We all are. Christ, I can't see us ever getting over this. I can't see Trengillion ever recovering."

"How are the Dukes?" Linda asked, placing each mug in the dishwasher.

"Pretty shocked," said Danny, "they're only kids, and they've taken it pretty badly. Duke Red was crying a while back and he's the one who usually acts the tough guy. Poor Polly. She was really nice. The Dukes and me had a nice long chat with her and Abby before last night's gig."

"And poor Abby," said Jamie, sympathetically, "she must be feeling dreadful."

"As are we all," said Linda, "I can't believe there is anyone in Trengillion who is feeling anything but shell-shocked this morning."

Around the village police made house to house enquiries, hoping someone might have seen or heard something suspicious the previous evening. For although they were convinced they had the right man regarding the murder of Polly Jolly, they were unable to come up with a feasible motive, hence it was imperative no stone be left unturned. Furthermore, they were aware the couple had only known each other for a few days, but this favourable fact, they concluded, was negated by Oliver Collins' dubious claim of memory loss.

The sun came out and the dull sky brightened as the police reached Coronation Terrace in the early afternoon. At Number Four, they found Trish Tilley eager to talk and suggest they question Windflower, for she had, after all, read the Tarot cards for Ollie and upturned the Death card. "What's more," she told them, "he was very sullen afterwards." The police, desperate to follow up any leads, went to Home Farm after they had finished visiting houses in the village. However, when they reached the farm they found Windflower and Sandy had already left.

"I'm afraid you've missed them," said Farmer, David Pascoe. "They went several hours ago. Judith, my wife, said they called at the house before they went, to buy some eggs and thank us for our hospitality. Poor Windflower was pretty upset apparently by the goings on last night because of the Card reading she did for young Ollie. Judith said the poor woman felt really guilty, but she told her not to be so daft."

The police officer nodded. "It's because of the Card reading that we wanted to question her. Our records show one of our officers spoke to her briefly last night but we didn't know of the Card reading then."

David shrugged his shoulders. "I would imagine it's of very little consequence anyway. I mean to say, that sort of stuff has gotta be nonsense, hasn't it? I'd be more likely to believe tealeaves or a crystal ball than I would a pack of cards."

The police officer nodded, but felt it would be inappropriate to agree verbally.

Sandy and Windflower pulled off the motorway near Exeter for a break. Windflower was feeling light headed, miserable, tearful and faint.

"I said you should have had breakfast before we left," scolded Sandy, looking for a place to park, "you ate very little yesterday, yet worked practically all day." He glanced sideways to look at her. "Christ, Sweetheart, there's more colour in that damn white van over there, than there is in your pretty little face."

Windflower smiled, weakly. "The lack of colour is probably due to very little make-up. Anyway, reading the Cards is hardly strenuous work, not physical work anyway, and I ate more than sufficient to keep my brain active."

"Humph."

Windflower leaned towards her husband and pecked his cheek. "Anyway, I expect you're more than ready for something else to eat. Your stomach seems to be a bottomless pit. What's more you ought to take a break: you've been driving for three hours already."

Sandy parked the car and caravan beside a glistening, silver Audi. The owner of the Audi, a tall, bald headed man wearing a black raincoat and sunglasses, looked askance at the aged, rusty, mud-splattered, Zephyr Six, as he retrieved a package from the boot of his gleaming car.

"She's a beauty, ain't she?" said Sandy, lovingly patting the Zephyr's roof, as he locked the driver's door."

The Audi driver's eyebrows rose, and making no verbal response, he closed the boot of his car and walked off towards the service station cafe.

Chapter Eighteen

After coming round in the London pub, Tally was taken to a back room by a concerned member of staff who insisted she had a brandy to bring back colour to her otherwise ashen face. Once colour was restored and she was able to stand, Jim thanked the kind barmaid for her hospitality and then holding Tally firmly round the waist, took her by Underground back to her brother's house in Hammersmith.

To Jim's relief, Wills and Lydia were wonderful, thoughtful, level-headed and of course concerned. They wanted Tally and Jim to stay overnight to enable Tally to get over the initial shock, but she refused; she wanted to get home as soon as possible. Wills was alarmed. He thought it very unwise for she was in no fit state to drive, hence he was much relieved when Jim said that he would drive all the way home.

Jim and Tally arrived back in Trengillion just before eleven o'clock that night, as persistent rain fell from the dark and gloomy sky. Greg and Elizabeth were still up and so Jim was able to leave Tally in the safe hands of her parents. He then walked home to Ebenezer House, after declining a lift from Greg; for he welcomed the opportunity to be outdoors despite the relentless drizzle.

Wednesday, June the sixth, dawned dull and damp. The long Bank Holiday weekend was over. The drizzle which descended from the gloomy grey skies continued until breakfast, and then the sun finally broke through the thick clouds and the damp roads dried up in the light easterly winds.

All too soon it was time for everything to get back to normal, and over much of the country, it did. But in Trengillion, life as it had been before the Jubilee celebrations had changed, possibly forever. The unwelcome presence of the media, the loss of a much loved comedienne and the arrest of a well-respected local lad, pushed all sense of reason, understanding and purpose to the outer limits. But for all the evidence against Ollie Collins, there was not one person in

Trengillion who genuinely believed it was as straightforward as the evidence suggested.

After a very poor night's sleep, Tally, who had heard on her return, a rundown of Monday evening's events from both of her parents, decided to walk down to the village to talk to Nick and Jill Roberts. She knew it was unlikely they would be able to add anything to that which she had already heard, but nevertheless deemed the horrendous, nightmarish incident might make more sense if she were to hear an appraisal from someone outside the family. She found only Jill at home. Nick apparently, had gone for a walk because he wanted to be alone.

Jill smiled sweetly as she offered Tally a chair. "He's rather cut up by all this," she said. "Poor Nick. I mean, he thought he'd left death and so forth behind. He witnessed some terrible things during his many years in the Force and all this has brought back bad memories. He always felt sorry for the families, you see, the blameless families of people arrested, that is. It always seems to be the innocent who suffer in cases such as this. Not that I believe Ollie is in any way guilty of taking poor Polly's life."

"Oh, I'm sorry," said Tally, still standing, "perhaps I'd better go before he returns."

Jill shook her head and held out her hands. "No, no, please stay. He's only just gone so won't be back for a while yet. I daresay he'll go up to the old mine: he likes it there. Would you like a coffee?"

"Only if you're having one."

"Actually, I was just about to do just that. Black, white, sugar?"

"White with no sugar, please."

"Same as me. So how are you coping? Please sit down. I feel so deeply, deeply sorry for you all."

Tally sat as Jill filled the kettle with water. "I still feel in a daze. And I feel so guilty because I wasn't here. Jim and I didn't know anything at all until yesterday afternoon. Of all things we saw it on a television inside a pub. My phone was dead, you see, because stupidly I'd forgotten to take my charger, and Jim hadn't even taken his phone. I can't believe I was so incredibly happy when everyone here was so miserable and sad. I should have known something was wrong. I shouldn't have gone in the first place. I feel as though I'm in some horrible nightmare."

Jill sat down while the kettle boiled. "You mustn't feel guilty, Tally. You couldn't possibly have known. None of us could. And if you had been here, then I'm sure the outcome would still have been the same. Oh dear, this must be awful for you, and what a horrible way to end, what I guess, must have been a brilliant couple of days."

Tally nodded. "It was, it was, and now I can only think of it with bitter remorse. And you, Jill, it must be dreadful for you as well, because you and Nick knew Polly prior to her visit here."

"Yes, yes, we did, and she was a very sweet, kind hearted person. That's why I was confident she'd take part in the Jubilee celebrations. She was the sort that would never hesitate to do someone a favour."

Jill stood as the kettle boiled. She then made the coffee.

Tally watched. "I'm glad she didn't have a husband or children, because it'd be even worse if she left behind a close family to mourn. Having said that, I suppose she still has living parents, because she wasn't that old, was she?"

Jill put the coffee mugs on the table and once again sat. "Her father is still living. Very much so, in fact, and he is about to remarry. Polly was telling me so in the pub the other night. Sadly though her mother passed away a couple of years back."

"Oh, Jill, whatever do you think happened? I mean, Ollie couldn't have killed her, could he? He wouldn't have killed her. I just don't understand. Mum's in a right state. Dad too. And I've not seen Auntie Anne and Uncle John yet. I don't think I could face them. But Jess, I must see Jess. She's been like a sister to me forever. And Ollie," The tears began to roll down Tally's cheeks, "Ollie's always been like a brother."

The weather forecast for Thursday, June the seventh, in the West Country was dreadful. The tail end of an Atlantic storm with gale force winds and gusts reaching sixty to seventy miles an hour was predicted along with frequent, heavy showers. Yet, in spite of the stormy forecast, Jim Haynes, decided to go to the Royal Cornwall Show in Wadebridge. He went every year on the first day and always enjoyed the atmosphere, the vast selection of merchandise for sale, the displays and the agricultural and horticultural events. This year, however, he wanted to go because of the crowds. He desperately wanted to lose himself amongst strangers and forget, for a day, who he was. Forget the horrible situation in Trengillion, and the fact there was nothing he could do or say to ease the torment poor Tally and her family were undergoing.

The Duchess of Cornwall was the Show's royal guest; she braved the elements and landed by helicopter near to the Showground in the midst of the relentless high winds. Jim watched from a distance, as the Duchess, dressed in a pale green jacket and skirt, walked amongst well-wishers, smiling, shaking hands, her hatless hair ruffled by the strong wind. It was after all, the third time he had seen Camilla in as many days. Her presence brought back snatches of happy memories, now sadly painful and lost in a seemingly endless whirlwind of gloom.

When the Duchess was no longer within his vision, Jim wandered around the huge, wet site looking for distractions, avoiding eye contact, hoping not to see anyone he knew. His interest was briefly riveted when he looked over colourful displays of fruit and vegetables. He almost enjoyed watching the cattle, and dairy cows in particular, as they paraded around the soggy, grassed show area. When he encountered the sheep, however, he found their conditions were less favourable than their bovine counterparts. While awaiting the verdict of judges in their pens, beneath a marquee continuously buffeted by ferocious winds, a safety inspection deemed the marquee unsafe and likely to collapse. Jim stared at the continuous flapping of the torn canvas, as the twelve hundred sheep inside, were led to the safety of waiting vehicles, where they were loaded on board ready for their premature journey home.

Jim likewise left the Show earlier than on previous years. Dejected and disheartened; the wind, rain and mud, only served to depress him further. He left just after three. His stomach was rumbling but he had no appetite for food.

Nearing home, as he drove his van through familiar country lanes, wild flowers, usually an attractive spectacle during May and early June, lay bent, twisted and crushed in the fierce, driving wind. Scattered across the roads, lanes and muddy grass verges, branches of battered foliage, torn from hedges, and vulnerable trees in full leaf, lay snapped, broken and sodden in the lashing rain.

By nine o'clock that evening, at high tide, the sea, wild, crashing and rolling, lashed heavily against Trengillion's steep cliff walls, and the Island was almost hidden beneath the white, thunderous waves.

Scum, frothy and foaming, resembling fermenting beer, fell onto the deserted shore, tearing at the rattling shingle as it slid, rapidly, beneath the relentless, breaking water. And on the grass verge by the lane, fishing boats lay sheltering, pulled there for safety earlier in the evening by fishermen and locals aware of the dangers of the high tide.

Standing was difficult in the strong, intense south westerly wind, yet everywhere, locals and holiday makers, shivering with hoods pulled tightly over heads and shoulders hunched against the cold, stood with cameras, video recorders, mobile phones and tablets as they attempted to capture the wild, amazing scene: familiar during autumn and winter, but seldom witnessed in early June.

On the top of the cliffs outside the front garden gate of Chy-an-Gwyns, Elizabeth, arms folded, cardigan pulled tightly across her chest and skirt flapping hard against the goose pimpled flesh of her bare legs, eyed the storm with quizzical, apprehensive doubt. "It's as though," she whispered, as salt spray rose from the crashing waves, dampening her clothes, face and windswept hair, and stealing breath from her quivering lips, "it's as though there is much anger in the spirit world this night."

The following day, Friday, June the eighth, the wind still blew with gusts up to fifty miles an hour, but at least the day was dry. There appeared to be no major storm damage and the sun occasionally shone. Meanwhile, Ollie appeared in court, charged with the murder of Pollyanna Jolly. He spoke only to confirm his name and address and was not granted bail.

Outside the court, angry crowds gathered and hurled abuse at the passing police van, kicking and thumping as it sped down the road chased by the media holding up cameras to the darkened windows.

Inside, Ollie, confused, a broken man, sat with his head bowed, his hands securely cuffed to a burly police officer.

Abigail, who had kept herself pretty much to herself since the death of her close friend Polly, returned home after Ollie's appearance in court. Justin and Morgana, although saddened by the loss of Polly, were not sorry to see Abigail go.

"There's something about that woman I don't like," said Morgana, as she hung the room key back on the hook, "something unnerving, almost spooky. She really does give me the creeps."

Justin tilted his head to one side and pulled a face. "Oh, come on Morgana, that's a bit harsh and I really can't see why you feel that way. I mean, for heaven's sake, the poor thing's had it rough this week. It can't have been easy having to answer police questions about the murder of a friend-cum-client. And with Polly gone there's been no-one here for her to confide in, or to give her the comfort she needed. No friends I mean. No-one close. I actually feel sorry for her. No wonder she's been at a loose end."

Morgana sighed. "Yes, I suppose you're right. But to be fair, I didn't really like her before the Jubilee do and poor Polly's death. You might say it was the opposite of love at first sight. But you're right, I am being unfair. She must feel awful."

Justin draped his arms around Morgana's shoulders. "That's better and sounds more like my dear wife talking."

Morgana half-smiled. "Poor Polly. Poor Ollie. I think had she lived the two of them might have had a future together. They looked the ideal couple and she clearly liked him very much."

Justin shook his head. "I doubt they would have had a future. The lives of celebrities and us normal folk are poles apart. Ollie wouldn't have been happy with a wife, partner, or whatever, who was always on the move, and Polly would never have given it all up to live down here in the back of beyond."

Morgana's eyes filled with tears. "And now we'll never know what might have been. Ill-fated Polly is no more, and poor, poor Ollie is likely to spend the best years of his life locked away, despised by thousands."

Chapter Nineteen

The Discordant Dukes stayed for the remainder of the week as originally planned, but when they returned home on the Saturday, Danny opted to remain in Trengillion. He knew there was little he could do to relieve the situation, but seeing Anne and her family distressed, confused and downcast, tugged at his heartstrings and he could not bear to leave them. Furthermore, he was trying to make himself useful. Anne, of course, had not worked since Ollie's arrest and so to help out his cousin Linda, he had been doing shifts on reception; a job he was very surprised to find he enjoyed.

Because the weather was fine, sunny and pleasantly warm, Danny took a stroll down to the beach after the departure of the Discordant Dukes. He had not seen Anne for several days and was keen to know if there was any more news regarding the death of Polly Jolly and to learn how she was coping. But rather than trouble Anne at home, he decided to go to the Pickled Egg where he knew her daughter, Jess, was only too happy to talk of her brother's case, as she wholeheartedly believed in his innocence. He found Jess kneeling on the floor making alterations to the menu on the chalk board. Janet was also present refilling half-empty salt cellars. He paused in the doorway before speaking.

"Hi, you probably don't know me, but I'm a very old friend of your mother ..."

"...Danny Jarrams," interrupted Jess, "of course I know who you are. Dad pointed you out to me at the Jubilee do. He told me you were the Dukes' manager, and that you used to be a pop star who Mum and her friends were dotty about many, many, many years ago."

Danny grinned. "Hmm, I think you could drop at least one of the manys, but thanks anyway. It's nice to be reminded I was once a desirable hunk."

Janet laughed. "You're still not looking too bad. A bit more portly, I guess, but you've still got your boyish good looks."

Jess stood up and rehung the chalk board on the wall. "Were you a fan of whatever they were called then, Janet?"

"Gooseberry Pie. Yes, of course, all the girls were."

To Danny's immense surprise he found himself blushing.

"Thank you for the compliment, it was the last thing I expected this morning. To be honest I wasn't sure how I'd find you, under the circumstances, that is."

Jess smiled sweetly. "My brother is innocent, Danny, and it's just a matter of time before everyone realises it and his memory is restored. Meanwhile, we must carry on as normal, keep soldiering on as they say. It's the only way and to prove our faith."

"I like your spirit, but I take it there is no more news."

Jess shook her head. "If there is then I'm not yet aware of it, but then it's early days yet. It's not even a week, although it seems like forever."

Janet agreed. "It does: the whole Jubilee weekend seems almost as long ago as Christmas."

Danny moved further into the cafe. "How's Anne, I mean, your mum?"

"As well as can be expected. But she doesn't seem to have as much trust in providence as me. I think she believes that Ollie will be found guilty and spend the best years of his life in prison. But he won't, Danny, he won't."

Sunday was wet. Not heavy rain, just drizzle. It also felt cold.

In the afternoon, Tally, all alone at Chy-an-Gwyns and not wishing to face the world outside, switched on the television to see if there was anything worth watching. As she flicked channels she remembered her mother had recorded the Diamond Jubilee Concert. With apprehension she found the recording, began to watch it and cried from beginning to end.

Her mother returned home as the Jubilee fireworks brightened the skies over Buckingham Palace. Tally listened as the car crunched over the gravel driveway and pulled up outside the kitchen door. She heard the car door slam and the back door open and close. There was a pause as Elizabeth wiped her feet on the doormat. She then called out, "It's only me Tally, where are you?"

"In the sitting room."

Elizabeth entered the room and dropped her handbag onto the sideboard. "Are you alright?" She saw the fireworks on the television screen. "Oh dear, you've been watching the Concert. Probably not the best of ideas.

Tally attempted to smile. "In a funny sort of way I think it's done me a little good. Seeing it, remembering it, has brought back so many happy memories." She suddenly laughed. "It's also just reminded me of the picnic." She got up from the settee and walked towards the door.

"Where are you going?" Elizabeth asked.

"You'll see. I'll be back in a minute."

Elizabeth heard Tally run up the stairs and open her bedroom door. Various bumps and rumbles followed. Shortly afterwards the door closed and Tally ran back down the stairs. On entering the room she handed a paper napkin to her mother.

"With all that has happened I'd forgotten I brought this back for you."

Elizabeth opened up the napkin and inside lay the cupcakes saved from the Palace picnic.

"Oh, Tally, how thoughtful, but they look far too good to eat."

Tally laughed. "Well, they did once upon a time, but I'm afraid they've got a bit crumpled and I daresay they're very dry now. I meant to give them to you as soon as we got back; as it is they've seen stuck in my bag along with everything else I've not bothered to unpack." Tally sat down. "Anyway, how's Granddad?"

"He's fine, dazed still, but fine. He, like the rest of us, feels there is no way Ollie is guilty and it's just a matter of time before the truth comes out. Bless him. He said he wishes Police Constable Fred Stevens was still around."

"Who?" Tally asked.

Elizabeth smiled. "Police Constable Stevens. He was the village bobby when I was a girl and he used to live in what is now the Ainsworths' place, the Old Police House. When he retired, he and his lovely wife, Annie, moved to the Lodge House just inside the main gates of the Penwynton Hotel. They bought it well before he retired and spent quite a while having it done up. I doubt you will remember him, but he was Jamie Stevens' father."

"I see," said Tally, thoughtfully. "It must have been nice having a policeman living in the village. Not that Trengillion is a hotbed for crime. Well, not usually anyway."

"It was nice. Comforting too, especially for us children and we knew we had to behave."

"Was Mr Stevens the last policeman Trengillion had then?"

"Sadly, yes. He was a nice man and I know Dad respected him greatly. Poor Dad: so many of his contemporaries have gone. I do hope he's never lonely. Anyway, at least he has us, and he said you must pop down and see him. You know he's always been very fond of you all and he's such a wise old thing. It might even help you to talk to him about Ollie."

Tally nodded. "I might just do that, after all I'm going to have a lot of time on my hands this summer."

Elizabeth frowned as she laid the napkin and cakes down on the pouffe. "I've not wanted to broach the subject before, but half term is over now, so are you going back to school tomorrow?"

Tally shook her head. "No, I've not been wanting to tell you because you might think me a coward, but the authorities have given me compassionate leave for the rest of the academic year. I had a letter saying so yesterday."

"I see, well, that's very good of them. I was a little apprehensive about you going back. It could have been a bit of an ordeal."

Tally half smiled. "I know what you mean. I just hope they won't say horrible things about Ollie. Not so much the teachers but the children. I can take the abuse myself but I couldn't bear to think of Ollie's name being spoken ill of. I suppose that's why they were so quick to give me time off. They might even think my presence would harm the school and be detrimental to the education of the children. I'm pretty sure some of the more malicious parents would say that was the case."

Elizabeth nodded. "Sadly, I have to agree. I just wish Ollie could remember something. I'm sure saying he has no memory of what happened is harmful because they don't believe him."

"If his memory loss was caused by trauma, as the doctors suggest, then when his mind is ready to deal with it, we'll find out what really happened. Meanwhile we must be patient, be confident and pray that his memory comes back long before they set a date for his trial."

On June the fourteenth, Jim Haynes donned his raincoat and gumboots. He locked up Ebenezer House and walked into the village to check on his vegetable plot at the allotments. To his disgust slugs and snails had nibbled at his lettuce, courgettes and butternut squash. Pigeons had feasted on his newly planted Brussel sprouts, and his potatoes had blight.

Jim cursed. The weather and pests were getting beyond a joke. The weather in particular. Flooding up country had wrecked the homes of many, and in Wales, a caravan park had disappeared beneath several feet of water. The previous day, three water boards in the South East had announced hosepipe bans were soon to be lifted, unheard of in mid-summer. And the night before, in the Jolly Sailor, Candy Bingham said she'd put the central heating on to dry the washing and it didn't even make the house feel too warm. All this and only a week to go until the longest day. But then 2012 seemed to be like no other summer. Not in Trengillion anyway.

Jim cut off the diseased leaves of the potatoes and stuffed them into carrier bags. He then tied up the tops of the bags and threw them into the back of the shed ready to burn when the weather turned more pleasant. Around the edge of his plot he then scattered organic slug pellets and put netting over the tops of his Brussel sprouts.

As time passed things did not improve. The following day brought more strong winds with gusts of up to fifty miles per hour. And when Jim went again to the allotment on Father's Day, Sunday, June the seventeenth, he found, to his dismay, the runner beans which had survived the destructive wind the previous week, looked sick following their second battering. Nevertheless, the sun was shining, the wind had abated and there was a distinct feeling of optimism in the air.

After completing a few chores Jim decided to go to the Jolly Sailor for a Sunday roast. He put away the tools he had been using in the shed along with his gumboots. He then locked the padlock on the shed door and put the key in its hiding place beneath a seed tray containing pieces of string in the greenhouse. Confident all was done, he closed the gate and wheeled his bicycle along the grass path to the lane and then cycled down the main road to the pub.

A few people were sitting at tables on the benches outside, mainly families with young children, when Jim arrived at the Jolly Sailor. Self-consciously he propped his bicycle up against the old toilet block wall and went into the pub through the open front door. He sighed, disappointed, as he glanced along the bar. Tally often worked on Sunday lunchtimes, but as he had feared, due to domestic troubles she was nowhere to be seen and nor were any other members of the family.

Jim ordered his dinner and bought a pint of dry cider; he then sat in the snug with his back to the window. On the next table sat Jill and Nick Roberts. Knowing they were neighbours of Ollie's grandfather, Ned Stanley, he asked, when Jill glanced his way, if there had been any developments in the Polly Jolly case.

Jill shook her head. "Sadly, no. Not that we're aware of anyway. Poor Ned. It's not a nice thing to have to come to terms with for any family member, but it must be even more difficult for someone his age. I feel desperately sorry for him. He looks so frail now. So tired. I feel partly responsible. Guilty even, as it was me who suggested and got poor, dear, Polly to come here for the Jubilee do. I wish I'd kept my mouth shut now."

Jim sighed. "I feel really bad about all this too. Being away I mean, when it happened. Poor Tally! It was a dreadful way to have to end what, until then, had been a brilliant couple of days."

"Have you seen her lately?" Jill asked.

Jim shook his head. "Cowardly, I know, but I've kept away simply because I wouldn't know what to say. I haven't seen her since we got back home."

Jill tutted. "That's a shame, Jim. You really ought to see her. She and the rest of the family need all the support they can get. And as regards what you say to her, well, it all depends on what your opinion is."

"What do you mean?"

"I mean, whether or not you believe Ollie to be guilty or innocent. After all, you must know Ollie a lot better than Nick and me, so if you believe him innocent, as we do, then talking to Tally shouldn't be too difficult. On the other hand, if you think Ollie murdered Polly, then conversation would be damn near impossible by my book."

Jim was taken back. "Good heavens! I've never for one minute thought him guilty. A nicer guy I couldn't wish to meet."

"Then for heaven's sake go and see Tally. Believe me, she'd appreciate it. She came to see us when she got back from London. She wanted to hear our side of things. She needs to talk, Jim. Needs to hear the opinion of others."

Nick nodded. "I agree with everything Jill has said. Go before it's too late."

"Too late?"

"Too late, inasmuch as every day the trial is getting nearer, and of course, the longer you leave it the more difficult it will be."

"But surely the trial won't be for several months," said Jim, "probably not even this year."

Nick groaned. "No, I don't expect it will. Sorry Jim, it's me being unrealistic. We're dreading the trial, you see, because we'll be prime witnesses for the prosecution, seeing as we were first on the scene. I have to admit it's starting to give me nightmares."

Jill sighed. "But let's hope it doesn't go to court. I have faith that it won't, but have to admit it's only a very small amount. Meanwhile, Jim, go and see Tally. Give her a bit of moral support. It's what she needs right now and I'm sure she's very fond of you."

Jim half smiled. "If only that were true."

Jill raised her eyebrows but Jim didn't reply for his dinner was ready and being laid on the table in front of him.

Jim found Tally alone when he arrived at Chy-an-Gwyns. Her parents, Elizabeth and Greg, he learned, had gone to see Ollie's parents, Tally's Auntie Anne and Uncle John. Jim was relieved. It was awkward enough having to face Tally, but would have been even more difficult had her parents also been present, for he had not seen them since he had arrived back with Tally from London.

Tally closed the door behind Jim. "Fancy a coffee? I was just about to have one."

"In that case, yes please. I had lunch at the pub along with a couple of pints and I must admit I actually feel quite light headed."

Tally led Jim down the hallway and into the kitchen. "Dutch courage, eh?" She said, reaching for the kettle.

Jim felt his face flush. "Well, no. That is to say, yes." he sighed. "What I mean is, I probably wouldn't have come up if I hadn't had a drink and spoken to Jill and Nick. They told me to come and see you. Oh dear. That sounds really bad. I'm so sorry."

"Sit down, Jim and don't be so daft. I think it's very brave of you to call even if you were browbeaten into it. I know it's a tricky situation and I was dreading meeting up with Jess for the first time. But I actually found talking to her a great help, and when all is said and done, Ollie is innocent and time will prove that to be the case. Meanwhile, we just have to have faith all will be well and hope he regains his memory."

Jim removed his jacket and hung it on the back of his chair. "I admire your confidence and trust in English justice, but how on earth will you be able to prove Ollie's innocence with all the evidence piled up against him? He can't even defend himself with no recall of the evening's events."

Tally made the coffee and sat down at the table opposite Jim. "Well, for a start, the prosecution can dig as deep as they like but they'll not be able to come up with a credible motive. I know it's said Jill and Nick Roberts caught him red-handed, but really that's not the case at all. He merely had the murder weapon in his hands. Polly was already dead. They didn't see him strangle her, therefore in no way did they catch him red-handed. So it seems obvious to me, and Jess too I might add, that someone else killed Polly. Ollie saw it happen, the trauma caused a severe loss of memory and he had the scarf in his hands when Nick and Jill appeared on the scene because he'd picked it up after the real murderer had scarpered."

"I can see where you're coming from, but I don't really see how someone could have strangled Polly with Ollie present. I mean, surely he would have intervened."

"I agree. And for that reason I think there must have been more than one person involved. Possibly even three or four."

"But who and why?"

"I don't know. I wish I did. But people in show business are very vulnerable. They get stalked by all sorts of freaks. And when you get an open event such as the Jubilee was, then all sorts of weirdoes could have been there."

"Hmm, you have a point. I suppose there is no record of just who bought tickets."

"Sadly not. And it makes it worse for you and me to try and recollect whether or not there might have been any odd bods around, simply because we weren't there."

Jim sighed. "Which makes us as good as useless."

Tally nodded. "And that, along with everything else, is very frustrating."

The following day, Polly Jolly was buried in the cemetery of the town where she had grown up. The funeral was covered by all television channels, and once again the face of Ollie Collins was flashed across television screens along with shots of the Penwynton Hotel and the gates of the Old Vicarage. Trengillion's response to the media, who came to the village, was to unite in solidarity, voicing their aversion to the charge, thus showing the faith they had in the man, who they strongly believed was wrongly accused.

Chapter Twenty

On Tuesday, June the nineteenth, Jamie Stevens woke up to see the sun streaming in through the bedroom window. He turned to comment to his wife on the pleasant change in the weather but found she was already up. Jamie cursed, he had hoped to be up and about before Linda in order to bring her breakfast in bed; it was after all their thirty sixth wedding anniversary.

Jamie sprang out of bed and opened the window which looked out onto the gardens at the back of the Hotel. One or two guests were quietly sauntering through the grounds enjoying the warmth of the sunshine, the fresh scents of a new day and the restful tranquility.

Leaving the window open he slipped into the en suite bathroom for a quick shower. When freshened, sweet smelling and dry, he dressed, combed his thick, wavy hair, and went downstairs to find Linda. She was in the conservatory watering the plants. He crept up behind her and gave her a hug. "Happy Anniversary, Lindy Loo. I see the sun is shining especially for you."

"It's shining for both of us; a tad different to thirty six years ago, eh?"

Jamie laughed. "Yes, what rotten luck that was. 1976, a year renowned for drought and we got married on what was probably the wettest day of the entire year."

"And I wore gumboots to get from the Hotel to the church. Hard to believe on a day such as this."

"I was going to take you breakfast in bed."

Linda smiled. "In which case you would have had to have risen very early. I woke just before five, was wide awake and so got up and watched the sunrise; it was quite breathtaking."

After returning the watering can to its rightful place in the cupboard, Jamie and Linda went to the kitchen where the chefs were busy preparing breakfast for the guests. Linda poured them both coffee which they took out into the gardens to drink in the sunshine.

Later in the morning, Jamie, determined to make the most of a dry day and wall to wall sunshine, opened the large doors of the shed near to the Mews accommodation and started the engine of the ride-on-mower. After meticulously checking no guests were strolling nearby, he drove out of the shed and onto the extensive lawns to cut the grass in the back gardens. When he had finished he drove down towards the pond, switched off the engine and walked down the steps leading into the wild flower meadow. No-one was about and so he sat on the grass bank listening to the gentle breeze whistling across the valley, tousling the petals of ox eyed daisies, vibrant blue cornflowers and the spiky magenta heads of meadow thistles.

Enjoying the warmth, Jamie lay back against the bank and looked up to the blue, almost cloudless sky. Had he really been married for thirty six years? It didn't seem possible. He didn't feel old enough. But the tell-tale lines on his face were a constant reminder that there were not many years left before he would be celebrating his seventieth birthday, and his once chestnut hair was now snowy white. Jamie laughed. Seventy indeed! But he had to concede the days when he was a boy, back in the late forties and early fifties, seemed a long, long time ago. His father had been the village policeman back then and his mother was a contented housewife, and both were so thrilled when he did well at school, achieved good GCE results and landed himself a job at the Midland Bank. Jamie sighed. Those days in the bank were now but a distant memory, for he and Linda had been running the Penwynton Hotel since Linda's parents, Mary and Dick Cottingham, and her aunt and uncle, Heather and Bob Jarrams, Danny's parents, had retired. And now they were all gone, and the Hotel belonged to Linda, Danny, and Danny's sister.

Jamie sat up. Looking at the bright sky was straining his eyes and causing them to run. He blinked several times, wiped his eyes on a handkerchief and then looked across the valley. Was he seeing things or was there a fox lurking by the lower hedge? He blinked again, knowing it was unusual to see foxes in broad daylight. Jamie rose, left the bank and walked quietly through the waving grass and flowers to take a closer look. To his amazement, his observations were correct. Before he was half way across the meadow the creature raised its ruddy head, took flight and disappeared with haste through the hedge and into a field of wheat beyond the boundary.

In spite of the swift departure of the fox, Jamie continued to cross the meadow, determined to see where the animal had made its hurried escape. By the assumed spot, he stooped to inspect the thick growth of twisted brambles, hawthorn, dog rose and elder. He found an opening secreted by a decaying fence post and hidden behind a clump of cow parsley. After examining the hole, Jamie stood and saw dangling from a clump of tangled briar, a tuft of red fur. Grinning, he tweaked it from the bramble, held it in the air and let the wind take it away, across the field and back towards the Hotel gardens. He then turned and walked along the perimeter of the field, beside the wild hedges, to avoid treading again on the flowers growing in the meadow.

As he approached the first corner his attention was caught by another sighting, this time something bright, shining in the sunlight amidst the heads of sweetly scented elderflowers. Jamie stepped into the undergrowth, plunged his arm into the foliage and pulled the object into daylight. To his surprise it was a mobile phone, a Nokia, the same model as he had owned many years before. He brushed off the debris and attempted to switch it on, but it was lifeless. Jamie's initial thought was that it must have lain in the hedge for many years, but its condition was good and it could not possibly have sat through the changing seasons and frequent deluges of rain. Confident he still possessed his old Nokia charger, Jamie dropped the phone into his pocket and continued on his way back towards the Hotel where he intended to charge the phone and see if he could establish to whom it might belong.

After dinner, Jamie went up to the utility room where he had left the Nokia mobile on charge. To his delight, the battery was full of life and the phone had a good signal. Excitedly he searched for any messages or numbers. To his disappointment the phone seemed little used. It contained no text messages and only one number was saved. After a few minutes' deliberation Jamie decided to ring the number just on the off chance he might be able to track down the owner. When the phone rang he held his breath. After five rings a female voice answered.

"Hello."

Jamie coughed to clear his throat. "Hello. I'm sorry to bother you, but you don't know me, at least I don't expect you do. The thing is, I've just found a mobile phone and I'm using it to ring you, because your number is the only one stored on it. Does that make sense? I'm hopeful you'll be able to put me in touch with the rightful owner, you see."

There was a pause before the voice on the other end spoke. "May I ask who you are?"

"Yes, yes of course, sorry. My name is Jamie Stevens and I, along with my wife, Linda, run the Penwynton Hotel in a village called Trengillion in West Cornwall."

"Jamie! No, surely not. It's me, Anne. Anne Collins. And I'm completely baffled."

"Anne! I thought the voice sounded familiar. Good grief, this is most odd."

"I'll say it is. Where on earth did you find the phone, Jamie?"

"It was tucked in a far hedge at the bottom of the meadow which borders David Pascoe's field of wheat."

Anne gasped. "You mean, near to where Polly was murdered?"

"Yes, well, no, not really. It was right down the bottom."

"I know where you mean, but someone could have thrown it over there"

"Well, yes, I suppose they could have. In fact there's no way it could have got there accidentally. I mean, I'm sure it hadn't been dropped or anything like that because it was too high up."

Anne sounded anxious. "But it doesn't make sense. Why would anyone throw away a perfectly good mobile phone?"

"Goodness knows. But more to the point, why do you think it has your number stored on it."

Anne's voice was little more than a whisper. "The number isn't for my phone, Jamie. It's Ollie's. The police gave his mobile back to us last week."

"Ollie's! Good grief. What on earth can this mean then? What I mean to say is, do you think it might have any bearing on Ollie's case?"

"I don't know. I suppose one way to find out is to hand it in to the police because there's no way we'll be able to find out who it belongs to. If you've no objections I'll pick it up in the morning and hand it in. On second thoughts, if you can spare the time, perhaps you ought to go with me because they're bound to ask all sorts of questions and will undoubtedly want to speak to you."

Jamie nodded. "Of course, Anne. I'll do anything I can to help Ollie, you know that."

"Thanks, Jamie. Although I've a nasty feeling the arrival of the phone might prove to be more of a hindrance than a help."

The following day began dry and fairly sunny, but by mid-morning grey cloud was rolling in from the west. Morgana, having attended a coffee morning in the village hall to raise money for the Christmas Lights, felt the first few spots of rain as she left the hall; and because she was not wearing a coat, she dashed home to avoid a soaking.

On arriving at the Jolly Sailor she was surprised to find amongst the morning mail delivery, a postcard from Windflower. On the front was a picture of Hope, one of the three theological virtues. The message written in neat childlike handwriting was simple but sincere.

Thinking of you all during these difficult days. Can't believe such misery has been inflicted on lovely people such as you all in Trengillion. And after such a joyous occasion too. Our thoughts are with you all.

With much love, Windflower and Sandy. X

Morgana, touched by Windflower's thoughtfulness, took the postcard into the bar and leaned it beside the brass pumps so that all could read the Tarot Card reader's sentiments.

Wayne Tilley armed with his digital camera set off on the morning of Wednesday, June 20th, for a walk along the country lanes. It was of course the longest day and he wanted to capture the Cornish countryside on his camera so that he could replicate the best pictures on canvas.

He left Coronation Terrace in the early hours before Trish was up and before he had breakfast. Hoping no-one would be about, he headed towards the narrow winding lane which ran between the school and the Old School House.

The morning was dry although not sunny, but as the light was good, Wayne knew it would bring out the true colours of the rolling countryside.

At the bottom of the hill he stopped, slid beneath the bars of a wooden fence and stood beside the stream. Mesmerised by the splashing water and the soothing sound as it flowed over rocks and mud before disappearing into the darkness beneath the bridge, Wayne lowered himself down onto a fallen tree trunk. Leaning forward he then took a series of pictures, his artistic nature aroused and delighted by the contrast between the brightness of daylight and the darkness of the rippling stream as it dimmed beneath the curved stone structure of the bridge.

Before returning to the road he glanced towards the trees and considered strolling through Bluebell Woods towards the Penwynton Hotel. He decided against it, for the trees were in full leaf, hence few woodland flowers would be blooming now springtime was past. Furthermore, due to all the recent rain, it was likely to be muddy under foot.

Back on the road he sat for a while on the bridge and looked through the pictures he had taken. He was pleased with the results and considered his early rise well worth the effort. But then he saw the dozens of pictures he had taken of Polly Jolly during her brief stay; many on the day she had died. He felt and heard his heart beat loudly as he slowly looked at every one. Most were taken during her performance at the Jubilee celebrations. One or two were taken inside the Jolly Sailor and a couple were of Polly sitting on the grass at the Hotel talking with Abigail. Wayne frowned; in the background, watching comedienne and agent, was the man he recalled seeing inside the beer tent - the tall man with a shaven head wearing a long black raincoat and with expensive-looking sunglasses perched on top of his bald head. Wayne wondered who he was but then conceded he was probably just a devoted fan such as he himself was, or to be correct, had been.

Wayne rose and dropped the camera into his pocket. Polly's death was not something he wished to think about, and so he continued his walk along the lane, his eyes misted with tears, trying hard to focus his thoughts onto searching for noteworthy scenery to photograph.

After breakfast on Monday, June the twenty fifth, Jim rushed around in the rain to get all his chores done by lunch time, for it was the first day of Wimbledon tennis and he was determined to watch as much of it as possible, every day during the fortnight. When he finally got to sit down with a mug of coffee and a ham sandwich, he switched on his television. To his delight the weather was beautiful in London. He laughed, for had the weather also been fine in Cornwall, he would have felt guilty sitting indoors.

There were no major upsets in the men's draw on the first day, but in the ladies' draw Venus Williams went out in the first round. By the end of the second day, two British men were through to the second round, Andy Murray, who won comfortably, and James Ward, who entertained the crowd with a thrilling five set match.

Three British women also went through to the second round, but only Heather Watson made it through to the third round where she was defeated. James Ward also lost his second match, but he went down fighting in another five set thriller against America's Mardy Fish.

Thursday brought a big shock. Rafael Nadal lost to Czech player, Lukas Rosol in a five set thriller. The roof was closed after the conclusion of the fourth set to avoid interruption when light inevitably faded. The match finished just after ten.

Meanwhile, up country, a tornado swept across Wales, the Midlands, and the North, leaving a trail of disruption. In some regions of Leicestershire, hailstones, the size of golf balls, fell violently, denting cars and smashing windows. Hundreds of homes were flooded and motorists had to be rescued from their vehicles. At one point the Environment Agency had ten flood warnings and forty seven alerts in place for England, mainly in the Midlands and the North. In Newcastle, the Tyne Bridge was struck by lightning. Many homes and businesses were damaged as an inch of rain fell in two hours, and the Olympic torch relay was briefly halted by lightning. At the famous Silverstone race track in Northamptonshire, the car park field was severely flooded and spectators were asked to stay away. Devon also suffered with flooding, Ottery St Mary in particular. And throughout the country several music festivals were cancelled. As the month drew to a close, June was declared the wettest since records began.

Chapter Twenty One

On Saturday evening, the last day of June, Trish Tilley sat at the bar in the Jolly Sailor, lamenting the fact that Polly Jolly's death had dampened the atmosphere in Trengillion. She was fed up with seeing everyone in the depths of despair. She was also fed up with the tennis.

"Do you like sport?" she asked Justin, as he refilled her glass with a double vodka and Coke.

"Absolutely, yes, and I'm really looking forward to the Olympics."

"Yuck! What with that lurking on the horizon and the sodding tennis, I've just about had enough. But at least we got knocked out of the silly, boring, Euro football rubbish, so blokes don't go on about that so much now."

"Good heavens, Trish, I didn't realise you were so unpatriotic," said Justin, dropping change into her hand.

"I'm not. Not when it comes to real things, anyway. It's just sport I don't like. All that leaping and running around makes me feel exhausted, and it all seems so pointless. Take grotty, old football for instance; the overpaid players spend more time hugging each other, spitting and fighting than kicking the ball. And as for rugby players, well, they look like thugs and they're always covered in dried blood and filthy mud. Athletes, especially runners and jumpers, are far, far too skinny, and the gymnasts, they must be made with rubber. And as for tennis players, well, they're all toffs."

Justin laughed. "Okay, so where does your patriotism lie?"

"Well, with things like Diamond Jubilees, of course. And you may find it hard to believe, but I'm very fond of the Last Night of the Proms too, because I like to hear all the good old pro-British songs, 'Jerusalem' in particular. I'm also very loyal when it comes to Remembrance Sunday. I never go car-booting on that day. I always wear my poppy with pride, and I always watch the service at the Cenotaph and stand for the two minutes' silence with a tear in my eye."

As an ex-sailor Justin was much moved. He reached down and patted her hand. "Can't agree with your sentiments regarding sport, Trish, but as regards the rest, well, you're a brick."

At ten minutes past eleven, Jim Haynes dashed into the pub. Reaching the bar, slightly out of breath, he stood beside the stool on which Trish sat sipping her drink.

"You been running?" Justin asked, as Jim slipped his hand in the pocket of his jeans for his wallet.

"No, I came on my bike. I thought it'd take too long on foot."

Justin nodded. "Your usual?"

"Yes, please."

"I take it you've been watching the Murray versus Baghdatis match. I managed to see a bit of it when I popped to our room for change, that'd be around nine, it was one set apiece then and they were just closing the roof. So did he win?"

Jim nodded. "Yes, and just in the nick of time. They're not allowed to play beyond eleven o'clock. It was quite amazing. Murray rattled through the fourth set in just twenty nine minutes and the match finished at two minutes past eleven. It was really thrilling."

"Good," said Justin, handing Jim his pint, "so we do at least have one player safely through to the second week."

Trish, after catching sight of her hair in the mirror behind the bar was eager to get in on the conversation and so quickly spoke up. "I like Murray," she said, convincingly, "if I'd known he was playing I'd have stayed in and watched him."

Jim was surprised. "I didn't know you liked tennis, Trish. So, who do you reckon will win this year?"

Trish squirmed, desperately trying to think of any name she might have heard of late. Suddenly one came to her as she recalled hearing his name on a recent News broadcast.

"Nadal," she said, proudly.

Jim frowned. "But he got knocked out on Thursday."

Trish laughed. "Yes, of course, silly me. Hmm….." she racked her brain hard but the only name she could think of was McEnroe, and even she knew he'd not played for years. Justin, amused by her predicament, came to the rescue.

"I expect it'll be Federer, he's desperate to win."

Trish nodded. "Yeah, I agree. Federer, I reckon he'll win."

"Would you like a drink?" Jim asked. "Then you and I can chat about tennis. It's nice to have something pleasant to talk about for a change, and I'd like your views on the women's matches. If I was a betting man my money would be on Serena to win."

Trish drained her glass. "Yes, please, vodka and Coke. I'd love to have a chat with you, Jim, because I also think, err, Serena will win the um, matches. "

Justin raised his eyebrows, and behind Jim's back, Trish winked, her eyes imploring his silence.

The second week of Wimbledon began with misty drizzle in Cornwall, but by Thursday it was brighter with a few occasional showers. It was also cool. But despite the mediocre weather, a reasonable number of early season holiday makers still descended on Trengillion; although it was suspected by locals that many of the Hotel's guests were visiting because of the publicity the village, and especially the Hotel, had received over the Polly Jolly case, and no doubt, they were hopeful of seeing the spot where she had met her untimely demise.

On Saturday, July the seventh, to the delight of Jim Haynes, Serena Williams, as he had predicted, won the Wimbledon ladies' final after beating Agnieszka Radwanska in a three set, rain delayed match, thus earning her a fifth Wimbledon singles title. Wayne Tilley watched the match while Trish took a long, hot bath. And when the match was over, she questioned him over the finer points so she could discuss it with Jim should she encounter him in the Jolly Sailor over the weekend.

On Sunday morning, Jim awoke to find sunlight streaming through his bedroom window on the upper floor of Ebenezer House. He got out of bed and crossed the room, enjoying the comfort of the carpet already warmed by the sun. He opened the window and looked out to the countryside beyond the curtilage of his graveyard. The morning sun shone on the outlying hills, and the sea, stretching to the distant horizon, sparkled a deep sapphire blue.

Jim eagerly rubbed his hands; there was much to do before lunchtime and chores were so much more easily accomplished if the weather was good.

After breakfast, he put the dirty dishes on the draining board along with the ones from the previous two days. Jim hated washing up and so only did it when he ran out of cutlery, plates, mugs or pans.

The first job to do was collect peppers, tomatoes and cucumbers from the allotment for the Pickled Egg, and then he must water and feed plants in the polytunnels. Jim slipped on his old trainers, locked up his home, took his bicycle from the shed and peddled down the road into the village. As he arrived at the allotments the church bells were ringing, beckoning worshippers to Sung Eucharist. Jim propped his bicycle against one of his three compost bins, took a carrier bag from his pocket and filled it, as instructed, from the list given to him by Jess over the phone the previous day. The task was finished as the last toll of the bell faded and the day grew silent.

Inside the Pickled Egg, Jim was surprised to find Tally sitting on top of a chest freezer talking to her cousin, Jess, who was preparing to open for lunch time. Tally greeted him warmly.

"Hi, Jim. Big day today," she smiled, swinging her legs. "Do you think he'll do it?"

Jim held up his hand. "Fingers crossed."

Jess looked puzzled. "Will who do what?"

"Will Andy Murray win at Wimbledon of course," said Tally.

Jess smiled. "Silly me, I should have known."

Jim looked at Tally. "Have you been watching the tennis then? What I mean is, I thought perhaps that under the circumstances you might not bother."

"The tennis has been a very welcome distraction," said Tally, softly, "but please don't think that means I don't care about Ollie, because I do. I care very much indeed. But in this country you are innocent until proven guilty, therefore at present, Ollie is still innocent. Isn't he, Jess?"

Jess nodded. "Absolutely."

"Can't argue with that," said Jim, "I just wish there were some new developments which might point towards his innocence."

Jess smiled. "Mum and Dad always taught us to be patient, you know, everything comes to he who waits. I'm one hundred percent sure all will be well in the end."

"But meanwhile poor Ollie is locked up," said Jim.

"Yes, but it's probably the safest place for him at present," said Jess. "I'm sure there are lots of nutters out there who'd like to take a pot shot at him given half a chance, and if he were to have been granted bail, they would have had ample opportunity. Poor Polly was after all very popular. I read in the paper only yesterday, that her grave has disappeared beneath a huge swath of flowers, and so they've asked, in future, that people leave their bouquets on an allocated patch of grass nearby."

"I read that too," said Jim, as he laid down the produce he had gathered on a table. "Anyway, I must be off as I still have several jobs to do." He turned to leave but then paused in the doorway. "Will you be watching the match, Tally?"

"Of course."

"Then why don't you come and watch it with me? It's so much more fun when shared and I'd appreciate your company."

Tally smiled. "If you don't mind, I think I will."

"You will, wow, brilliant! Come round whenever you're ready, I should be back home by twelve at the latest."

Jim wasted no time returning to the allotments to water the produce growing in his polytunnels and in order to get the job done more quickly he even postponed feeding the plants, a chore he was usually rigorous about. Mentally promising them faithfully he would give them lashings of food and lots of loving care and attention the following day, he leapt on his bicycle and peddled up the road at high speed.

Once his bicycle was back inside the shed, Jim tackled the dirty dishes, grabbed the vacuum cleaner from the cupboard under the stairs and ran it over the living room carpet. He then wiped over dusty surfaces with a damp cloth and dashed into the bathroom for a quick shower. Only when he was satisfied that he, and the room, looked respectable, did he relax.

At ten minutes past twelve, Jim heard Tally's car pull up in front of the chapel gates. Eagerly, he went to the door to welcome her. She waved as she walked up the path.

"Not too early, am I? I was going to have lunch before I came up but thought instead it'd be nice to have something to eat while the match is on, and so I ran home and grabbed a couple of microwave meals from the freezer." She arrived at the door. "I hope you've not eaten yet, and I hope you like Chicken Jalfrezi too."

Jim moved back so she could step inside. "No, I've not eaten and yes, I do like Chicken Jalfrezi. Come in and make yourself at home."

"Thanks. I hope the weather's fine in London, it's starting to cloud over here."

Jim looked at the sky as he closed the door. "So it is."

The weather in London was fine and the match began in full sunshine, but at the beginning of the third set, when Murray and Federer were one set all and one game all, the rain began and the covers went on.

"Perfect," said Tally, rising to her feet, "I was beginning to feel peckish, now if you're game we can microwave the curries while they close the roof."

Jim nodded. "Ideal. Would you like me to do the honours?"

"I think I can manage, but you can make us both another coffee."

After the lengthy break during which the retractable roof was closed and air conditioning was pumped out to acclimatise the environment from an outdoor to an indoor stadium, the match finally got underway again. But sadly it concluded at the end of the fourth set with a win for Roger Federer who had been desperate to claim his seventh Wimbledon title in order to equal the record set by Pete Sampras.

To the surprise of many, Andy Murray was very emotional, tearful and exceedingly gracious in defeat, and possibly for the first time since he had appeared on the tennis circuit the hearts of a nation went out to him. He found it difficult to speak as he fought to hold back the tears in the brief interview with Sue Barker after the presentation. His girlfriend, Kim cried and so did his mother, and inside Ebenezer House tears streamed down Tally's face too.

Jim smiled. "It's only a tennis match, Tally. Federer was just too good today, but don't worry, Murray will win before long, mark my words.

Tally wiped her eyes and attempted to smile but the tears continued to flow. "It's not just the tennis, Jim, it's everything," she sobbed, "everything's so horrible at present, and poor Ollie should have been home watching the tennis. He loves Wimbledon. Life is just so unfair."

Much stirred by her sudden spell of emotion, Jim moved closer, took her in his arms and stroked her hair. He wished he could confidently assure her that all would soon be well, but knew it would be unwise to utter words of hope when he had no grounds to justify such a statement.

Chapter Twenty Two

By mid-July the weather was the most frequently raised subject in the British Isles. Farmers were depressed; crops rotted in flooded fields and the price of vegetables was predicted to rise should the bad weather continue. On the high streets, shops reported bad sales figures, especially for summer wear, and in garden centres, summer bedding plants lingered unsold, along with barbecues, watering cans, hoses and garden furniture.

The weather took its toll on the holiday trade too. In Trengillion and other seaside resorts, bookings were cancelled, tourists returned home early, and the hours of seasonal workers were cut. Furthermore, it was announced that because of the lack of sunshine, the nation's health was at risk due to a Vitamin D deficiency.

Yet in reality the nation had much to smile about, for the Olympic flame was nearing the end of its long journey and the Games were just around the corner.

The third week of July began misty and damp, with the mist not clearing until the afternoon. On Wednesday it was so dense in places that it was impossible to see from one side of a field to the other. The forecast, however, promised change. A fairly good weekend was predicted; the weather would be dry, but not hot, and by Tuesday the weather should be more in keeping with what might be expected for the time of year. The nation heaved a sigh of relief. Just in time for the Olympic Games.

On Friday, some schools in Cornwall, but not in Trengillion, broke up for the summer holidays. Parents were impressed, for usually the weather began to deteriorate at the beginning of the long school holidays, hence it was a welcome change to witness conditions in reverse.

The weekend, as predicted, was glorious. On Saturday it was sunny and warm and on Sunday the weather was actually hot. Everyone was in a happy frame of mind. They went to the beaches in droves determined to make the most of the heat should it prove to be short lived. And before long it seemed difficult to imagine feeling cold and watching rain water run down the road like a fast flowing stream.

Gardeners too, rubbed their hands with glee. Flowers lifted their battered heads towards the sun and buds opened. Plants lost the bedraggled, tatty, appearance caused by the wind, rain, slugs and snails. Refreshed by the respite, they took on a new lease of life.

Meanwhile, in the capital city, Londoners welcomed the Olympic flame, cheering it through crowded streets, over bridges, through Greenwich Park, around the London Eye and Wimbledon. It seemed crazy to those living in Trengillion that it was already nine weeks since the torch had begun its epic journey in Cornwall.

On Tuesday, July twenty fourth, Trengillion School also broke up for the lengthy summer holiday. The weather was still very hot, but regrettably the forecast predicted conditions were set to turn cooler by the weekend.

On Friday, July the twenty seventh, the nation watched on their television sets the opening ceremony of the 2012 Olympic Games. There was the threat of a possible shower, but the weather, for once, co-operated and it kept fine throughout the evening's outstanding spectacle.

Danny Boyle was the man behind the opening ceremony and his efforts were hailed as a triumph by most of the world-wide audience. The extravaganza which lasted for several hours, began with the history of Britain, rural Britain, a green and pleasant land. It then moved on to the Industrial Revolution, chimneys belched out smoke, and actor Kenneth Branagh, as engineer, Isambard Kingdom Brunel, read from Shakespeare's *The Tempest*.

The founding of the NHS was depicted by dancing doctors and nurses in old-fashioned uniforms, with children bouncing on three hundred beds.

Music, included a medley of greatest hits from British pop over the decades. In memory of the fifty two people who lost their lives in the London bombings, referred to as 'seven seven', which occurred the day after the announcement that London had won the bid to hold the games, Emile Sande, movingly sang 'Abide With Me,' gracefully accompanied by fifty two dancers.

To the amazement of many, the Queen also took an active part along with actor Daniel Craig, the current James Bond, who duly met the Queen at Buckingham Palace and accompanied her to the Olympic Stadium by air, where they landed together by parachute, or so it seemed.

Anne absentmindedly watched the Opening Ceremony with a heavy heart. She knew Ollie had been looking forward to the Olympics for a long time and she very much wished he was sitting beside herself and John, cheering, as she knew he would have, had fate not been so cruel. However, she was able to console herself that at least he would be able to watch some of the Games from behind locked doors, and in doing so it might, for a while, take his mind off his imprisonment and give his brain a much needed chance to relax and hopefully even restore his loss of memory.

On Saturday, the day after the Opening Ceremony, the weather was fine, but it ended with no medals for Team GB. On Sunday, it rained and Team GB won two medals: a silver for cycling, and a bronze for swimming. Monday the thirtieth, and the men's gymnastics team won a bronze. On Tuesday, a silver medal was won for an equestrian event. The nation began to despair, four days gone and no gold medals.

Wednesday, August the first, was a fine, dry and bright day in Cornwall, but despite the sunshine, many of Cornwall's inhabitants remained indoors during the morning, glued to their television sets to watch Penzance girl, Helen Glover, and her rowing partner, Helen Stanning, race beneath overcast skies at Eaton Dorney. And to the delight of thousands, the girls won with ease, gaining a well-deserved, first gold medal for Team GB.

After the win of the two Helens, the gold medals rapidly began to accumulate, and on Super Saturday, August the fourth, Team GB won six gold medals, three in less than an hour during the evening events at the Olympic stadium. To mark each achievement, the Post Office painted post boxes gold in each of the winning medalist's home town or village.

By Sunday August the fifth, Team GB were third on the Medals' Table and at the All England Tennis Club's ground at Wimbledon, Andy Murray, once again had to face Roger Federer, this time in the Olympic tennis, Men's final. The match began at two o' clock, four weeks to the day since the Wimbledon final when Murray was defeated and his dreams shattered.

The weather was bright and sunny in London, and the Centre Court roof, which was closed for the earlier ladies doubles match, won by the Williams sisters, remained open.

To the relief of the crowds, both at Wimbledon and at home watching the tennis on television, the Murray versus Federer match began well for Murray. He appeared in good form, made very few errors and to the delight of the tennis loving spectators, he won the match effortlessly in three straight sets, thus earning yet another gold medal for Team GB.

But for Andy Murray there was no time to celebrate, he had another match to play: the mixed doubles' final with Laura Robson. Although both played skilfully, they were eventually defeated by the favourites from Belarus and were duly awarded silver medals.

In Cornwall, the weather produced prolonged showers, to the delight of Jim Haynes who was able to watch both matches without a feeling of guilt. He clapped and cheered throughout, overjoyed by the outcome, but regretted that Tally, who had a bad cold, was not with him to relish the delight of Murray's big win.

During the afternoon on Monday, August the sixth, a silver Volvo saloon pulled up outside the post office in Trengillion and from it stepped a grey haired man wearing gold rimmed spectacles, beige chinos and a pale yellow, short sleeved shirt. After locking the car he went into the post office where Post Master, Stephen Pascoe was sorting parcels ready for their imminent collection; his wife, Nessie, was also present, placing newly arrived greetings cards into a rack. As the stranger closed the door Stephen laid down the parcel in his hand and asked how he might help the new arrival.

"I'd be very much obliged," said the stranger, politely nodding to Nessie to acknowledge her presence, "if you could direct me towards the Old Vicarage. I've driven through the village twice but haven't yet spotted it. I assumed it would be near to the church, you see."

Stephen grinned. "Well, it is and it isn't, near to the church, I mean. That is, it's near to the church if you take a short cut over the recreation field, but by road it's a bit further. I'll show you."

Stephen walked out from behind the counter and led the visitor outside. "If you go back along this road here you'll come to a junction on the left-hand-side from which runs a short narrow lane.

Go down there and you'll see the Old Vicarage gates on the left, opposite the entrance to the allotments field."

The stranger smiled and shook Stephen's hand. "Thank you very much. I shall call there straight away."

Without another word he climbed back into the driving seat of his car, started the engine, released the handbrake and drove off up the road.

"Who do you reckon he might be?" Nessie asked as Stephen returned indoors.

"I don't know," said Stephen, mystified, "but I think I'll ring the Old Vicarage and warn Anne and John just in case the man is from the media."

But a gut feeling told Stephen he was not. Besides, the media were unable to say much since Ollie had been officially charged with the murder of Polly Jolly and the case was *sub-judice*.

Inside the Old Vicarage, Anne was decorating the spare bedroom: not because it needed doing, but because it was something to do and it whiled away the time. On hearing the phone ring, she climbed down the step ladder, laid the paintbrush on an old plastic carrier bag, peeled off her rubber gloves and went into the bedroom where the extension phone rested on her side of the bed.

"Hello," she said, with unsurprising reticence.

"Anne, it's me Stephen, at the post office."

She heaved a great sigh of relief. "Stephen, is everything alright?"

"Yes, but I just wanted to warn you that you're about to get a visitor. I don't know who he is, but he called in here a few minutes ago asking for directions to the Old Vicarage."

Anne winced. "A man. What is he like?"

"Elderly, well into his seventies I would guess, but he seemed nice, if that makes sense. Not rough, in fact if anything I'd say he seemed rather cultured. He's driving a silver Volvo, not that that is any indication as to his character."

Anne smiled. "Dad has always believed you can tell a lot about a person by the car he drives. Not quite sure how, but that's what he's always told us."

"Hmm, so what's the verdict with Volvo drivers, I wonder?"

"God only knows." Anne replied, suddenly aware of the sound of a vehicle crunching over the gravel driveway. "But whoever he is, he's nearly here and so I must go."

"Do you want me to ring anyone to get them round for moral support?" Stephen hastily said before she hung up.

Anne smiled. "That's very sweet, Stephen, but I'll be alright. I'm sure I have nothing to fear from an elderly gentleman."

Trish Tilley, bored witless by the Olympic Games, switched off the television and made herself a cup of milky coffee. "Roll on Sunday," she muttered, reaching for the biscuit barrel, "and then everything will be back to normal." She paused, her thought momentarily with Ollie Collins, "Well, near normal anyway."

With coffee and a plate heaped with custard creams, Trish sat at the kitchen table to consume her refreshments. She sighed. So many damn names to remember. So many different events too. What an impossible task. What's more, why on earth was she bothering? Jim Haynes had no more interest in her, romantically, than had the man in the moon. But she had to admit she had enjoyed the evening in the Jolly Sailor several weeks ago when he had talked to her about his beloved tennis. She just wished she knew which events, other than tennis, interested him at the Olympic Games, so that she didn't have to try and keep up to date with them all.

As she drained her cup, she suddenly remembered Linda Stevens' cousin Danny, the bloke who managed the Discordant Dukes. She had heard that he was still in Cornwall to help Linda out while poor Ollie's mum took time off because of the trouble. She grinned. It might be worth her while trying to get to know him. After all, he wasn't drop dead gorgeous now, even if he had been in the past, so he shouldn't be too fussy about who he knocked around with. What's more, if she could get him in her thrall for just a fortnight, then her precious hair would be safe.

Delighted with her idea, Trish contemplated how best to achieve her new goal. Bumping into him in the pub wasn't really an option because she had only ever seen him in there once since his arrival in early June. The Hotel would be a better bet, but for what reason could she go there? She mulled over a few ideas. After a few minutes she clapped her hands with glee. She would go to the Hotel and ask if they had found a diamond earring of great sentimental value which she had lost, but not realised was missing until she got back home on Jubilee night. And she had, of course, not been up to ask about it before because of the tragic events of that night. Thrilled with her latest plan, she rose to put her empty mug on the draining board. As she reached the sink, Wayne walked through the front door, camera around his neck. "I've just seen some old bloke going down the Old Vicarage drive. I wonder who he can be."

Trish shook her head. "You're so nosy. It could be anyone, probably a lawyer or some dude who wants John to build him a garage." She grinned, "On the other hand, the stranger might even be a doctor. Anne's depression might be worse in which case she'll be off work for much, much longer, meaning Linda's cousin will have to stay here even longer."

Inside the Old Vicarage, Anne watched from behind the curtains in the big room as the unknown visitor stepped out of and locked his car. She then went into the hallway to await hearing the doorbell ring. She counted to fifteen before she answered.

"Mrs Collins," said the stranger, politely bowing.

She nodded. "Yes."

"You don't know me, but please allow me to introduce myself. My name is Gus Richardson. I am a retired businessman and I live in Somerset."

"Oh," said Anne, nonplussed.

He smiled. "The reason for this visit is to do with a mobile phone found in the grounds of the Penwynton Hotel. I believe you are aware of it."

Anne nodded, intrigued. "Yes, you'd better come in."

"Thank you."

They went into the big room where Anne invited Gus Richardson to sit. "I do, of course, know of the mobile," Anne said, "It was brought to my attention by the person who found it, and together we took it to the police station. But I was told they had no reason to believe the person to whom the phone was registered had anything to do with Polly Jolly's death."

Gus nodded. "And quite rightly too. It was registered to me, you see, but I never bought it, and I was nowhere near Cornwall the day

Miss Jolly died. In fact I've only ever been to Cornwall once before in my life, and that was many moons ago when I was a boy. The police, needless to say, have checked out my alibi, which thankfully is very reliable. I was one of the judges at a talent show that evening and so there are many who will vouch for that."

Anne frowned. "So why was the phone registered in your name? And what was it doing in the hedge of the meadow behind the Penwynton Hotel? It doesn't make sense."

"I agree and that's why I'm here. To see if you're able to help enlighten me at all. I've been meaning to come down for a while, but a bout of gout put a stop to that idea. I'm here now though."

"So I see. Would you like a cup of tea or coffee?"

"Tea would be nice, thank you."

Anne rose. "Perhaps you'd like to come with me to the kitchen. It's a lot brighter in there as it gets the afternoon sun."

When the tea was made both Anne and Gus sat at the kitchen table.

"If you don't mind me saying so, this is a very nice house," said Gus. "How long is it since it was the Vicarage?"

Anne shook her head. "Not sure of the exact year because it stood empty for a few years before we bought it and that was in 1977. My husband is a builder and so he did all of the renovations himself."

Gus nodded, approvingly. "And a very fine job he's done. I love old buildings: they're so much more gratifying than new."

Anne smiled. "Although I think new places have their good points, being draught proof for instance, and not suffering from damp."

"Hmm, I suppose that's right, but I'm a sucker for character and there's nothing like a big, old, open fireplace, like here in the room we were just in."

"Oh, yes, I have to agree with you there," said Anne, "my grandmother always loved an open fire and so do I. In fact, I doubt there are many people who don't like them."

"Especially if they don't have to clean them out," laughed Gus.

Anne smiled sweetly. "So, getting back to the subject of the phone. Let me see if I have this straight. A mobile phone was found by Jamie Stevens, who runs the Penwynton Hotel with his wife, Linda. The phone had only one number stored on it, and appears to have made only one call, that being to my son Ollie on the night Polly Jolly died, and that call was unanswered. The police, after Jamie and I handed in the phone, traced it as being registered to you, but you have never been to Trengillion before in your life, and you knew nothing of the phone until you were approached by the police."

Gus Richardson nodded. "Not only have I never been here, but I'd never even heard of the place until the unfortunate death of Miss Jolly."

Anne scowled. "But it really doesn't make sense."

"I agree."

"Mr Richardson, may I ask you a blunt question?"

"Gus, please. And yes, of course."

"Gus, do you believe my son killed Polly Jolly?"

Gus put his head to one side. "Taking all things into consideration, such as I have never met either your son, or Miss Jolly, and I know nothing of this location, then I would say it's difficult for me to judge. However, because there seems to be no motive and the fact this mobile phone business is baffling me, and the police also I might add, then I think I'm quite justified in saying no, I don't believe your son is guilty."

"Absolutely," said Anne. "I think if we were to find out who really bought the phone then we might be getting near to the truth. I mean to say: for some reason someone must have registered it in your name to hide their true identity."

Gus laughed. "I can see where you're coming from but I'm not sure how finding out who bought the phone might help." Anne sighed. "Besides," Gus continued, "it was probably an old employee of mine who did it for a prank."

"But why?" Anne asked.

"I don't know," said Gus, "perhaps they lost the phone before they had a chance to use it properly, but if so it seems odd the only fingerprints on it were those of the Hotel proprietor."

"Jamie's, yes I heard that too."

"And another thing that baffles me is how whoever it was that owned it, knew your son's number, and why they phoned him."

Anne shivered. "It must be someone he knows," she said.

Gus nodded. "And that someone quite obviously knows me too.

Anne sat musing over the conversation with Gus Richardson long after he had departed. She racked her brain, wished there was some way she could round up everyone who had been at the Jubilee celebrations so that he could see if there was anyone present he recognised. At first she accepted this was impossible, but then suddenly, she remembered her son-in-law, Clive. Clive had spent a great deal of time over the Jubilee weekend taking pictures of the celebrations with his digital camera, and according to Jess he had taken hundreds. Hoping he might be able to help she went round to see Clive in the evening after he had returned home from work. To her delight he offered to put all the pictures taken onto a disc so that she could post them on to Gus. This she did a couple of days later after first phoning Gus to establish his postal address.

Chapter Twenty Three

By the end of London 2012, Team GB were third on the Medals Table having won twenty nine gold, seventeen silver and nineteen bronze medals. Sixty five in total, and substantially more than their original target of forty eight. Inside the Old Vicarage, Anne and John watched the closing ceremony of the Games on television, although both agreed that in comparison with the opening ceremony it was positively mediocre.

"Too much singing and not enough comedy," sighed Anne, rising from the settee, "I'm going to have a hot chocolate, would you like anything?"

"I'll have a coffee please."

"Okay."

John reached for the remote control. "Shall I see if there's anything worth watching on the other channels?"

Anne shook her head as she opened the door. "No, we must watch it, after all it really is a must-watch event and I want to see the Games end, because, in spite of our misery, they really have been marvellous, and for someone not over keen on sport such as myself, I actually feel very proud."

After Anne returned with the drinks they watched more of the Ceremony and as the Spice Girls entered the stadium standing on the tops of London's black taxi cabs, they heard the phone ringing in the hallway.

"I'll go." said John, rising.

"No, no, I'll go," said Anne, jumping up, "you've had a busy week working and I've been positively lazy."

"You've been decorating."

"Not with any urgency," she laughed.

John sat back down and Anne went into the hallway. "Old Vicarage," she said, after picking up the receiver.

"Mrs Collins, Anne," said a familiar voice on the other end of the line.

"Yes."

"It's me, Gus Richardson."

"Oh, hello, Gus."

"Hello, Anne. I'm ringing to thank you for the pictures. They arrived yesterday but I've only just got round to looking at them."

Anne felt the hairs on the back of her neck rising. "And do you recognise anyone?"

He laughed. "I recognised you, of course, and the unfortunate Polly Jolly, but there is another face which seemed familiar. I may be wrong as I've not seen this person for several years, not since I dismissed him from one of my factories for serious misconduct. And it's difficult to explain to you which pictures he's on because there are several. And so for that reason I shall visit you again tomorrow, if I may, to point him out."

Anne felt faint. "May I ask the name of this person you recognise?"

She heard a groan from the other end of the phone line. "If only I knew. But for some reason his name escapes me, his surname that is. I do remember his Christian name though. It was Nigel."

Shortly after breakfast on Monday, Trish Tilley, eager to put her latest plan into action, informed Wayne she was going into Helston to do some shopping. Wearing her favourite outfit and most seductive perfume, she then left the house, climbed into her van and drove up the road towards Penwynton Hotel. As the huge Hotel gates came into view, she slowed down and steered the vehicle sharply right, through the open gates and onto the crunchy gravel driveway. Feeling slightly nervous, she drove slowly past the old Lodge House and down the long driveway, pleasingly bordered on either side by huge hydrangeas in full blossom. At the foot of the Hotel's front steps she parked her van, stepped out and with the aid of the wing mirror checked that her appearance was acceptable. She then climbed the steps and peeped around the open double door into the vestibule.

To her surprise there appeared to be no-one on the reception desk. She went inside and hesitantly looked around. She frowned. Perhaps Danny was not working after all and Linda, on duty, had just popped to the loo. Trish was just about to make a rushed exit when she heard footsteps approaching along the black and white tiled floor. She looked up and to her utter dismay saw Anne.

Anne smiled. "Trish, hello, what brings you up here?"

"Oh, hello, I, err, um, that is to say, I lost an earring on the um, night of the Jubilee do. Oh dear, I shouldn't be bothering you with such trivia, you must think me frightfully insensitive bringing that night up, but I didn't realise you were back working yet, Anne. I'm sorry."

"Ah, that's very sweet of you, Trish, but I'm not actually back yet. I'm only here because I came to see Linda and Jamie about something."

"Oh good. I mean, it's nice to see you out and about. So, who…who do I need to ask about the earring?"

"Linda: she'll be back in a minute. She just popped upstairs to see one of the guests who's been taken ill. Nothing serious, I believe, just a nasty cold. She's taken up some paracetamol and hot lemon."

Trish began to back away towards the doors. "Oh dear, perhaps I ought to pop back another day."

As her voice faded they heard footsteps on the stairs and Linda appeared around the corner.

Anne turned to greet her. "Linda, Trish is here because she lost an earring on the Jubilee night and wonders if anyone handed it in."

Trish attempted to smile, but not very convincingly. "Yes, it's a…um…diamond earring of great sentimental value. Had it been costume, I wouldn't dream of bothering you about it. I didn't realise I'd lost it, you see, not until I got home that night and was getting ready for bed. Needless to say I didn't come up the next day because of well, you know. Anyway I'm here now."

Linda shook her head. "As far as I know no-one has found an earring and the police were very thorough searching the grounds. In fact I reckon they looked at every blade of grass for miles around. But just in case it should turn up, can you describe what was it like?"

"What? Oh, yes. Well actually I can do better than that, I can show you its mate."

From her handbag she lifted a small box, opened the lid and showed the one earring inside. She felt a pang of guilt knowing the other lay inside the drawer of her bedside cabinet.

"Oh dear, it's really pretty," said Anne, sympathetically. "I hate it when I lose an earring. One's completely useless on its own."

Trish quickly closed the box and dropped it back inside her bag. Clearly agitated, she stepped from foot to foot. "Anyway, if you don't have it here, I'll be off and leave you in peace."

"Okay," said Linda, "but we'll keep a look out, won't we, Anne? And I'll tell Jamie and the rest of the staff."

Trish smiled. She felt guilty. "Thank you. Will you be returning to work soon then, Anne?"

Anne nodded. "Yes, next week. Danny went back to London this morning so my services will soon be required again."

Trish's face dropped. "Danny's gone back."

"Yes, the Dukes have several important gigs coming up and he felt it was time he went back and gave them some support," said Linda. "He also felt it was time to relieve his mate who has been managing the lads for the last couple of months. We shall all miss him. He's been a tremendous help."

"Before you go, Trish," said Anne, "do you know anyone who was at the Jubilee do called Nigel?"

Trish shook her head. "Nigel. No, should I?"

"Not really," said Anne, "and I won't explain now because it's a very long story."

Inside Chy-an-Gwyns, Elizabeth picked up six library books and her handbag and went out to the car. The books were due back and as she had already renewed them twice by phone, she thought it was time they were returned. She didn't really want to go into Helston, but hoped a change of scenery and getting away from the village for a while would do her some good. At least she thought the drive might help but she wasn't so sure about mixing with people. Most people in Trengillion wanted to believe that Ollie was innocent but this was not the case with people with whom he and the family were not acquainted. At the Old Vicarage, following Ollie's appearance in court, the family had received numerous hostile letters and several menacing phone calls.

To Elizabeth's relief the library was quiet. She took the books over to the computer and scanned them as returned. When done, she leaned them neatly beside others on a shelf, but as she turned to leave, her books toppled over causing one of the other books nearby to tumble onto floor. Elizabeth tutted and dutifully picked it up.

When she saw the book's title, she was overcome with a sudden surge of hope and optimism, as if a lingering mist was being lifted from her eyes. In a state of quandary, Elizabeth stared at the book resting on the palm of her hand until her vision blurred. Its title was *Hypnotism*.

Detective Inspector Peck was not a happy man. All evidence in the Jolly case indicated Oliver Collins was a guilty man, but common sense told him he was not. Oliver came from a good family. He did not blow his mind with drugs or excessive alcohol. He was gentle by nature, hard-working and well liked. Furthermore, there didn't seem to be any feasible reason for him to take the life of Polly Jolly, at least not so far as he could see. But all the evidence was against him. He could not, or would not, account for his movements that night. No-one else appeared to have had contact with Polly Jolly after her performance, and everyone who was there was able to produce an alibi. Inspector Peck slapped his desk, hard. He'd been in the Force for twenty years and had seen things that would turn the hair of most folks white overnight. He'd dealt with thugs, murderers, armed robbers and drug dealers, and he'd never had any doubts as to whether people he'd charged had been guilty or not. At least not until now.

He stood, walked over to the window and watched the people walking along the street below.

"Oliver Collins is no more guilty of murder than any one of them," he muttered, "but how the hell do I prove it and start a search for the real killer? At present with such an open and shut case there's no reason to even look elsewhere. Yet I know damn well the real culprit is currently a free man, or woman, and no doubt laughing at our ineptitude."

A knock on the door caused him to turn. "Come in," he bellowed.

"Excuse me, sir," said a young police sergeant, "but there's a Mrs Castor-Hunt on the phone. She wishes to speak with you regarding the Jolly case, if that's convenient."

The inspector sighed and nodded. "Put the call through, Higgins. I'll speak with the lady."

Chapter Twenty Four

Inside the house she and Sandy rented in Reading, Windflower Saunders kicked off her shoes and sat on a kitchen chair glad to be home and off her aching feet. She yawned. Trade had been brisk in the supermarket café where she worked and the long walk home had tired her. But she didn't mind, she had two days off now before she had to go back.

Once she felt rejuvenated, she filled a kettle, poured a little of its contents into a pot where parsley grew on the kitchen windowsill and then boiled the rest for a mug of tea. With tea in hand she returned to the chair at the kitchen table to drink it.

The daily newspaper was lying on the table; she picked it up and skipped through the pages. There was a lot written about the Olympics and an in depth analysis of the closing ceremony. She sighed: all other stories seemed dull after the excitement of the Olympics. She closed the paper, folded it and then laid it back down on the table.

Sipping her tea, she glanced towards the top of the work surfaces and spotted amongst old post and clutter, a wallet of photographs. She quickly rose and eagerly picked them up, knowing they must be the pictures taken during their touring holiday, for Sandy had dropped the film into the chemist before going to work on Saturday morning. She sat back down, withdrew the photographs from the wallet and shuffled through them. When she saw one of herself she laughed out loud. The aging make-up she and Sandy had worn was very convincing.

When she had viewed all the pictures she returned them to the wallet and looked wistfully across the table where her Tarot cards lay beside a vase of yellow chrysanthemums. She had enjoyed the holiday, but how dreadful it was that it should have had ended so tragically. Poor Polly. Fancy being murdered by someone with whom she had seemed so happy. Windflower shuddered, recalling the night the Cards had foretold death. She had tried to convince Ollie the card didn't have to mean death in the true sense of the word, but it more likely indicated the end of something and the beginning of something new. How cruel. She was right and yet she was also wrong, for the Card had meant death; it had also meant a new beginning. A life locked up in a prison cell. Windflower's eyes suddenly brimmed full of tears. Poor, silly, Ollie. Whatever could have happened to cause the lad to commit such an outrageous, deadly act? She shivered and prayed, not for the first time, that the Cards were not responsible for unhinging his mind.

Windflower glanced at the clock. It was half past three. Wearily she rose from the chair and crossed the room to the fridge. She looked inside hoping for inspiration for the evening meal. Uninspired, she cooked some pasta, opened a jar of sauce and a tin of tuna, mixed them together with a few vegetables and then topped the mixture with grated cheese. She looked at the clock. It was another two hours before Sandy was due home from work. She put the pasta bake in the oven but didn't switch it on. She then went out into the garden to bring in the washing which was tangled badly around the rotary drier due to the fresh westerly wind.

Upstairs in the bathroom, she dropped the laundry basket onto the floor ready to fold and put away the washing into the airing cupboard. As she turned she caught sight of her reflection in the mirror above the wash basin and smiled. Thank goodness she was not really as old as she had appeared in the photographs downstairs. She stepped closer to the mirror and brushed her fingers across her smooth cheeks. No sign of any wrinkles yet, thank goodness. No signs of grey hair either amongst her dark brown curls. She sat down on the side of the bath and her thoughts drifted back to the touring holiday, paid for by the money she had made reading the Cards: a talent she had learned from her mother. Windflower laughed. It was such a clever idea of Sandy's to dress up like old hippies. It had been fun too. She had always enjoyed experimenting with make-up and had learned the skills of aging from a friend who worked in the make-up department of a television company. She giggled, recalling the time Tally Castor-Hunt had knocked on the door of the caravan. They saw her coming and both had hidden because neither was wearing make-up and her black wig was hanging on a hook by the door.

As she stood to sort out the washing the telephone rang in the hallway below. She ran downstairs to answer it.

"Hello."

"Mrs Saunders?"

"Yes."

"Is Sandy home?"

"No, sorry, he's not back from work yet."

"What! But he hasn't been at work today. I'm his mate, Mike. I've been trying to get hold of him all day. They said in the office he rang in sick this morning and I wondered what's up, but he's not answering his mobile."

Windflower scowled. "I've not been back from work very long myself, Mike. And I haven't seen Sandy since first thing this morning and he seemed alright then. His car isn't here and neither is he, but he must have been out at some point and come back again because he collected our photos from the chemist. I had assumed he picked them up during his lunch break and popped them back here so that I could see them when I got home, but now I'm confused."

"I see. Well, he must've been skiving then. When he does come in will you get him to give me a ring? He knows my number."

"Of course, Mike."

"Thank you. Bye then."

"Bye."

Windflower put down the receiver. Sandy never went out without his mobile phone and he wouldn't have forgotten it, unless, perhaps, he'd left for work in a hurry. She frowned. But according to Mike he'd not been to work because he wasn't well. Windflower was baffled. Where the hell was he?

Inside the kitchen of Chy-an-Gwyns, Elizabeth made up a mug of hot chocolate, dropped in several dollops of cream, put on her thick cardigan and went out onto the cliff tops where she sat looking across the ocean towards a large vessel sailing slowly across the horizon. The wind was fresh and the afternoon air felt cold. To keep warm she wrapped her fingers around the hot mug and the heat from the rising steam warmed her face.

Sipping the creamy chocolate drink, she pondered over her trip to the library and the book which had for no apparent reason fallen onto the floor. Was it a sign, an omen? The more she thought about it the more convinced she was that hypnotism was the ideal way to help Ollie relive the evening Polly had died and by doing so prove his innocence. The problem was, how could she convince anyone else, and would it ever be possible to get permission from the authorities to put Ollie under hypnosis? She groaned. To her it was the obvious way to get to the truth, to dig into his lost memory. She closed her eyes and said a little prayer. Her only hope was that Detective Inspector Peck would prove to be as helpful and supportive as he had sounded on the phone.

As Windflower put away the washing in the airing cupboard, she turned over in her mind possible locations which might give a clue as to the whereabouts of her husband, Sandy. None the wiser after puzzling for several minutes, she returned downstairs and switched on the oven to cook the pasta bake. As the whirr of the oven's fan picked up speed, Windflower thought of her own mobile phone. Without hesitation she took it from her handbag and rang Sandy's number. To her amazement, she could hear the familiar jingle of Sandy's ring tone close by. She turned and looked on top of the microwave. Her husband's mobile phone was there, vibrating with her incoming call.

Normally, Windflower would never dream of meddling with her husband's phone, but hearing it ring made her suddenly feel inquisitive. Why hadn't Sandy been to work? He certainly wasn't ill. And why hadn't he come back for his phone? Surely wherever he was he must have realised he'd forgotten it by now. Unless, of course, he'd not long left the house.

Windflower lifted the phone from the microwave. She checked his incoming calls. No-one had rung, except Mike, several times, and herself moments before. She put the phone down on the table and then picked it up again. Texts. She must check his texts. To her surprise there were two from Abigail. She read the first. *At last. Gr8 news. Bet UR heartbroken. LOL. x*

Windflower frowned. Confused. She read the second. *Come over later. Be home by 1. x.* Even more confused she checked the times. Both messages had been sent that morning just before half past eight, which was the time Sandy normally left for work.

Windflower sat down. Why would Sandy go to see Abigail instead of going to work? What was great news? Windflower stood. There was only one way to find out. She must pop round to Abigail's house and ask. She switched off the oven, put on her most comfortable shoes and reached for her handbag. As she flung it across her shoulder it knocked into her Tarot cards sending them cascading to the floor. Windflower knelt to pick them up. All were face down except one. The lovers. In a daze she left the kitchen, walked through the hall and out into the warm balmy air. She locked the door, dropped the key into her bag and walked off down the road in a state of unease.

Abigail lived on the other side of town. Normally they would take the car when they went to visit, but the car was gone, and so Windflower, feeling too weary to walk, decided to catch a bus. She strode off to the bus stop forgetting her feet ached. She was on a mission. A mission to find out the great news. To her relief a bus pulled up shortly after her arrival.

Sitting on the lower deck she looked from the window and pondered over possibilities as to the news, but could come up with nothing feasible. After all, she and Sandy had only known Abigail since June when they'd all met for the first time in Trengillion's pub, the Jolly Sailor. And since then, after discovering they all lived in the same town, they had kept in touch and had made frequent visits to each other's houses.

Windflower left the bus when it stopped outside the school near to Abigail's house. The road seemed quiet. The school was closed for the summer holiday and there were very few pedestrians on the narrow pavements. She walked on past a park and a development of new houses. As she turned at a junction by a corner shop she spotted the Zephyr Six parked outside Abigail's house. Windflower quickened her pace, looking forward to sitting down with a cup of tea, hearing the news and enjoying a chat. Windflower smiled. Abigail had laughed when they had told her that the hippie outfits were to create an image. She cursed, wishing she had popped the pictures in her handbag.

Windflower arrived at Abigail's house where a wooden gate, painted orange, was tucked neatly between brick walls which bordered the front garden of the Victorian semi-detached house. The gate was closed. As Windflower lifted the latch, her arm brushed against honeysuckle cascading from a wooden trellis on top of the wall, filling the air with its sweet perfume. Delighted by the scent, Windflower snapped off a sprig and pushed it into the button hole of her cardigan.

After closing the gate Windflower walked up the path towards the house. She climbed four red tiled steps and approached the front door. But as she raised her hand to knock, she instinctively stopped. Something told her to go round the back. She left the front door steps and followed the paving slabs around to the rear courtyard, where ferns and grasses rustled in the breeze. No-one was outside, but the French doors were wide open. She crept inside and stood in the large dining room. On the mahogany table lay a newspaper, folded inside out. Windflower glanced at it as she went into the wide hallway.

Sunlight, shining through the curved, stained glass window, above the front door, cast colourful patches onto the hall's diamond shaped Victorian tiles. Windflower stood where the light beams fell. Above her head hung two paintings of tropical beaches. She paused and listened. From above she heard laugher, and then voices. Quietly, Windflower kicked off her shoes and slowly climbed the stairs, holding her breath until she reached the top. After stepping from the last tread, she tip-toed onto the landing and turned her head towards the sound of voices. Abigail's bedroom door was ajar. The dressing table mirror reflected the room inside. Windflower's heart sank. Her lips trembled. In the bed sat Sandy, bare-chested, laughing, with one arm tightly around Abigail's naked shoulders. He reached out with the other arm and picked up a bottle. Abigail giggled as he topped up the glass in her hand. Both were drinking champagne.

Chapter Twenty Five

Windflower was preparing a salad to accompany the pasta bake when Sandy returned home at his usual time, half past five. She smiled and tried to act as though everything was normal. "Hello, love, did you have a good day?" she asked, as he removed his jacket and sat down at the table.

"Yes thanks." He picked up the photographs. "Have you seen these? They're really good, aren't they?"

Windflower nodded. "Yes, I did look through them and I particularly liked the one of Abigail. She looks very pretty."

"Really, I can't say that I'd noticed." He shuffled through the photographs. "Ah, you must mean this one. I suppose it is quite a good snap, not that I even remember taking it. What's for dinner? I'm starving."

"Pasta bake, but I'm a bit behind so it won't be ready for another half hour yet. Did you know you left your mobile phone here today?"

"Did I?" With a scowl, Sandy reached for his jacket and fumbled around inside the pockets.

"Yes. It's on top of the microwave."

Sandy stood, picked up the phone and sat back down at the table. "Hmm, I didn't even miss it. I wonder if I've had any calls."

Windflower's confidence strengthened. "Not since I've been home. Other than me, that is. I rang it, you see, because I didn't know where you were."

Sandy leaned back in the chair. "What do you mean?"

"I mean, I know you've not been to work today because your mate Mike rang the house phone because he was concerned about you. He told me you rang in sick this morning."

Sandy's face twitched and his eyes glazed over. Windflower sensed his brain was working overtime looking for an excuse. Suddenly he smiled. "Actually, that is right, I've not been to work today, but that's because I really was feeling a bit queasy this morning and so I phoned in sick. After a while I felt a bit better though and so went out to pick up the pictures." He attempted to laugh. "Seeing them made me rather wistful. I thought it'd be nice to have another holiday and so that's where I've been this afternoon; at the travel agents looking to see what's on offer."

Windflower raised her eyebrows. "Oh dear, poor you. I'm surprised you went out if you were feeling rough though, especially when you normally do anything like that online."

"Yes, and umm, you're right. But I had a headache, you see, and didn't think staring at a bright screen would do it much good. So I decided to pop down the road, get some fresh air and let someone else's eyesight take the strain."

"And?" Windflower asked.

"And," repeated Sandy, puzzled.

"Yes. What did you come up with?"

"What? Oh, err, well…nothing actually. That is to say, I couldn't really book anything without consulting you first, could I? So I thought I'd leave it for another day."

Windflower smiled sweetly. "How thoughtful. But we can't really afford a holiday, can we? Not unless we intend to finance it with my Card reading, and I don't know that that would be feasible abroad."

"Probably not. Anyway, what time did Mike ring?"

Windflower wrinkled her nose. "Half three, four, I can't really remember but it was soon after I got back from work."

Sandy rose. "Okay, well I'd better ring him back."

From inside the hall Windflower heard Sandy laughing and talking to Mike. Were it not for the scene she'd witnessed in Abigail's bedroom her mind would have been at ease. As it was she was anxious and eager to get to the bottom of the relationship between her husband and Abigail.

"I've told Mike I'll meet him for a pint, if that's alright with you." Sandy said, as he returned to the kitchen. "It'll only be for a couple of hours so I won't be late."

Windflower shrugged her shoulders. "Of course I don't mind. Sharon's back in *EastEnders* tonight, and I know you don't particularly like the programme, so I'll be able to watch it in peace."

After dinner, Sandy changed and went off down the road to join Mike for a drink at the pub on the corner. Windflower sat down to watch *EastEnders* but her concentration was non-existent; her mind kept wandering.

Upstairs, inside the bottom of the wardrobe, Windflower knew Sandy kept a file, bulging with old letters, photographs and old papers to do with his family. She suddenly felt compelled to go through it, but she didn't really know why. After all, his past would have no relevance regarding his attraction to Abigail. Nevertheless, she felt it might give her an insight into questions churning around in her mind. There might even be hidden notes or letters from Abigail, popped in of late: perhaps even correspondence from other women with whom he might have had a dalliance in the past.

Florence was in bed when Jess got home from work, hence before she removed her coat, she went upstairs to kiss her daughter goodnight, but to her dismay Florence was already fast asleep. Returning downstairs she joined Clive in the kitchen. He was making a curry. Something he always did on a Monday night.

"Glass of wine, Jess?"

Jess looked at the bottle. "I shouldn't, but I will. I'm feeling shattered today."

"Been busy?"

"So so."

Clive poured wine into her favourite glass. "Why don't you go and sit down on the settee and enjoy a bit of comfort. Dinner's nearly ready, I just have to do the rice."

Jess rose. "I think I will. Is there anything worth watching on telly tonight?"

Clive shrugged his shoulders. "No idea, I've lost interest now the Olympics are done, but the paper's in there if you want something to look at."

Jess took her wine and left the room. Clive tipped grains of rice into a saucepan and poured on cold water from the tap.

In the sitting room Jess picked up the daily newspaper, placed her glass on the coffee table and curled up on the comfortable settee. The news was dominated by the closing ceremony of the Olympic Games. Jess yawned. She had watched the grand finale and so wasn't that keen to read about it. With little interest she half-heartedly turned the pages, until suddenly, on page seven, the name Polly Jolly caught her eye. Jess sat up straight. The article told of the death of Polly's uncle, a wealthy man called Geoffrey Gower. It claimed his premature death was accelerated by the murder of his beloved niece. It also told how Polly was to have inherited his vast fortune, but since she had predeceased him, it was likely the money would go to Polly's only cousin, the son of Geoffrey's deceased older brother, with whom he had never seen eye to eye.

Jess dropped the paper. Gower. At long, long last she knew of someone who would benefit from Polly's death. Someone with a very strong motive.

Ollie looked pale. His eyes lacked sparkle, and he appeared to have lost weight. So thought Detective Inspector Peck as Ollie was led into the interview room where he waited alongside a hypnotist called Charlie Morrison who had a string of impeccable recommendations.

Ollie was told to sit at the table facing the inspector and the hypnotist. The police officer who had escorted Ollie from his cell waited beside the door.

"Is there anything wrong?" Ollie asked, his eyes darting back and forth between the two men opposite.

Detective Inspector Peck half-smiled. "No, there's nothing wrong, Oliver, in fact quite the opposite. We're hopeful that this interview will actually help you."

"Help me," said Ollie, resting his elbows on the table, "how can anyone help me? I don't understand."

The inspector leaned forward. "This isn't exactly run-of-the-mill, Oliver, in fact we've had to plead hard to get permission to do it. But we, which is myself and Charlie here at my behest, would like to hypnotise you and see if you being in a trance might shed some light on just what happened on the night of June the fourth."

Charlie sat beside the inspector, smiling. He looked friendly but Ollie, with fists clenched to stop his hands from trembling, eyed him with suspicion. He shook his head firmly; his bottom lip quivered.

"I...I don't think that's a good idea," he muttered.

Charlie reached out and touched Ollie's arm. "I won't harm you, Oliver. Hypnotism is quite painless, there are no side effects and you'll not be asked anything other than to recall what happened on that fateful night."

A look of fear appeared in Ollie's eyes.

"What are you afraid of, Oliver?" the inspector asked.

"I, I…don't know," he muttered, frowning, "I really don't know. But for some bizarre reason the thought of hypnosis fills me with dread. I don't understand."

A reassuring smile from the inspector calmed him. "We shall not harm you, Oliver. I promise you that. Please believe me, we have your interest at heart."

The hypnotist nodded.

Ollie bit his bottom lip. "Alright, gentleman you can hypnotise me but I really don't think it will achieve much."

The inspector informed Ollie that the interview would be recorded. He then handed over the operation to Charlie.

Once Ollie was in a hypnotic state, Charlie spoke, his voice calm and soothing. "It is the night of the fourth of June, Oliver. The band, the Discordant Dukes, are playing and you are with Polly Jolly."

Ollie tilted his head to one side and smiled. He was in the gardens of the Penwynton Hotel. The evening was cool, rain was expected, but he didn't care: Polly, sweet, dear Polly, was by his side.

Charlie spoke again. "You and Polly have wandered away from the crowds and are walking towards the pond and the rose pergolas."

Ollie nodded. "My dad helped make the pond, and he paved the area around it too, many years ago, before I was born." He paused. "I can smell the roses and the honeysuckle. Their scent is quite strong. Polly thinks it's all very pretty."

Charlie leaned forwards. "Good. And what is happening now you've reached the pond."

Ollie smiled. "Polly looks so beautiful. She always looks beautiful. We have passed the pond and are sitting on the steps talking. She is admiring the meadow. It is a blaze of colour. She likes wild flowers, especially poppies. There are poppies on her scarf. Poppy was Polly's mother's name."

Ollie paused and looked at his hands.

"Carry on," said Charlie.

"I am asking her about being a comedienne. She is telling me of a very rich uncle who was her mother's twin. He will leave all his wealth to Polly. Poor Polly, she is sad. She is very fond of her uncle, but he is dying. He has lung cancer and is in a hospice."

"You're doing well, Oliver," said Charlie, giving the thumbs-up to Detective Inspector Peck, "what is happening now?"

Ollie smiled again. "I am leaning forward to kiss her. I don't want her to go. She is going to Manchester in the morning with Abigail." Ollie frowned. "Shush, we can hear footsteps. Now they have stopped. Someone is coughing near to the pond. Damn, we are not alone."

"Who is it, Oliver. Can you see? Who is near the pond?"

Ollie grinned. "Sandy. It's Sandy." Ollie laughed. "Sandy is saying, 'Whoops, sorry to interrupt. I didn't realise there was anyone down here.' Polly is laughing too. Sandy is asking if he can sit down with us on the steps. Polly is saying yes. She likes Sandy and is asking where Windflower is. He is saying, she is sleeping because she's had a very busy day."

"Excellent, Oliver, you are doing exceedingly well. What is happening now?"

"He is talking. Sandy does a lot of talking. He's making us laugh. He's telling us he used to be a circus performer. He's worked all over the country in seaside places and even abroad. When he was young, in his early twenties, he was a trapeze artiste, but he had to give that up after a nasty accident. He fell from the swing, bounced off the safety net and damaged his shoulder. Eventually his shoulder got better but he'd lost his nerve, and so he learned all sorts of other things instead, including hypnotism. I'm laughing now, and telling him it's not possible to hypnotise people. Hypnotists are conmen. Polly is laughing too."

Charlie smiled. "Oh, really! And what does Sandy say to that?"

"He says hypnotists are not conmen and he'll hypnotise me to prove it, and I'm saying he can try all he wants but he won't succeed."

"Go on," said Charlie, slowly.

Ollie's eyes, wide open, yet dazed, stared blankly into space. He frowned. "Sandy is saying, 'You will remember nothing. You will remember nothing'." Ollie began to tremble. "I remember nothing. I remember nothing."

Charlie stood, walked around the table, knelt beside Ollie and firmly gripped his shoulders. "It's alright, Oliver, it's alright. I say you can remember. For the love of Polly, lad, you must remember."

Ollie's lips quivered. "I can hear music. My mobile phone is lying on the steps and it's ringing. My phone has stopped ringing. I'm picking it up and then I'm dropping it. Polly is lying on the steps. Her face is blue. Her beautiful face is blue. Her scarf is in my hands. Polly! Polly, wake up. Someone is here. Someone is near the pond. It's Nick and Jill Roberts. Nick is by my side. He's feeling for Polly's pulse. He is shaking his head. No! No. Polly is dead. Polly is dead."

Ollie was panting, trembling and breathing heavily. Tears trickled down his flushed cheeks and beads of perspiration formed on his creased forehead.

"Oliver, is Sandy still there?" Charlie asked, "Is he still with you?"

"No, no, I can't see him, he's gone."

"Where has he gone?"

"I don't know."

"Oliver, who killed Polly? Was it you?"

"No, no it wasn't me. I loved Polly. I would never hurt her. Somebody ring for an ambulance. Please, somebody ring for an ambulance."

Windflower knew little of Sandy's family. His mother died shortly after they had first met and he'd not seen his father since his parents had parted and then divorced when he was just a child. For that reason Sandy never mentioned or talked about his father who had re-married, except briefly on one occasion when he read in the Obituaries that his father had died. She was surprised, therefore, to find a family tree for Saunders amongst the contents of the file. After all, if Sandy wanted nothing to do with his father's family, why would he keep such an item? She carefully unfolded the huge scroll of paper and laid it down on the plain grey carpet. Sandy's name was at the bottom of the tree, below that of his mother, Gillian. Windflower frowned. Puzzled. The names made little sense. After careful examination the penny dropped. Saunders was Sandy's mother's maiden name. After the divorce she must have reverted to that name and changed Sandy's name likewise.

Intrigued she wondered as to the identity of Sandy's father, as he was not included on the family tree. Windflower tipped out the entire contents of the file onto the floor. Somewhere there must be documents to establish Sandy's name at birth. Eventually she found what she was looking for. A newspaper cutting revealing details of his birth to parents, Anthony, and Gillian Gower, nee Saunders. "So," she said, much surprised, "before the change, Sandy was a Gower." Windflower laughed, glad Sandy's mother had made the change. "After all," she giggled, "Windflower Gower is almost as bizarre as Polly Jolly."

Inside his Bayswater flat, Digger Potts, a tabloid newspaper hack, chewed on the end of his ballpoint pen. He'd been very interested in the Polly Jolly murder case, perhaps more so than the rest of his colleagues, because he'd not only been in Cornwall, on holiday, when her death had occurred, but he'd actually been in Trengillion at the Jubilee do. But despite his being on the scene, he'd still gleaned no more information than his colleagues. However, hearing of the death of Polly's seriously rich uncle, renewed his interest. He felt sure there had to be a link between Polly's death and Geoffrey Gower's little known about nephew. He phoned a friend. A private investigator whose ruthless means usually obtained quick and accurate results. By the end of the day he'd learned that Nigel Gower lived in Reading with his wife. He worked in a sweet factory from nine 'til five, three days a week; drove an old Zephyr Six; went under the name of Nigel Saunders and everyone knew him as Sandy. Without hesitation, he put on his long black raincoat, slipped his sunglasses on top of his bald head, picked up the keys to his silver Audi, and left the flat.

Charlie woke Ollie from the hypnotic state he was in when ordered to do so by Detective Inspector Peck, who realised there was little more to be gleaned from Ollie who was clearly distressed. When Ollie came too, Charlie was wiping beads of perspiration from his brow. His face was flushed and very hot.

"May I have a drink of water, please?" He asked, as his breathing slowed. "My throat feels hoarse.

Detective Inspector Peck nodded to a police constable standing by the door. He returned within minutes and handed a paper beaker to Ollie.

"What happened?" Ollie asked, after taking several gulps of water.

"You no more killed Polly than I did," said Charlie, carelessly.

The inspector peered over the top of his spectacles and tutted.

Charlie took in a deep breath. "Sorry, Inspector."

Ollie's eyes flashed; he looked and felt apprehensive.

There was a knock on the door and a police sergeant entered the room.

"Sir, there's a newspaper man called Mister Potts on the phone. He says he has information which you might find useful regarding the Jolly case."

Detective Inspector Peck's eyelids flickered as he rose. "I shall be back shortly," he said, following the sergeant towards the door, "Please bear with me."

Chapter Twenty Six

Sitting alone at an empty table in a bleak interview room guarded only by a middle aged woman police constable standing with hands behind her back beside a solitary door, Abigail Armstrong reflected on the unsettling situation she was in. A tall man, who had informed her he was called Detective Inspector Peck from Devon and Cornwall Constabulary, had grilled her with a continuous string of awkward questions, but she'd remained tight-lipped throughout the ordeal. Now she was left alone with her minder to consider his words and decide whether or not she would co-operate on his return. Were she to do so, then he would, he said, do everything he could to see she was treated fairly.

Abigail placed her elbows on the table, rested her chin in the palms of her soft hands and stared blankly at the plain wall opposite. To co-operate would mean confessing her involvement with Sandy and her knowledge of the subsequent murder of Polly Jolly.

Abigail sighed. It had all seemed such a good idea when they'd first hatched up the plan. Now doubt began to creep into her faltering mind, even though she was confident there was no incriminating evidence at all to indicate their participation.

Above the door a round, white-faced clock ticked noisily, counting the seconds as they slowly passed. Abigail wondered how long Detective Inspector Peck would leave her to stew, or as he put it, come to her senses. He had gone, so he said, to question Nigel Saunders further.

Nigel Saunders. Abigail leaned back in the chair and whispered his name, a name she had known since secondary school days when they first met as classmates at the age of eleven. For some reason they hit it off, but as so often happens once school days are over, they lost contact and their paths didn't cross again until quite by chance they bumped into each other in Tesco one rainy Saturday afternoon. Sandy told her that his wife, Windflower, was working, so they went for a drink in a pub nearby and their renewed friendship blossomed from there. But as time passed, friendship wasn't enough and eventually they became secret lovers, meeting in dark pubs and cafes at the other end of town often at weekends when Windflower was working.

It was as they drank cider one afternoon in Abigail's house while Windflower was waitressing at the busy supermarket café where she worked, that he told her he was cousin to Polly Jolly the comedienne. At first Abigail was in awe, but when she learned of the vast fortune Polly was to inherit from her wealthy sick uncle, her attitude changed from awe to fascination.

Abigail worked for a theatrical agency and had heard on the grapevine that Polly was often at loggerheads with her own agent, a bossy, pompous man who was notorious for going over the heads of his clients and forcing them into gigs against their will. Abigail suggested to Sandy it might be possible for her to form a friendship with Polly and ultimately earn her trust and offer to become her agent. Sandy had grinned - a wicked, mischievous grin. He thought it an excellent idea, for if Abigail were to succeed they would have complete control over Polly Jolly's movements and could ultimately plan and organise her demise.

Everything went to plan. Abigail became Polly's agent and their relationship appeared to all, including Polly, to be very amicable. However, Polly was timid about informing Abigail she had been asked by an erstwhile neighbour, Jill Roberts, to perform at a Diamond Jubilee celebration in Cornwall for a very modest fee. She expected Abigail to disapprove and create a scene. She was surprised, relieved and overjoyed therefore, when her new agent expressed approval and even uttered delight regarding the opportunity of taking a few days' break by the coast.

When Abigail informed Sandy of the arrangements he was equally thrilled. A rural location well away from media attention, during a jam-packed bank holiday weekend, sounded the ideal setting in which to dispose of his unwanted mollycoddled cousin.

It was Abigail who bought Polly the scarf which would eventually take her life. Abigail bought it from a market stall and told Polly it would bring her luck. Polly was superstitious, hence from that day forward she wore it religiously for every performance. As her popularity increased, she firmly believed the good fortune was due to Abigail's lucky scarf.

While Abigail and Polly made preparations for their trip to Cornwall, Sandy did likewise. He suggested to his young wife, Windflower that they take a relaxing touring holiday around the West Country where she could earn a few bob reading her beloved Cards, should she so desire. And as driver, he planned to make sure they ended up on the Lizard Peninsula, in a place called Trengillion, where Abigail said Polly was to perform at the village's Diamond Jubilee celebrations.

Windflower was ecstatic about touring the West Country and when Sandy suggested they hire an old gypsy-style caravan and dress as old hippies, she thought it a thrilling idea. She was, however, a little reluctant at first, about wearing aging make-up. After all, she was a good fifteen years younger than Sandy and her skin was fair and blemish free. Sandy's skin, on the other hand, showed signs of wear. As a smoker and a sun-worshipper, many tell-tale lines were already in place.

Abigail grinned. Little did silly, naïve Windflower know the real reason for the disguise. It was planned as a precaution. Sandy doubted his cousin Polly would recognise him as they had not met since they were tiny children, but there was always the slight possibility there might be some family resemblance which might cause her to ask questions.

Everything had gone according to plan. Inside Trengillion's pub, Abigail had the Cards read by Windflower purposely so they could form a friendship. And Sandy had put on an amazing performance pretending they were all meeting for the very first time. Windflower was astounded when she learned from Abigail they all lived in Reading and they agreed they must meet up again when the holiday was over.

It was originally planned that Sandy would take Polly's life after he'd lured her away some time after her performance at the Jubilee celebrations, ideally when the Discordant Dukes were playing and holding the attention of the multitudes. Abigail would be Sandy's alibi and vice versa. Windflower would be out of the way, her drink having been laced with crushed sleeping tablets. There was, however, a change of plan when Polly conveniently formed a liaison with Ollie Collins. Ollie, Sandy deemed, would make the perfect scapegoat. And so a second, more daring plan, was hatched.

As luck would have it Polly went straight to Ollie after her successful performance. They talked for a while and then left the crowds and walked through the gardens down towards the pond and the meadow. Sandy gave Abigail the thumbs up and quietly slipped away while everyone watched and listened to the Discordant Dukes. When he returned he told her excitedly the plan had worked. The deed was done. He had successfully hypnotised Ollie, strangled Polly and then woken Ollie from his trance by ringing his mobile from an old phone in which he'd put a new sim card under the name and address of Gus Richardson, an erstwhile employer he didn't much care for.

Leaning back in the chair Abigail crossed her legs beneath the table and smiled - a self-satisfied, smug smile. There was no need for her to co-operate with Detective Inspector Peck. There were no witnesses. There was no evidence to link herself and Sandy to the crime. Detective Inspector Peck could question her until the cows came home, but she would not crack. She would not tell. And when everything blew over Sandy would claim his rightful inheritance and be rich. He would leave silly little Windflower and together they would move abroad and spend the rest of their days living in the sun on a tropical island.

When Detective Inspector Peck returned he was not alone. Abigail took little notice of the man by the inspector's side. She was determined to say nothing. The inspector sat. The man did likewise.

"I hope you don't mind Charlie being present," the inspector said, casually, attempting to hide a smirk.

"Of course not," said Abigail, haughtily, her face lit by a self-satisfied smile, "I have nothing to say to you or anyone else you care to bring along." She turned her head towards the wall to emphasise her lack of concern.

"Good," said the inspector, "but for the record, I ought to tell you Charlie is a hypnotist."

The smile half vanished from Abigail's face. She turned her head, her cheeks noticeably pink. "A hypnotist! How silly. Surely you jest."

Detective Inspector Peck slowly shook his head. "No, Ms Armstrong, I do not."

Abigail felt the palms of her hands break into a sweat. She must keep calm. "And?" She muttered, nervously.

"And," said the inspector, "Charlie hypnotised Oliver Collins yesterday afternoon."

The colour drained from Abigail's face. "May I ask for what purpose?"

"The purpose, my dear Ms Armstrong, was to try and establish the truth."

Abigail laughed, nervously. "How absurd."

The inspector smiled. "Absurd you might think, but the process did achieve its objective. You see, through great duress the lad was able to relive the dreadful night on which Polly Jolly died, and I'm sure you'll not be surprised to learn that he and Polly were not alone at the time."

Abigail felt dizzy. Her world was falling apart. She saw contempt in the inspector's eyes. And as the implications sank in, she realised he had won.

Abigail Armstrong speedily confessed. Detective Inspector Peck was delighted. Although of course he did not divulge the fact Ollie was unable to say, under hypnosis, just who had killed Polly Jolly. Once Abigail's confession was recorded. Nigel Saunders and Abigail Armstrong were separately charged with the murder of Polly Jolly and taken into custody. Later that afternoon back in Cornwall and in a state of shock, Ollie was told he was free to go.

When Tally heard the news following a phone call from her Auntie Anne to her mother, she could think of no-one she wanted to convey the good news to more than Jim. Leaving her mother to ring Wills in London, Tally grabbed her jacket and ran from the house down the cliff path and into the village. She did not stop until she reached the allotments, where instinct foretold Jim would be working.

Jim was hoeing between rows of onions when he became aware of someone screaming his name. Recognising the voice, even in its crazed state, he leaned the hoe on the side of a water butt and walked towards the gate of his vegetable patch.

Seeing him, Tally ran along the grassed path, waving her arms, screaming louder still. "It's Ollie, Jim. It's Ollie. Oh, Jim, he's been released."

Puzzled, Jim strode forward to meet her. "Released, I don't understand."

Reaching him she flung her arms around his neck and kissed his cheek. "Ollie has been released because someone else has confessed. Isn't it splendid news? Auntie Anne rang Mum a few minutes ago before she left to pick him up. Mum's over the moon. She partly solved the mystery, you see, because she came up with the hypnotism idea."

Jim laughed as Tally released him from her embrace. "When you've calmed down you can explain, as I'm rather in the dark. I mean, hypnotism. What's that got to do with anything?"

Tally laughed and took both his hands in hers. "Let's go to the Jolly Sailor. I could do with a drink and then I'll explain. I'm sure there will be lots of people in there too who will want to know just what's what, including Justin and Morgana."

To Jim's delight she continued to hold his hand as they left the allotments and walked together through the village to the Jolly Sailor.

Chapter Twenty Seven

On Tuesday morning, Elizabeth Castor-Hunt sprang out of bed, slipped on her dressing gown and ran down the stairs with a spring in each step. As she filled the kettle, she sang, and as she crossed the kitchen to get milk from the fridge, she danced. Ollie was innocent. Ollie was free. Ollie was home, she sang the words with happiness and enthusiasm. Life had never felt so good.

After breakfast she put the dirty dishes in the dish washer and then went upstairs to shower and dress. She put on her favourite skirt and favourite jumper, brushed her hair and sprayed lashings of perfume around her neck and on her wrists. She then returned downstairs, picked up a small package and an envelope from the mantelpiece, took the car keys from the hook in the hall and went outside. She felt a little guilty as she climbed into the car, conscious she ought to walk for the sake both of environment and her figure, but she convinced herself it was likely to rain and therefore to take the car was perfectly acceptable. She started the engine and drove along the drive singing happily to the car radio.

Outside Rose Cottage she parked the car, got out and walked up the garden path clutching the card and small package. She was a little apprehensive. For her father's eighty sixth birthday, unable to think of anything original, she had bought a silver ballpoint pen on which she'd had his name engraved and she wasn't convinced it was a good choice.

After entering the back porch she opened the door leading into the kitchen. "Don't get up, Dad, it's only me," she called.

But Ned was already on his feet. He had heard the car and was straightening the cushions on the settee, left squashed by an earlier visitor.

"Happy birthday, Dad," she said, giving him a hug, "can't believe you're eighty six. You're marvellous for your age."

Ned beamed. "Thanks, Liz. I must admit I'm very lucky to have got through life without too much illness and trauma, well, apart from the last twelve months, that is. It didn't do me much good losing your dear mother, but I feel she's still here keeping an eye on me and that helps."

Elizabeth smiled. "Yes, I'm sure she is and so is Grandma." She handed Ned the card and present and then sat down beside him on the settee. "I hope you like it."

To her immense relief Ned said he was delighted.

"Do you really like it?" Elizabeth asked, "I mean, you don't think it's too flashy?"

Ned shook his head. "Not at all. You know, I've never had a pen with my name on before. I think it's smashing, Liz, and I'm so glad you've had it engraved Ned Stanley and not Edward. No-one has called me Edward for as long as I can remember: other than in an official capacity that is."

Elizabeth heaved a deep sigh. "Wow, I'm so glad. I was going to make you a birthday cake too, but Jess beat me to it. Whoops! I really shouldn't have said that because it's meant to be a surprise."

Ned grinned. "And surprise it was. Jess dropped the cake in on her way to open up the Pickled Egg this morning."

"She did. Where is it?"

"In the kitchen on top of the work surface beside the sink. I'm surprised you didn't see it."

Elizabeth jumped up and walked into the kitchen. "Well, I'll be damned. How on earth did I miss seeing that? And what a beauty. Jess really is a clever old stick, but it seems a shame to cut it."

"That's what I thought," Ned said, as Elizabeth returned to the living room, "And I suppose I ought to cut it today, especially as I'm getting a few visitors calling. But I want everyone to see it intact first."

"In which case," said Elizabeth, "I'll rally together the troops and we'll pop round this evening and help you eat it, after all there is much to celebrate."

"I thought you celebrated last night."

"We did, but it was only a quiet affair, just me Greg, Tally, Anne, John, Tony and Jean. Jess couldn't get away because she was icing your cake, and Ollie, bless him, is still in a daze and not ready to start celebrating yet."

"I'm not surprised," said Ned, "after all being found innocent only takes away half of the pain and anguish. Poor lad, he's been to hell and back and it will probably take a very long time til he's able to come to terms with Polly's death."

"Yes, you're right of course and we must all treat him with kid gloves for a while. Nevertheless, I shall try and get him to come here tonight: he mustn't be left on his own to brood too much, and talking often helps. It has to be said, he spent a lot of time on his own locked up awaiting trial, so he's already had more than enough time to mull things over. It must have been awful though not being able to remember what happened that night and seeing no-one believed him."

Ned nodded. "How about you making us both a coffee."

Elizabeth jumped up. "Good idea. And do you have any biscuits in the tin? I'm feeling quite peckish."

"Yes, there are some chocolate digestives, but I doubt you'll want them: too many calories, I believe."

"You're right, of course, but chocolate digestives are my favourite."

Ned's raised his eyebrows. "You've finished with the dieting then."

"Only on days when there are no cakes and chocolate biscuits around."

Ned grinned. "You sound like Gertie. She's always twittering on about weight and cake, not that I'm complaining."

"Has Gertie been round to see you yet today?"

Ned shook his head. "Not yet, but she did ring first thing to say she'll be round this afternoon. She's bringing me a chocolate éclair. We were talking about cream cakes the other day, you see, and I happened to say I used to love chocolate éclairs many, many moons ago. Bless her. She said she'd take a trip into Helston this morning to get me one. How's that for dedication?"

Gertie arrived with a box of four cream cakes just after three o'clock.

"I had to get four Ned because I couldn't decide which to have for myself. So, as you can see, I bought a chocolate éclair, a cream doughnut, a French horn and a vanilla slice, and I only had a small sandwich for lunch to make sure I had room left."

Ned opened the box which Gertie had placed on his lap as she removed her coat.

"Happy birthday, by the way. Fancy you being eighty six. It's a good age, Ned, and I must admit you don't look a day over seventy."

"That's because your eyesight isn't what it was, Gert, but thanks for the compliment anyway. I just wish I felt like a seventy year old."

From her handbag Gertie took a birthday card. "You open that while I put the kettle on. We can't eat cream cakes without a nice cup of tea. And then we can discuss the latest news about Ollie."

Ned opened the card which, as he anticipated, was saucy. He laughed, both at the card and Gertie's message.

Inside the Old Vicarage, Anne put down the phone after she had rung Guy Richardson to tell him of Ollie's release. Guy had intended to visit Trengillion on the Monday, but a return of the troublesome gout when he had woken that day, had prevented him from doing so. As it turned out, his help had not been needed, but Anne was delighted to confirm his identification of Nigel Saunders was correct, and had Ollie not been hypnotised and the truth learned that way, then Guy's information might also have ultimately led to the arrests of Sandy and Abigail.

"I'm amazed and disgusted," said Guy, "by the lengths people will go to for money. It's quite sickening."

"I agree, and such evil doings inevitably swallow up many innocent people along the way."

"Sadly, yes. By the way, how did Nigel Saunders get hold of your son's mobile number?"

"Easy," said Anne, "Abigail confessed she went through the numbers on Polly's phone one day while Polly was showering. She knew it was there, because Polly and Ollie had frequently sent each other texts."

The following night there was a party in the Jolly Sailor to celebrate Ollie's release. At first Ollie was reluctant to attend. After all, he had suffered much over the preceding weeks and was still mourning the loss of Polly. But eventually Jess persuaded him to go. She reminded him people had never lost faith in him and many had worked tirelessly to try and prove his innocence. In attendance were

Ollie's two remaining grandparents, his father's mother, Gertie, and his mother's father, Ned. Both sat in the snug reminiscing.

"We've seen a few parties in here, haven't we, Ned? And I think we could teach these youngsters a thing or two."

Ned smiled. "We certainly have, and I don't think any of them, parties that is, have ever topped my first in 1952. Do you remember, Flo Hughes' sixtieth, Gert?"

Gertie's eyes sparkled with girlish glee. "How could I ever forget? It was one of the happiest nights of my life. Your mum looked stunning and the major couldn't keep his hands off her. And you danced with me. I was over the moon."

"And you wore a frock your mum had made especially for the do. In which, if I might be permitted to say, you too, looked stunning, Gert."

"Fancy you remembering that. You old flatterer."

"And it was your mum, if I remember correctly, who was dancing with drunken Albert Treloar when he lost his balance and fell into Sylvia's record player and broke it. There were a lot of unhappy people when the music and dancing stopped."

Gertie giggled. "But not for long. Your mum soon got the party going again with her séance thing. Blimey! She scared the life out of us all when she got hold of that politician chappie."

Ned sighed. "But let's not recall events that happened soon after that, and spoil our happy memories."

Feeling warm, Gertie unbuttoned her coat. "When you first got here, Ned, did you ever think you'd spend the rest of your days here?"

Ned reached for his glass and took a sip of real ale. "No, Gert. I certainly did not. In fact during the first couple of days, until I met you, I didn't think I'd even stay the course of my convalescence. I was dreadfully lonely, you see, and felt like a fish out of water."

Gertie reached out and linked her arm through his. "Funny old thing, fate."

"Indeed it is," Ned agreed.

"And if you were able to live it all again, is there anything you'd change, apart from the Jane affair, that is?"

Ned thought for a while and then said, "I've been happy all these sixty years, Gert, and apart from wishing people we've known hadn't met an early demise, there's little I've had to complain about. In fact the only thing I regret is Raymond Withers changing the name of this place to the Sherriff's Badge. I really resented him doing that, but then at the same time, the Ringing Bells Inn was a name that belonged to Frank Newton and so I suppose in a way, it was right the name was changed. The Ringing Bells Inn belonged to our generation, didn't it? And apart from us they've all gone."

"Sadly, yes. So what do you think of the name Jolly Sailor?"

Ned laughed. "I think, Gert, it just about sums up the way things are today, and is very much suited to our current landlord."

Chapter Twenty Eight

"What's the matter, Morgana? You seem very distant this morning."

Morgana looked away from the sitting room window of the Jolly Sailor where she'd been staring into space. "I don't know. Well, that is to say, I do. It's Mum and Dad. Everything that's been going on here this summer has made me realise the importance of the family. I've not seen any of my family at all this year. And, well, I sort of miss them."

Justin, doing paperwork, laid down his pen. "Then you must go and see them. Take a week away, or more if you want. I'm sure Tally will give me a hand now all the awful business over Ollie has been cleared up."

Morgana smiled. "That's very sweet of you, Justin, but I wouldn't dream of leaving you during the summer season."

"The summer season's nearly finished, love, once Bank Holiday is over things will quieten down dramatically."

Morgana shook her head. "I know, but I still won't leave you. I'd not be able to enjoy myself anyway, because I'd feel guilty."

"Then we'll both go in the autumn, even if we have to close the place for a week."

Morgana half smiled. "You can't do that. It wouldn't be right. A public house should never close on any day other than Christmas Day."

Justin frowned. "Look at me, Morgana."

When Morgana lifted her head Justin saw there were tears in her eyes. "You really are homesick, aren't you? Homesick for Wales."

Morgana nodded. "Yes. Oh Justin, I feel so confused. If the truth be known, I want to return to my homeland and stay there forever. I want to walk along the streets I knew as a girl; have coffee with Mum and Dad in the house where I grew up and hear the lilt of the Welsh accent. I know it's very selfish of me. I mean, I love Trengillion and I know you do too, but it..."

To Justin's surprise Morgana began to cry. "You don't want to leave me, do you, Morgana?"

She shook her head and attempted to laugh. "No, of course not. I couldn't live without you. You're the best thing that's ever happened to me. If only we could be in two places at once, but we can't, can we?"

Justin smiled. "My dear, dear, silly Morgana. If you want to go back to Wales then you shall. We'll both go. We'll sell the Jolly Sailor and perhaps even get a nice little pub, near, or in your hometown. How does that sound?"

Morgana gazed lovingly at her husband. "Would you really do that for me?"

Justin rose from the chair, crossed the room and took her in his arms. "I love you, and if you're no longer happy here, then I'm no longer happy, and it's time to move on. I'm not saying I won't miss this place, because I will. After all, I've been here for thirteen years. But all good things must come to an end and a change is as good as a rest. Besides, the good people of Trengillion might welcome a change themselves."

Morgana smiled. "I doubt it. They'll never have as good a landlord as you."

"They will," said Justin, "because I shall make sure whoever we sell to is worthy of this fantastic, friendly village."

Morgana laughed. "Selling might take quite a while then."

Tally woke early on Friday morning. It was her birthday and she had much to consider. She was another year older, yet still she felt she was not following the path fate meant her to pursue. Wanting time to think, she left Chy-an-Gwyns after breakfast and walked along the cliff path to the Witches Broomstick. Above the tourist attraction she stopped, sat on rocks, hugged her knees and contemplated her options.

The obvious choice was of course to return to teaching when the new term began in September. The School had, after all, been very good in giving her compassionate leave following Ollie's arrest and she did very much like her work colleagues. But teaching was not something she wished to do for the rest of her working life.

The next option was to find herself a wealthy husband and become a housewife and mother. The idea appealed but only slightly. Anyway, Trengillion wasn't exactly bristling with handsome millionaires and as she seldom went outside a ten mile radius of the village and much of that was in the sea, the likelihood of that idea coming to fruition seemed extremely remote.

She contemplated returning to college. She could take up nursing, the law, become a potter, a fashion designer, an actress or a politician. She laughed. Nothing really appealed.

Above, a flock of seagulls swirled and hovered. Tally lifted her head and watched. As they veered out towards the sea she felt a splat on her arm. Tally looked at the sleeve of her jumper and laughed. Seagull droppings were said to be lucky.

"If that's your way of saying happy birthday, then thank you," she giggled, rising to her feet. She then headed for home to change her top.

Ollie Collins, after much soul searching, was at last enjoying his freedom. Although he was still being sought after by the media each offering him vast amounts of money to tell of his relationship with Polly Jolly and the consequences thereof, Ollie would not tell. The story was too painful and he refused to make a single penny out of Polly's tragic death.

On Tally's birthday, as he sat on Denzil's bench watching the waves relentlessly crash onto the sea shore, he saw a young woman crossing the shingle. She seemed to be heading his way. When she reached him, she stopped. Ollie eyed her with suspicion. "If you're from the media then I've nothing to say," he snapped, turning away his head.

She half smiled, clearly nervous, and tossed her dark brown curls. "I'm not. You obviously don't recognise me, do you? I must say, that's a relief."

Ollie frowned and shook his head.

She sat down on the bench by his side. "I, like you, have suffered much of late, but without doubt your pain is far greater than mine."

From her pocket she took a pack of cards. "This is a clue."

"Windflower," whispered Ollie, sliding along the bench away from her, "they're Windflower's Cards, but…"

"…and I am Windflower."

Ollie frowned, confused, unable to speak. The woman broke the silence. Her voice quaked and quivered with emotion. "Ever since the day you picked out the Death card I've been riddled with guilt, Ollie. But never, never in my wildest dreams would I have guessed the cruel sequence of events which were to follow."

"Windflower," stammered Ollie, "it can't be you."

"It is."

Ollie looked at her and suddenly angered by her presence, began to rise. "Well, what the devil are you doing here? You've got a damn cheek, I must say."

Windflower's bottom lip trembled. Tears filled her eyes and she grabbed his arm. "Please don't go. Stay. I've come to apologise."

Ollie dragged his arm from her grasp. "Apologise! So what part did you play in the little charade?"

"I didn't play any part. It all came as an enormous shock to me. Who Sandy was, I mean. But I feel I still must apologise for his dreadful behaviour, Ollie. Because deep down I should have known, should have been more alert, less trusting even."

Ollie shook his head. "I don't believe you. You must have known he was Polly's cousin."

Windflower stood up. "I didn't. I'd not the slightest idea. His mother's maiden name was Saunders, you see. When she and her husband, Sandy's father, divorced, she changed her name back to Saunders and that of her son, Sandy too. But I didn't know that. I didn't know his father was a Gower. I assumed he was a Saunders. I didn't know about the name change until a few weeks back. But even if I had known, I wouldn't have connected him to Geoffrey Gower. Sandy tricked me too, Ollie. And I feel so unclean. So used. But having said that I didn't even know a man called Geoffrey Gower existed."

Ollie lifted her chin and looked her in the eye. A sudden pang of pity replaced anger. "I don't suppose for either of us life will ever be the same again," he whispered.

"No. But at least you have a loving family around you and a wonderful village where you have lots of sympathy and support. I don't want to sound hard done by, but I've lost everything. My husband. My self-respect. And now I'm on my own, I shall even lose my home."

"Your home?"

Windflower nodded. "Yes, it's rented, you see. I shall not be able to afford to live there on my own. Not that I want to. The memories are too raw."

She tried not to cry.

Ollie gently pulled her arm and they sat back down on the bench.

"How long are you in Trengillion for?"

"I don't really know. I came down by train yesterday. No way would I drive the old Zephyr. I stayed in Helston last night. Trying to pluck up courage to come here, you might say. I shall probably stay for a couple of days and then go back and try to pick up the pieces." She half smiled. "Not that I have a job to go back to. I left the café where I worked, you see. Most people were kind and sympathetic to my face, but I knew behind my back they were saying nasty things and so were my neighbours. Customers too kept coming in and pointing at me. I don't think anyone believes me."

"I do," said Ollie, "I believe you."

She smiled. "Then I don't care about anybody else."

"Have you arranged lodgings here yet?"

Windflower shook her head, "I thought I'd try the pub. Justin and Morgana seemed really nice."

"Yes, they are. They'll be sorely missed when they're gone."

"Gone. I don't understand. Gone where?"

"To Wales, I think. Morgana comes from there and I've heard she wants to be nearer her family."

"Oh."

"Is Windflower your real name?"

She nodded. "Yes. My parents were into the hippy thing back in the seventies, but funnily enough, I've never really minded."

"It's a pretty name."

"Thank you."

Ollie stood up and held out his hand to help Windflower up. "Come on. You're going to stay with us at the Old Vicarage."

Confused she rose to her feet. "But I can't. I mean, your parents. They must hate me. It would be too embarrassing."

Ollie grinned. "I can assure you Mum and Dad won't mind a bit. In fact they'll be pleased to see you. Especially when they hear your side of the story."

"But…"

"No buts. Come on."

Ollie took her hand and led her over the compressed sand towards the road.

"By the way. How did you know I'd be on the beach?"

Windflower smiled. "When you've been doing the Cards as long as me you get to know many things by instinct."

"Yet you never suspected your husband of deceit."

Windflower lowered her head to hide her quivering lips. "No, but I never wanted to believe you were guilty either, even though the evidence was all against you. I said as much to Sandy many times but on reflection, I realise he was always quick to change the subject. He pretended it was too painful to talk about. I thought he was being sensitive. What a cad. And what a fool I was."

Tally, having changed her top, was drinking coffee with her mother, Elizabeth, at Chy-an-Gwyns when they heard the distinct click of the letterbox.

"I expect the postman has brought me stacks of birthday cards," said Tally, rising. "I'd better go and see."

"Well, there should be at least one," said Elizabeth. "Wills may have forgotten in the past but Lydia's red hot when it comes to remembering birthdays."

Tally returned with the morning's post. "Two for me, one for you and two for Dad."

She opened the first, obviously from Wills and Lydia. The second confused her. She opened it and to her immense surprise found it was from Jim and inside was a Lottery ticket and a message saying. 'Hope this will enable you to follow your dreams'.

"Oh, that's really sweet," said Tally, showing the card to her mother. "Not that the ticket will win. Life just isn't like that."

Tally took the cards into the drawing room and placed them on the mantelpiece beside those already received. The Lottery ticket she tucked beneath the brass carriage clock.

"Have you anything planned for today?" Elizabeth asked.

Tally shook her head

"Then perhaps Dad and I could take you out for a meal."

Tally nodded. "On the other hand, we could just go out for a drink. It would be nice to pop in the Jolly Sailor, especially if this is likely to be Justin and Morgana's last summer, and I never feel much like drinking when I've eaten out."

"I quite agree. I always eat too much when out anyway. They always have such mouth-watering desserts on offer."

"Good. That's settled then. I'll text Jess and Ollie and get them to join us. Perhaps you could get Granddad to pop along too."

"I'm sure he'd like that. In fact I'll nip down there now and ask him. I could do with stretching my legs."

When Elizabeth returned she handed Tally a birthday card from Ned. Tally opened it. Inside was a cheque for fifty pounds.

"Oh Mum, he shouldn't give me that much. Are you sure he can afford it?"

"He's fine, Tally. The house is bought and paid for and his pensions are more than enough to cover day to day expenses. Food doesn't amount to much when you get older, so I'm told."

Tally put the cheque beneath the clock along with her Lottery ticket. The card she placed on the mantelpiece with the others. But as she turned away she caught sight of the message she'd already read, written inside Jim's card. Something made her pause. Made her think. She felt a sudden surge of excitement. She grabbed the card. Of course, it was the way he had written his capital H. Not straight and uniform like most people, but with a curl on the bottom of the second vertical line. She dropped the card on the settee and ran upstairs. From the drawer of her bedside cabinet she pulled out a pink envelope. Inside it was the mystery Valentine card. She looked at her name and address written in capital letters. The H for Hunt had the same curl as the H for Hope in her birthday card. Tally ran downstairs and compared the two. There was no doubt in her mind. Jim Haynes had sent the Valentine card and no doubt the red roses too.

"I'm just popping out," Tally shouted to Elizabeth who was in the kitchen, "won't be long."

Elizabeth heard the front door slam. Puzzled she walked into the drawing room. On the settee she saw the birthday card and the pink envelope. Suddenly the penny dropped. "Well I never," she whispered. She laid the cards back down on the settee, clasped her hands and looked heavenwards, a beseeching expression in her rapidly watering eyes.

Tally ran through the village to the allotments. Jim was not there. As she fled from the allotment field she saw her Auntie Anne opening the gate at the top of the Old Vicarage driveway, her bicycle by her side.

"Auntie, please may I borrow your bike? That's if you've finished with it. I won't be long."

"Of course. But what's the rush? Nothing wrong, I hope."

Tally laughed, as she mounted the bicycle. "No, everything's fine. In fact it couldn't be better. I'll tell you later."

Tally peddled along the road towards Ebenezer House faster than she'd ever ridden a bicycle in her life. She felt ecstatic. Jubilant. As though the mist which had shrouded her vision was finally lifting. She could see her future. A future in which Jim played a huge part.

Jim was outside the front of Ebenezer House watering tubs of flowers. He raised his eyebrows as Tally leapt from the bicycle, opened the gate and ran up the garden path.

"Are you all right, Tally? You can't have won the Lottery because it's not been drawn yet."

"Oh, but I have. Well, not exactly. I've won a different type of lottery. It was you, Jim, wasn't it? You sent me the Valentine card."

Jim was so surprised he sat down on the wooden bench beside the front door of his home.

"Yes. But how come you've found out? It was months ago?"

"It's the way you write your capital Hs. The curl gave it away. But why did you never say anything? And to think we went away together too. It's crazy."

"Well, actually, I did make up my mind that I'd tell you when we got back from London. I mean, we got on so well, didn't we? But then of course, the Ollie thing happened and I just thought perhaps you and I weren't meant to be."

"Fiddlesticks," said Tally, falling to her knees in front of him. She took his shaking hands in hers. "Jim Haynes, I know it's not February the twenty ninth, but it is still a leap year, and right now I feel justified in pushing my luck. Will you marry me?"

The gathering in the Jolly Sailor had a double celebration that evening, Tally's birthday and the announcement of her engagement to Jim. And the following day, Jim, overjoyed with the change of events, drove Tally into Helston where he bought her a diamond engagement ring.

Tally likewise, was delighted with life. She was beginning to see the future with more clarity and although there was still an uncertainty over her career direction, she did at least know with whom she would be spending the rest of her days.

Inside the Jolly Sailor, a few days later, as Jim returned to the snug with drinks, he found Tally absently gazing into the empty fireplace.

"You're miles away, sweetheart. What are you thinking of?"

Tally raised her head and smiled. "I was just day dreaming: imagining you and I owning and running this place. I'm dreading Justin and Morgana going. I'm sure I shall never like the new people, however nice they might be. But then perhaps it's just because I hate change."

Jim took up her hand and squeezed it tightly. "Would you really like to be landlady here?"

Tally nodded. "Hmm, I would. I feel very attached to the place. Almost as though I belong."

"In that case I shall sell my house, get a bank loan and buy it for you."

Tally laughed. "That's a lovely gesture, but I'm afraid the bank loan would have to be huge and with houses not selling and pubs closing left, right and centre, I'd think to get a loan on such a risky business would be damn near impossible."

Jim sighed deeply. "I suppose you're right. At best my place would be worth only two hundred and fifty thousand, and I know with this place being a free house, Justin'd looking for around six hundred thousand, which is quite reasonable, I think, considering the location."

Tally nodded. "Don't laugh, but I've started doing the Lottery on a regular basis. I do it online and I'm in a draw every day of the year. So the law of averages says I must surely win something."

Jim laughed. “Yeah, a tenner, that’s the most I’ve ever won and that was years ago. And the ticket I bought you for your birthday was no good. But how come you’re in a draw every day?”

“I’m in the National Lottery draw on Wednesdays and Saturdays and the Plus five draws the other five days.”

“And how much could you win with the Plus five?” Jim asked. “I’m not familiar with the set up there.”

Tally giggled. “As little as two pound fifty, and as much as two hundred and fifty thousand.”

Jim pulled her close and kissed her. “I love your optimism, Tally, but I think if you really want this place we’ll have to come up with a more realistic plan.”

A week later the Jolly Sailor was advertised for the first time and with its publicity came several couples interested in buying the place. None though was in a position to buy nor had any experience in running a public house.

“Time wasters,” spluttered Justin, as a couple attracted only to the appearance of the place and with no interest in the business side of things, left the premises. “They couldn’t run a pub to save their lives.”

Meanwhile on the front wall of Ebenezer House a ‘for sale’ board was erected by a local estate agent, and inside Jim was phoning his bank to arrange a meeting regarding a loan. An appointment was made for early September.

August Bank Holiday was wet, but two days later the rain cleared just in time for the beginning of the London Paralympics. And on August the thirty first, the last day of the month the weather was lovely, no wind and lots of glorious sunshine.

Inside Number Four Coronation Terrace, Trish Tilley looked at the calendar hanging on the kitchen wall beside the window, with utter loathing. August was as good as over: she had not found herself a boyfriend and now it looked as though her precious hair was facing the chop. Hoping he might agree, she had earlier suggested to Wayne, before he had gone out walking, they call it quits, so neither would have to face the forfeits agreed. But to her dismay he had laughed, and actually said he was looking forward to seeing his hair a different colour. Trish quietly fumed. But then considered, if the choice of colour was to be hers, perhaps she could teach him a lesson and dye his hair something ludicrous like shocking pink, purple, or even green. She shook her head, because the agreement was he would cut her hair, and she knew if she made him look daft then she'd end up with a short back and sides.

The morning looked like dragging and despite the weather being bright and sunny, Trish had no motivation to make good use of it and go outdoors. Instead, she sat and moped. She was still moping when Wayne arrived home.

"What's up with you?" he asked, as he reached for the kettle, "you look proper fed up."

"I am."

"Really. Why?"

"Pretty obvious isn't it? I don't want to lose my hair."

"Ah! Coffee for you?"

"Yes, please."

"It's funny you should mention hair, because I've been thinking." A look of hope flashed across Trish's face. "Yes, I've been thinking, that rather than you dye my hair and I cut yours, we ought to make appointments with Rebecca Williams and have our transformations done properly. What do you think?"

Trish's face dropped. "Can't we forget the whole thing? There's nothing wrong with your ginger top."

Wayne shook his head. "No, we agreed, and a deal is a deal. Mum and Dad always told us we must never go back on our word."

"Oh yeah, but they meant over serious things, not silly hairdos."

Wayne shrugged his shoulders. "I take it your answer is no then. To having Rebecca do our hair, I mean."

"Do what you want, I don't care."

Wayne grinned as he pulled his mobile phone from the pocket of his trousers, and within minutes he was talking to Rebecca at her hairdressing salon.

Chapter Twenty Nine

At ten o'clock on Friday morning, an hour before opening time, a rather grand car pulled up on the cobbled area in front of the Jolly Sailor. From it stepped a couple in their mid to late fifties. Morgana watched from the window of the dining room.

"The Watkins are here," she called to Justin who was in the kitchen hoping to grab a quick coffee before the arrival of potential purchasers. "They're not exactly spring chickens, but they look like they might be worth a bob or two."

Justin groaned and switched off the kettle. "In which case I expect they'll be looking for something to do in their retirement and think running a little pub will be the perfect thing. Silly sods."

Morgana laughed. "Time will tell, I'll go and let them in. It looks like they're coming to the side door."

To Justin's surprise the Watkins were very businesslike. They were familiar with the licensed trade having been involved with it throughout their working lives. For twenty years John Watkins had worked for a large brewery, after which he had started his own business in the Midlands brewing real ales which soon became well established and popular. That business was now sold.

After looking over the premises, John let it be known, he and his wife, Audrey, were extremely interested in purchasing the Jolly Sailor. Morgana, somewhat overwhelmed by the meeting, suggested they return to the snug bar for coffee.

The sun was streaming through the window of the snug as John and Audrey took their places on the window seat and Justin pulled up a stool.

"We're in a very good position to buy," said John Watkins, nodding his thanks to Morgana as she placed coffee on the table in front of him. "Not only have we sold the business but we've sold our home too. Our furniture is in store and we're currently touring the West Country looking for our idea of the ideal pub. It has to be freehold, of course, and I have to admit this place is pretty damn near perfection."

"But we'd have to change the name," said Audrey, stirring a heaped teaspoonful of sugar into her coffee. "You know, to something a bit more modern and appropriate. I hope you wouldn't take offence."

Justin shook his head. "Of course not. I changed the name myself when I came here. The Jolly Sailor reflects my past. I was in the Navy, you see."

John grinned. "So what was it called when you bought it?"

"The Fox and Hounds. I changed it because I didn't approve of fox hunting. Still don't. I also thought it an inappropriate name for a coastal pub. At least the Jolly Sailor relates to the sea."

"Hmm, yes, I suppose it does," said John.

"Have you a name in mind?" asked Morgana.

Audrey leaned forward. "Personally, I'd like to call it something completely different. Something no other pub is called. The Nip and Nosh or the Scoff and Tipple. Something like that."

John winced. "Anyway, that's of no importance at present. I'm prepared to make you a very good offer here and now, but before I do I really think Audrey and me ought to go away and discuss things. We've also got another place to look at this afternoon, but it's not by the sea, so I don't think for one minute it'll be of any interest. We'll go and see it though, if only for the sake of courtesy."

"Yes, of course," said Justin, "we understand."

All rose and shook hands.

"I expect we'll be back. And if we are, we'll book a room and stay the night, if that's okay."

"Of course," said Morgana, "we have a double room vacant: the Gibsons, a nice couple from Darlington, left early this morning."

Tally and Jim went to the Jolly Sailor in the evening to discuss Jim's meeting the following Monday with the bank. When they heard from Morgana of the possible sale, both were shattered. Jim was already somewhat down-hearted because only one of the two parties who had made appointments to view his property that day, had actually turned up.

At half past seven the door of the Jolly Sailor opened. Audrey Watkins wafted into the bar followed by her grinning husband.

"If it's still available, we'd like to book a room for the night, there is after all much to discuss."

"The other pub was not to your liking then," said Morgana.

Audrey shook her head. "Not a patch on this place. I've said from day one I want to be near the sea."

They took stools alongside the bar, near to Jim and Tally, who sat looking glum. Tally in particular was fighting hard to hold back the tears.

Without beating about the bush John bluntly told Justin he was prepared to pay the asking price as long as the sale could be over and done with as quickly as possible.

"It's my birthday on October the twelfth," said Audrey, "my fifty-fifth. We'd like to be in by then so we can have a bit of a do."

A little later that evening Jim walked Tally home to Chy-an-Gwyns. She was very down-hearted. Nothing he could say or do cheered her. Her dreams were in tatters.

Elizabeth was watching the News when she reached home. Greg was sitting at his laptop. Tally sat down on the settee with a disillusioned groan.

Elizabeth picked up the television's remote control and turned down the volume. "You're home early, Tally, is anything wrong?"

"Everything," she spluttered.

Elizabeth switched off the television.

"It's the Jolly Sailor," said Tally, with a deep sigh, "ever since Justin told me he was going to sell up, I've felt I must buy it."

"What! But how on earth might you be able to do that, it'd be far more than you could ever borrow."

"I know, that's why I'm avidly doing the Lottery."

Greg pushed aside his laptop and rose from the table. "You can't be serious, Tally. What about your job? From all accounts I've heard you're a damn good teacher."

"But it's not what I want to do for the rest of my working life. I'm sorry, Dad, but I've always considered teaching a stop gap. You know, something to do until I decided where my real passion lays."

"Well, I don't really know what to say," said Elizabeth. "I suppose we could help if you're that serious, but we'd not be able to put our hands on the sort of money Justin is likely to want. What does Jim think of your idea?"

Tally smiled. "Dear Jim. He's all for it. In fact he put his house on the market earlier this week and the 'for sale' board went up yesterday. He's already had one lot of people viewing it; another couple should have come but they didn't turn up. So I wouldn't be going in for it alone, Jim and I would take it on together. He rather likes the idea of a pub, especially the Jolly Sailor."

Greg nodded. "Well, if Jim can sell the old chapel, we'll see what we can do about raising some money. But don't get up your hopes too high, Tally, selling houses seems to be a tricky business these days, and it's madness to even think you might win anything substantial on the Lottery."

Tally smiled. "Thanks, Dad. But sadly, it's probably already too late. That's why I'm so fed-up. Justin already has likely buyers. They were in the pub this evening, full of enthusiasm and feeling very pleased with life. Hateful pair!"

"Then that's that," said Elizabeth, shaking her head, "there's nothing we can do. Perhaps it might be worth looking elsewhere though, if Jim sells his house."

"No. Nowhere else will do. I have to have Trengillion's pub, Mum. It's meant to be. I don't know why, but it is. In fact, I shall not give up hope until I know all is lost and Justin has finally signed it over to someone else, and he and Morgana have departed for Wales."

Audrey and John Watkins enjoyed Friday evening at the Jolly Sailor. They chatted with the locals, bought rounds of drinks and listened to accounts of the Polly Jolly case, which, because of the Trengillion connection had dominated many thoughts throughout the long summer months. Finally, weary from the day's activities, they bade Justin and Morgana goodnight and climbed the stairs to their room on the front of the building.

"Well, love, do you think you'll be happy here?" John asked, as he bent to untie his shoe laces.

Audrey nodded. "Unquestionably. The locals are very nice, although one or two might become bores in time. On the whole though, they're alright."

"Hmm, I thought so too. That young woman sitting at the bar with a scruffy looking oik when we first arrived seemed a bit of a sourpuss though. She kept giving us the evil eye. Did you notice?"

Audrey shook her head as she briskly removed her make-up. "Can't say that I did. It was probably your imagination."

"No, I don't think so. She definitely seemed to bear a grudge or something like that. Anyway, it doesn't matter. If she chooses not to patronise us when we take over, it'll be her loss."

After rubbing anti-wrinkle cream all over her face, Audrey climbed into the double bed and snuggled down beneath the duvet. "Shut the window before you get into bed, John," she yawned, "there's a bit of a draught."

Inside her room at Chy-an-Gwyns, Tally sat up in bed. Frustrated by a deepening feeling of helplessness, she was unable to sleep. Repeatedly, she tossed things over in her mind, but deep down knew there was no reason to suppose the Watkins' purchase of the Jolly Sailor would not go ahead, and with no money of her own to put in a better offer, there was absolutely nothing she could do to prevent the sale. Tally thumped the pillow. Her lips trembled, she burst into floods of tears and eventually cried herself to sleep.

Down in the valley, the Watkins slept soundly in their room on the front of the Jolly Sailor. The night was calm and the dark, velvet sky was littered endlessly with millions of bright, twinkling stars. Beneath the stars, the waves of the tranquil sea, gently tumbled and splashed onto the shingle and sand; each wave falling, hushed, as though eager not to disturb the sleeping village.

In the trees behind the Jolly Sailor, a lone owl hooted as the clock's chime in the ancient church tower struck two. Suddenly, for no apparent reason, Audrey Watkins awoke. She peered over the top of the duvet and looked into the room where a shaft of moonlight rested on the foot of the bed. She shivered. She felt uneasy. All was not right.

Against the window, something outside scraped against the clear glass. Audrey pulled up the bedclothes beneath her chin and leaned forward. The curtains juddered. Audrey jumped. Without taking her eyes from the window, she reached out for John and shook him violently, digging her long painted nails into his fleshy arm. John awoke, groaned and scowled at his wife. "What the hell are y…?" His words faded away as the top sash window dropped with a hefty crash. John promptly sat up and moved closer to his wife. A dark shadow drifted across the shaft of moonlight. Simultaneously, a picture slipped from its hook on the chimney breast and fell onto the chest of drawers below, cracking the glass and sending fragrant petals, bark, hips, seeds and the aromatic peel of potpourri, floating to the floor like falling snow.

From the dressing table, Audrey's hairbrush swiftly rose and took flight across the room, smashing into the wall and crashing onto the carpeted floor. Audrey stifled a scream. Her hair stood on end. "Do something, John." John remained still. Frozen to the mattress. Too numbed to speak. Too afraid to move a muscle, apart from a quick twitch of his nose as the delicate perfume of sweetly scented violets wafted through the chilled, ice cold air.

The room fell silent as an invisible weight appeared to settle on top of the duvet covering Audrey and John's feet. Both watched in horror as they felt the weight sliding towards them, visibly creasing and crushing the bedclothes as it moved closer, trapping their legs and halting their breath. The weight neared the top of the duvet. Audrey and John instinctively leaned back. As they rested their heads on the wall, something soft, like a hand, a smooth cold hand, reached out and touched their faces. They heard faint laughter, a giggle, and then a soft voice whispered, "Go home." The weight lifted from the bed. A swift breeze flashed across the room. The top sash of the window closed and the room fell eerily silent. In a daze John reached out and switched on the bedside lamp. Audrey's hairbrush was back on the dressing table. The fallen picture was hanging on the chimney breast, and the potpourri was back in the bowl. John looked at Audrey. Her face was white.

Tally awoke feeling low-spirited. She groaned when recalling the reason why. With very little enthusiasm she stepped from her bed, but when she opened the window and breathed in the fresh air, she was overwhelmed by a sudden wave of optimism. With elbows resting on the window sill she gazed out to sea and relished the sound of the waves gently crashing onto the cliffs below. It was the beginning of a new month: her favourite month, September. The sun was shining casting golden beams across the cliff tops and the garden below. Leaving the window wide open, she picked up clothes from a wicker chair and went to the bathroom for a shower.

Elizabeth was buttering toast when Tally entered the kitchen.

"Morning, love. I've only just realised it's back to school for you next week, suddenly, I don't know where the summer's gone."

Tally dropped a teabag into a mug and switched on the kettle. "A cup for you, Mum?"

"No thanks."

"We're back on Monday, and have to go in then for the usual meetings and preparation for the coming year. I wish I had a little more enthusiasm. As it is, I'm dreading it."

Elizabeth nodded sympathetically. "I suppose it's only to be expected. You're probably a bit apprehensive because you're bound to be asked about the extraordinary case of your cousin. I mean, with any story that has made headline news it is bound to raise a lot of interest and people are always keen to say they've spoken to someone involved."

Tally groaned as she sat down at the table with her tea. "I hope not, because it's not something I like to discuss with people who don't even know Ollie. But hopefully everyone will be so wrapped up in the new term and their foreign holidays that they'll have forgotten I wasn't even there for much of last term."

"Hmm, anyway, I'm sure you'll have plenty to do today, but if you can spare the time, I'd really appreciate it if you could drop some washing down to Granddad. I'd do it myself, of course, but I really want to make the most of this dry day and tackle the weeds in the garden before they strangle all my flowers."

"Of course I will. I was going to pop into the village anyway. That is to say, I'm going to see Jim. Poor thing, I was pretty miserable last night and he bore the brunt of my bad mood. I must go and say I'm sorry."

Elizabeth smiled. "I'm pleased to see you're in a better frame of mind this morning. I suppose you've come to terms with the situation."

Tally shook her head. "Not really. But for some reason everything seems better today and I feel optimistic, and you know what they say, if you want something badly enough then you'll get it in the end."

Elizabeth raised her eyebrows. “You’re still hoping to get the Jolly Sailor then, despite the fact Justin has buyers?”

Tally laughed. “Where’s Granddad’s washing?”

“In the hall. But surely you’re not going yet, you’ve not eaten anything.”

Tally jumped up and reached for her sandals on a rack beside the back door. “I’m not hungry. But I’ll grab something later when I’ve seen Jim.” She picked up the bag of washing from the hall and then opened the back door. “Bye Mum. See you later.”

Tally walked down to the village by way of the coastal path. At the bottom she stopped on the lane which ran across the top of the beach and looked down towards the sea. She sighed. It didn’t matter how many times she saw the sea, it never failed to thrill her. Had she not been carrying her grandfather’s washing she would have wandered down to the shore and thrown a pebble into the oncoming waves. Instead, she turned and continued with her walk; the sea could wait until she was on her way home.

As she left the beach she noticed, Cove Cottage, the house in which she had spent her childhood, said, ‘Sold’, on the estate agent’s board. Wondering who might have bought Iris Delaney’s cottage, she continued along the lane, past the Pickled Egg, not yet open, and on up the steep incline towards the village. On reaching the Jolly Sailor, she was surprised to see Audrey and John Watkins outside, putting luggage into the boot of their car. Tally stopped walking and watched as they climbed into the car seats; neither looked very happy. In fact, on reflection, Tally considered, both looked utterly miserable. John slammed the driver’s door shut and as he opened the window he caught sight of Tally and glared at her angrily. “You’ll be very pleased to know we’re off now and we most certainly won’t be back.” He then started the engine and roared off through the village dramatically exceeding the speed limit.

Tally stood perfectly still, baffled by the outburst. Desperate to know the reason for the sudden change of heart, she went into the Jolly Sailor by way of the side door to seek out either Justin or Morgana.

Justin was coming down the stairs as she closed the door. “Hi, Tally, what brings you here on a Saturday morning?”

"Curiosity," she said, "what goes on with the Watkins couple? I've just seen them drive off and in none too good a mood."

Justin scratched his head. "Search me. They were fine last night, exuberant in fact, but when I saw them this morning, John said they were withdrawing their offer and heading for home. They wouldn't even stay long enough for breakfast. I'm beginning to think they're both crackers."

A broad smile crossed Tally's face. She shivered in spite of the warm feeling surging through her body.

"What's so funny?" Justin asked.

"Nothing. I wonder what made them change their minds."

Justin shrugged his shoulders. "God only knows. They mumbled something about cold hands and falling pictures. I've no idea what they were talking about and I don't suppose I ever shall."

Ned was sitting on the settee with the telephone on his lap when Tally went in with his washing.

"Were you just about to make a call?" Tally asked, after they had greeted each other.

Ned shook his head. "Actually I've just answered one. Your brother; he rang to ask me to go and stay with them in London for a week or so."

"Really, that's a splendid idea, Granddad. You'll be able to take a trip down memory lane."

Ned smiled. "Bit too old for that I think. I daresay I'll not even be able to recognise most places. Nothing stays the same for long. Anyway, I told him I'd think about it. It won't be for a month or so yet. Probably mid-October. The weather's often good then and there'll be less people about. I should imagine the place is still pretty busy at present with the Paralympics and all that."

While Tally was putting away Ned's washing in the drawers upstairs, Jill from Ivy Cottage next door called in with a pot of strawberry jam she'd made following a visit to a pick-your-own farm. Tally, happy that Ned had company, declined the offer of coffee as she was keen to see Jim and relay the news regarding the early and astonishing departure of Mr and Mrs Watkins.

As Tally approached Ebenezer House, she saw Jim standing by on the roadside talking to a young couple. Before she reached the chapel gate they got into their car and drove off, waving.

"Well, would you believe it?" Jim laughed, taking Tally's hand, "they were the couple who didn't turn up yesterday. She, Mrs Hope, that is, slipped on some rocks over on the north coast yesterday afternoon and they spent the rest of the day in A and E. The estate agents had closed by the time they got out so they decided to leave it until today to make contact with me direct and convey their apologies."

Tally opened her mouth to speak but was too dumbfounded to put her muddled thoughts into words.

Jim grinned. "Don't you want to know what they thought of the place?"

Tally raised her eyebrow. "They looked round then?"

"Well yes, of course. After all that was the original purpose of their visit."

"And?"

"And they loved it, Tally. They love the fact it was once a chapel. Loved the location and I think they quite liked me."

Tally felt her heart quicken. "And do they want to buy it?"

Jim nodded. "They said they will definitely be making an offer on Monday when the agents open. Oh, Tally, I could kick myself. If only I'd put the house up for sale earlier. Now it's too late and I'm not sure I want to leave here if the Jolly Sailor's been snapped up."

Tally burst into tears. "But it hasn't been snapped up, Jim. The sale has fallen through already. John and Audrey Watkins have gone, threatening never to set foot in Trengillion again."

"What! But that's crazy. They were potty about the place last night and couldn't wait to get in."

Tally wiped her eyes. "I know. Something obviously happened to make them change their minds. Oh, I knew when I looked from my window this morning that today was going to be good."

"Well don't get your hopes up yet. Even if I can sell the house I shall still have to convince the bank manager taking on a pub is a good idea, and I don't think that will be easy. We are after all, talking about a three hundred and fifty thousand pound loan."

Tally linked arms with Jim. "Where there's a will and all that. Anyway, how about lunch at the Jolly Sailor? We can discuss its future and I'm actually starving because I've not had any breakfast."

Jim nodded. "Good idea. I like your optimism and we might even be able to find out a bit more about the Watkins' sudden departure."

"I doubt it," said Tally. "Justin was miffed when I saw him and there's nobody else much who might have an inkling."

Jim looked at his watch. "Actually, it's much too early for lunch so come in for a coffee and I'll toast you a teacake to keep the wolf from the door."

Chapter Thirty

On Monday morning, despite the fact that she had to return to work, Tally awoke feeling even more optimistic than she had over the weekend. She and Jim had spoken with Justin and Morgana during the Saturday lunchtime visit and Justin had been delighted by the prospect of handing over the pub to local people rather than strangers. There was, however, still the meeting with the bank to overcome and Jim needed to receive a firm offer from the Hopes.

By lunchtime the first of the two hurdles was overcome. Tally found a text message from Jim when she looked at her phone in the staff room. The Hopes had made a very good offer. Their own place was already sold, Jim had accepted the offer and already it was in the hands of solicitors.

"One down and one to go," whispered Tally, "I only hope Jim's encounter with the bank manager is as fruitful."

As Tally returned her phone to her handbag, it bleeped. She picked it up and read the text message. It was another from Jim, this time asking her to wish him luck. The appointment with the bank was for half past two and already he was feeling nervous.

Tally sent a message back and then dropped her phone back into her bag. As she zipped it up, a sudden thought struck her. She hadn't checked the Lottery numbers for a couple of days. She found the website and groaned. As usual she'd won nothing in Saturday's Lottery draw, which she was surprised to see, had been shared by five winners. She laughed. She didn't even have one number.

A fellow member of staff called across the room. "Tally, I'm making tea, would you like a cup?

Tally put down her phone. "Yes please."

Outside Ebenezer House, Jim climbed into his van wearing his one and only suit. He felt uncomfortable, not just because he was wearing a collar and tie, but also because he lacked confidence when talking over money matters. Tally had wanted to go with him, but since she didn't have an account with Jim's bank, he thought it might be counter-productive. Besides, the new academic year was beginning and Tally had to go in to school.

He arrived in Helston at five minutes to two. Too early for his appointment, he decided to go for a quick coffee to steady his nerves, even though he knew a large scotch would have a far more therapeutic effect. In the coffee shop Jim took his coffee to a window seat and looked out into the street where one or two shoppers drifted by.

At two twenty seven he walked into the bank feeling like Daniel entering the lion's den. On announcing his arrival he was ushered into the interview room. A kindly looking man shook his hand. As he sat his mobile phone rang. Jim ignored it.

"Do answer it," said the bank man, pushing aside papers on his desk, "it might be important."

Jim laughed. "I doubt it." He took the phone from his pocket. The caller was Tally. Jim was miffed. Tally knew his appointment was at two thirty, so why would she choose such an inopportune moment to ring. Furthermore, she was back at school and so should be otherwise engaged.

He put the phone to his ear. "Tally, what's wrong, where are you?"

"At school, but don't worry, there's nothing wrong, in fact quite the opposite. Listen, sweetheart. I checked the Lottery results at lunchtime, but because I got distracted, I didn't get round to checking the Plus Five results for last night until I remembered a few minutes ago. Oh, Jim, you'll never believe this, but I've got all six numbers and have won two hundred and fifty thousand pounds. Isn't that wonderful? Now you only need to borrow one hundred thousand."

The weather for the first week of September remained as beautiful as the month had begun, it was even hot in some locations; the south east in particular. Several evenings produced breathtaking sunsets and the cool evening air was filled with the comforting smell of the first fires of autumn. The good weather continued for the entire duration of the Paralympics.

The following week, on a wild and windy Wednesday afternoon, Trish, her newly styled, short, layered hair, part-covered by the hood of her jacket, and Wayne, his confidence boosted by the shade of his mid-brown hair, strolled down to the sea to watch the waves crashing onto the shore. However, before they reached the beach they stopped; on the front garden path of Cove Cottage, a couple were unloading furniture from a small self-hire van.

"Need a hand?" Wayne asked, seeing the female member of the couple struggling with the back end of a two seater sofa.

The male at the front nodded. "Yes please. Friends helped us load up but it's a bit tricky trying to shift heavy things with just the two of us."

Wayne stepped forward and quickly took the back end of the sofa, leaving the much relieved female to let go and lick her aching fingers. When the sofa was safely indoors Wayne insisted on helping unload the rest of the van, and Trish likewise helped with the smaller things. When the van was empty the new arrivals asked Wayne and Trish to join them for a much earned cup of tea.

"That's very kind," said Trish, "but we don't want to be in the way."

"You won't be in the way," said the female stranger, "we've all the time in the world to get things straight."

"What about the van?" Wayne asked, "I see you're from Plymouth. Do you have to get it back tonight?"

The male newcomer shook his head. "No, we're taking it back in the morning. By the way, our name is Woodman, Simon and Melanie Woodman."

"Pleased to meet you," said Wayne, shaking hands with Simon and Melanie, in turn. "I'm Wayne Tilley."

"And I'm Trish Tilley," said his sister, doing likewise.

When they were all inside and the front door was closed, Melanie searched through cardboard boxes marked kitchen, for the kettle and mugs. Once found, she filled the kettle and took milk and sugar from a Sainsbury's carrier bag. When the tea was made they went into the sitting room where Melanie and Simon sat on boxes, after insisting Wayne and Trish have the sofa.

"So," said Trish, "would it be rude to ask what brings you to Cornwall?"

Melanie looked at Simon and giggled. "Shall we tell them?"

"Might as well. It's no secret."

"Simon is a writer," said Melanie, with pride. "His latest book is being made into a television series. The money from it has enabled us to give up our rented place and buy what we've always dreamed of, a cottage by the sea in Cornwall."

"Wow," that's brilliant," said Trish, "you've come to the right place. There are lots of arty types in Cornwall. In fact Wayne is an artist."

Wayne blushed. "Not a well-known one, regrettably. I paint land and seascapes and sell them to tourists."

"Is there a living to be made in that?" Melanie asked.

"Just about. Luckily our house is bought and paid for so we only have the normal everyday things to budget for. You know, Council tax, heating, water and so forth. And Trish is a market trader, so we manage to keep our heads above water."

"Selling anything in particular?" Melanie asked.

"Jewellery," said Trish, "costume jewellery."

Simon grinned. "You two should get together then. Melanie makes jewellery, and damn good she is at it too."

Trish raised her eyebrows. "Really! I'd love to see some of your work."

"And so you shall when we've got everything unpacked."

Simon laid his empty coffee mug on the hearth slate."

"What's the pub like here?"

"Smashing," said Trish, "Justin and his wife, Morgana, are really nice."

"They won't be here for much longer though," said Wayne, "because they're in the throes of selling. But fortunately the buyers are locals, so hopefully there won't be too many changes."

"And what's the food like?" Melanie asked.

"Really good. They have a proper chef called Maurice and he's been here for years. Ever since Justin came here, so I believe."

Simon looked at his watch. "In which case, if you've nothing else planned, would you like to go round there with us for a meal. Our treat."

Wayne looked at Trish who nodded. "Yes," he said, "we'd like that very much. But I insist we buy the drinks, and before we go, do you think I might use your loo?"

"Of course, help yourself," said Melanie, "it's upstairs, first door on the right, if I remember correctly."

"Thanks."

Melanie picked up the mugs to return them to the kitchen. "We must get your husband to show us some of his paintings sometime, Trish. It'd be nice to have a few local scenes to enhance our walls, wouldn't it, Simon?"

"Husband?" Trish muttered, confused.

"Wayne," said Melanie, baffled by her confusion.

As the penny dropped, Trish began to laugh. "Oh, no, Wayne isn't my husband," she giggled, "he's my brother. My twin brother in fact."

Melanie dropped the mugs down onto an upturned chair. "I don't believe it. How utterly amazing. Simon and I are twins too."

To the delight of both Tally and Jim, Andy Murray reached the final of the US Open tennis tournament. His opponent was Novak Djokovic, and in the late hours of September the tenth, he won, and attained his first Grand Slam title.

By mid-September the weather had turned considerably cooler, but no-one minded, it was dry and for that people were extremely grateful. For the first time in ages, tubs, pots and hanging baskets actually needed watering, and washing could be left on the line without housewives keeping watchful eyes on the weather.

In greenhouses throughout the village, gardeners were glad to discard tomatoes and peppers which had suffered with the poor summer. Only the cucumbers had produced reasonable crops. Jim had fared a little better due to the aid of oil heaters in his greenhouse and polytunnels. The cost of running them, however, had reduced his profits. All in all, the summer had been a disaster for all but umbrella manufacturers and sellers, and the wettest since 1912: although it wasn't as cold as the previous year, 2011.

And Britain wasn't the only country with disastrous weather. In Russia crops were destroyed by flooding, and in the United States, crops were decimated by drought.

Inside her rented Reading house, Windflower sat on the floor by the fire amongst stacked cardboard boxes, screwing up old bills, documents and photographs of Sandy. It was the last day she would spend in that house. The following day she would leave to begin a new life in Cornwall.

When the last of the papers curled up and fell back, blackened and charred, amongst the cinders, she leaned back against the settee and closed her eyes. She tried hard not to think of Sandy with hatred, bitterness and repulsion, but it was not possible. The wound was too deep and the pain too acute. And as for Abigail, Windflower found it hard to believe that anyone, any woman, could befriend another, the objective being murder, purely for the sake of greed.

Windflower pulled her laptop from the seat of the settee, switched it on and checked her emails. There was nothing new in her Inbox and so she read, yet again, the last she had received from Ollie.

Windflower.

It's all arranged. Accommodation is waiting for you in one of the Mews flats behind the Penwynton Hotel, along with a full time job as receptionist.

Mum has been saying for some time that she ought to give up work but has been reluctant to do so because she didn't want to leave Linda and Jamie in the lurch. Danny helped out while she was off, but of course, it was only temporary and when he went back to London, she returned to work, but her heart wasn't in it, and she confessed to having enjoyed her free time, despite the fact my fate then hung in a balance. So please, please, don't think of yourself as a burden, but more of a Godsend.

I shall be with you on Sunday morning, September the twenty third, to pick you up and your belongings. I shall be leaving here in the early hours so should be with you by breakfast time.

Try to keep smiling.

Much love. Ollie. x

Sunday the twenty third was wet, cool and windy. Branches blew off trees still in near full leaf, and autumn flowers: chrysanthemums, Michaelmas daisies and dahlias, brutally battered by the wind, lay twisted and broken, on the sodden earth. Only the strong stemmed Japanese anemones stayed erect in the buffeting winds. But

Windflower didn't care. She saw the weather as a dramatic gateway to her new life.

Her accommodation in the Penwynton Mews was modest but well equipped, with a small amount of furniture and central heating. Windflower loved it from the moment she first stepped over the threshold. The furniture was quaint, and the décor was tasteful, and it was hers for as long as she liked.

Chapter Thirty One

By late September, the sale of the Jolly Sailor to Jim Haynes and Tally Castor-Hunt was well underway. The transaction was being handled by the solicitor's office in which Tally's father, Greg worked, hence every effort was being made by his colleagues to get the sale over and done with as quickly and smoothly as possible. The final selling price was five hundred thousand pounds. Justin had been advised to ask for six, but he considered Tally and Jim the perfect couple to take over the pub, and because of Tally's many years of dedication and devotion, he wanted to make the price affordable.

Ned, after much deliberation, finally agreed to take a trip to London to stay with Wills, Lydia, and baby Ned. The chosen date was Saturday October the sixth. Elizabeth drove Ned to Penzance station to catch the early, six fifty, train. It was still dark when they arrived and much of the station was unrecognisable due to large stretches of its structure being shrouded by scaffolding.

Elizabeth escorted her father onto the train, made sure he was in the correct seat and his luggage was safely on the rack above. Two minutes before the train was due to depart, and after she had instructed him not to attempt to leave the train until Wills had boarded it at Paddington, she left and waved from the platform until the train was out of sight.

On Friday, October the twelfth, Justin and Morgana had their farewell party at the Jolly Sailor. The following day they would be moving to Wales leaving the pub behind in the capable hands of Tally and Jim.

The evening began on a sombre note. Justin and Morgana had been familiar faces behind the bar for a long time and many were sorry to see them go. But after a few drinks, the atmosphere became more joyful: after all, it was only right that the departing licensees took with them happy memories of a cheerful and appreciative past clientèle. However, as the evening drew to a close it was Morgana who became emotional, not only because they were leaving but because it seemed many loose ends, romantically speaking, were being tied up. As she filled glasses for a round of drinks requested by Wayne Tilley, she could not but help notice a glint in his eyes she had never seen before. Since the arrival of the Woodman twins at Cove Cottage, it seemed that they and the Tilley twins were rarely out of each other's company. Morgana was delighted: they all seemed so happy. And then there was Ollie. Whoever would have guessed the outcome of the ordeal he had encountered earlier in the year: not only in the proof of his innocence, but his now open relationship with Windflower, the former wife of the man who had set him up.

Wayne Tilley paid for his drinks and left for the table by the door where, Trish, Melanie and Simon waited. Morgana heard the laughter, saw the smiles and her eyes filled with tears.

"No regrets, I hope," said Justin, as she turned and he saw her face.

She shook her head. "No, what you see are tears of happiness. I could never have left here if things were not so wonderful. I think the timing of our exit is just right."

The following morning Morgana and Justin, having seen the last of their possessions placed in a large removal van, handed over the keys to Tally and Jim. All four then gave each other hugs and kisses, uttered good wishes and vowed to keep in touch.

"Promise you'll come back and see us soon," said Tally, as Morgana climbed into the passenger seat and Justin closed the boot.

"We promise," said Morgana, "we'll pop back in the spring."

Before he climbed into the car, Justin squeezed Tally's hand. "I shall miss your lovely smile, Tally. I don't think the good people of Trengillion realise just how lucky they are to have you two taking over."

Tally bottom lip quivered. "I promise we won't let you down. All the good work you have done is safe with us. We shall change very little. And Maurice will have a job here for as long as he wants."

Justin kissed her cheek, shook hands with Jim, quickly jumped into the car and then drove off. And before the car was even out of sight, Tally was in floods of tears.

Jim put his arms around her shoulder and kissed the top of her warm head. "Come on, sweetheart, there is much work to be done."

Inside the Jolly Sailor, Jim locked the door, for the pub was to remain closed during lunchtime, and then open up again in the evening when Tally and Jim had everything under control.

"It always seems so different in here when the bars are empty," said Tally, "eerie, ghostlike and so quiet apart from the ticking of the clock, the wind whistling in the chimney and the flickering of flames in the fireplace."

"When it's lit," said Jim.

Tally smiled. "Yes, when it's lit."

Jim pulled Tally towards him and kissed her. "So, will you be happy here, my darling?"

"If it's possible, then today is both the happiest and saddest of my life. Sad, because Justin and Morgana have gone, but happy, because you and I have the rest of our lives together in the best pub, in the best village, in the whole wide world."

Ned's ten days in London passed by rapidly and all too soon it was his last full day. When asked how he would like to spend it, he opted for a visit to Hyde Park. Initially, Wills thought the trip might be too much for his aged grandfather, but Ned was adamant.

"Touched as I am, Wills, by your thoughtfulness, I must go. I want to go. For when all is said and done it's the last chance I'm ever likely to have."

The morning was beautiful. Several people were out riding bicycles available to hire throughout London and fondly known as Boris Bikes after London Mayor, Boris Johnson, under whose auspices the scheme had been put into action, although the initial idea was that of the previous mayor, Ken Livingstone.

"If only I were twenty years younger," said Ned, wistfully, watching as a stream of blue bicycles passed by, "In fact I'd probably have had a go as recently as ten years ago."

"You really need a bike to see all of the park," said Lydia, pushing baby Ned in his buggy, "it's a fair old way on foot, as I'm sure you'll be more than aware."

Ned nodded. "I've walked round here many a time in my youth and I'm pleased to see that much of it is still recognisable."

After reaching the Serpentine they veered off to the right and wandered along a path, beneath trees slowly changing from green to autumnal colours. Crunching through fallen leaves reminded Ned of his younger days, the wildlife in particular, as pigeons, ducks, starlings and even magpies strutted across the grass alongside grey squirrels.

"It's possible to see parakeets here, especially on the other side of the Serpentine," said Wills, indicating with a wave of his arm. "That's where I've seen them anyway. They're especially prevalent at roosting time."

"I've heard mention of them before," said Ned, glancing up to the trees, "but how does a bird that looks more suited to a warmer climate survive in the UK?"

"They actually originate from the foothills of the Himalayas," said Wills, "so they don't need it to be all that warm to survive, and there's plenty of food for them here in the park. You know, nuts, berries and seeds."

Lydia noticed Ned's pace was slowing. "I should like to sit for a while," she said, tactfully, eying a vacant bench, "then we can all take in our surroundings and enjoy this fine spell of weather."

There was a little rain overnight in London but by morning it was gone and so dawned another fine day, although the wind was a little blustery in comparison with the previous day. Ned looked at the calendar. "October the sixteenth, I can't believe I've been here for ten days: the time really has flown."

"That's good," said Lydia, handing Ned a mug of tea, "it means you must have enjoyed yourself."

"Oh, I have. It's been wonderful. Truly wonderful, and I shall have much to tell the rest of the family when I get home."

Lydia leaned forward and kissed his cheek. "You must come again."

But Ned shook his head. "I don't think so. I want to remember London as I've seen it these last few days. As time goes on I'll get more and more decrepit and even less agile. If I couldn't get around I'd be a dreadful burden and I have vowed, just as my mother did, that I shall never be a burden to anyone."

After saying his goodbyes to Wills, Lydia and baby Ned, at Paddington Station, Ned boarded the six minutes past three train to

Penzance. He was travelling first class, his family had insisted; they wanted him to enjoy as much comfort as he was able for the five and a half hour journey.

Once he was seated, Ned nodded politely to an elderly woman sitting on the opposite side of the aisle. And after the train had pulled out of the station, he opened up the book of crossword puzzles Lydia had bought for him to pass away the time. As he was puzzling over what at one time he would have considered an elementary question, complimentary refreshments were brought round on a trolley. Ned had a cup of tea and an individual packet of shortbread biscuits. He then continued with the crossword.

After a while his eyes began to ache. Frustrated by his lack of concentration and inability to answer the questions, he laid down his personalised pen and looked from the window. As the train pulled into Newbury station, it jolted slightly, his pen slid across the table, fell to the floor and rolled across the carpet towards the feet of the lady sitting opposite reading a magazine. Obligingly, she picked it up. When she saw his engraved name, a puzzled expression crossed her face.

"Ned Stanley, how strange. Sorry, you must wonder what on earth I'm talking about." Laughing, she handed the pen back to Ned. "But, you see, it's a name I've never forgotten."

Thanking her, Ned took the pen and clipped it inside the pocket of his jacket. "I'm intrigued, please tell me more."

The woman laughed. "Ned Stanley was a teacher my dear, late father met on a train many, many years ago when he was coming down to Plymouth to visit us. I remember the name so well, because Dad often wondered how he was, your namesake, I mean. He was going to Cornwall, you see, to convalesce, because he'd been ill."

Ned felt the muscles in his throat tighten. "Good God, David Braddley."

The woman removed her reading glasses and lay them down on the table. "I don't believe it. Surely you're not the Ned he spoke of. Not after all these years. It's too much of a coincidence. Good gracious, I've gone all goose-pimply."

Ned laughed. "Yes, I'm he, and it was sixty years ago. February to be precise. King George had just died and the country was in mourning. I remember it like it was yesterday. Your dad was going to stay with you because your mother had gone to Scotland to stay with her mother who was ill."

The woman shook her head, shocked and bewildered. "That's right and I should have realised the year, especially with it being the Queen's Diamond Jubilee."

Ned nodded. "And you, I was told, were a teacher too, back then, and married to a boat builder."

She laughed. "That's correct, but needless to say I retired from teaching many, many, years ago. And my husband has been gone for five years now, God rest his soul. I still live in Plymouth though, well in that area anyway. We moved to Kingsbridge when, Jed, my husband, finally retired. My name's Agnes, by the way, Agnes Denner."

Ned leaned across the aisle and shook her frail hand. "As you already know, I'm Ned Stanley," he grinned.

"So, Ned, are you Cornwall bound again today?"

"Yes, but not to convalesce. I live there now, and have done so since Christmas 1953."

A broad smile crossed the face of Agnes Denner. "Ah, so would I be correct in assuming what Dad always hoped, that you met Miss Right in Cornwall?"

Ned wrinkled his nose. "Well, yes and no." He then proceeded to tell Agnes Denner of his first visit to Cornwall and how he had met his late wife, Stella Hargreaves.

Between Castle Carey and Taunton, the train passed by flooded fields where ducks swam on the short-term ponds alongside grazing sheep, and overhead a few grey clouds, slowly began to appear in the previously blue skies. By the time the train arrived in Plymouth and Agnes and Ned bade each other farewell, it was dark.

As the train crossed the River Tamar, Ned looked from the window but there was little to see in the dim lights. He sighed: it all seemed rather dull after the bright lights of London.

Eventually, tired of seeing his own reflection in the dark window, Ned pulled the curtain, closed his eyes and took a nap.

He slept for one and a half hours and awoke as the train neared the station at Redruth. Ned pulled back the curtain. Outside looked even darker. He shivered, feeling chilled after his sleep, and so reached up to the rack above his seat and took down his overcoat.

After putting it on, he slipped the crossword book into a carrier bag and laid it down on the table.

The train stopped at Camborne, and then St Erth. Ned felt a pang of delight; he was nearly home. Feeling the need to stretch his legs, he left his seat and walked to the end of the carriage, where his suitcase rested on the luggage rack. By the door he looked from a half open window. The breeze tousled his hair and took away his breath. He was mesmerised by the view, for as the train neared the bridge at Marazion, St Michael's Mount appeared in the distance, lit up like a fairy castle on an island not far from the shore. The train went under the bridge and then ran alongside the sea. The sea, at high water, was rough; a strong wind was blowing and he could smell its pungent ozone. The train slowed as it neared Penzance station and Ned hung his head from the window. He could feel the salt spray of the sea on his face as the train hissed, squeaked, rattled and groaned, until finally, it stopped, several yards from the buffers. Before Ned had a chance to alight, the door of his carriage was opened and Anne was by his side insisting that she help with his luggage.

Although he was tired, Ned chatted happily, telling Anne of his meeting with Agnes Denner, the joy of holding his great grandson, and the many changes that had occurred in the area he had once, long ago, called home. It was not until they were in the car and heading towards the Marazion roundabout that Anne reluctantly burst Ned's bubble.

"Dad, I'm afraid I have some bad news." Ned froze, very much aware of the tremor in his daughter's voice. "It's Mother-in-law. She has a nasty chest infection. The doctor says she ought to go into hospital, but she won't. John, Tony, and Sue have all tried to persuade her, but she's adamant that if her time has come she wants to be in her own bed. We were hoping you might be able to change her mind, but I think it's too late now. She's fading fast."

Ned sat in silence for a while before he finally spoke. "I shall visit her as soon as we get home, Anne. She's the only one of our generation left. I must see her."

Ned found Gertie propped up in bed by four plump pillows. She smiled feebly when he entered the room and held up her hands to him.

"Ned. Come sit by my side."

Ned sat on the bed and took her warm hands in his. "Don't leave me, Gert. Please don't leave me."

She smiled. "We had some good times, didn't we, Ned? We've lots of happy memories, and between us, you, me, Stella and dear Percy, we produced a lovely family."

Ned gripped her hands as tightly as his weak hands permitted. He nodded. "Yes, Gert, between us we've produced a family to be proud of."

"You know, I've been thinking a lot about the past lying here drifting in and out of sleep. And if I've never told you before, then I must tell you now, that when I heard you'd got the job as headmaster of the school, all those many, many years ago, well, it was one of the happiest days of my life."

Ned felt a lump in his throat. "Mine too."

The door quietly opened and Susan entered with a tray holding cups of tea and a plate of biscuits. "I thought you might be thirsty, Ned, after your long journey. And Mum needs to keep up her liquid intake, don't you, Mum?"

Gertie eyed the tray. "Yes, but I've no craving for food, Sue."

Ned half smiled. "I never thought I'd live to hear you say that, Gert."

She gave a feeble laugh. "And I never dreamt I'd ever say it."

Ned stayed until Gertie's eyes began to flicker and it was obvious she was on the verge of sleep. He then rose, kissed her cheek, and vowed he'd return the following morning to see her.

Chapter Thirty Two

Gertie passed away that night in her sleep. She did not suffer. Susan found her when she went in to make sure all was well at five o' clock in the morning. She told her brothers, when conveying the news, the room in which their mother had died, was filled with a strange eerie quietness. A peaceful serenity unlike anything she had ever before encountered.

It was Anne who broke the news to Ned. "I'm so sorry," she sobbed, "it's been a horrible homecoming for you, hasn't it?"

Ned nodded. "Poor Gert. She was only eighty. She should've lived for many more years yet."

"I agree, but she had a good life, didn't she? And was very much loved."

"And she'll be sorely missed. Oh, Anne, I suddenly feel very old. So very, very old."

Anne tried to smile. "It's been a bitter blow for all of us. Poor Sue. When she saw how much her mum perked up during your visit last night, she thought perhaps she was on the mend. But it was just a blip. Almost as though she'd hung on and saved her last bit of energy for when you came home. John reckons she was determined to see you again. She said you'd become her best friend since everyone else had gone."

The weather for the remainder of the week was mild, bright, windy and sunny, but by the weekend it changed to dull, damp and drizzly with mist and little or no wind.

The first three days of the following week were damp, drizzly and dreary too, but on Thursday, a fresh easterly wind blew and everywhere dried up. The sun even shone for a while.

Saturday, October the twenty seventh, was a sunny, dry and blustery day with a cold wind blowing down from the north. In Scotland and along the east coast of England, snow had fallen during the night and many parts of the country woke to a frost, but not Cornwall. Cornwall, as so often happens, was frost free.

Around Trengillion, most trees had shed their leaves, the cherry tree in the front garden of the Old Police House, much admired by villagers in the spring, was bare; but the lilac tree in the front hedge of Rose Cottage, still had many green leaves around the blackened heads of long dead blooms.

In the front garden of Number Two Coronation Terrace, Michaelmas daises, chrysanthemums, fuchsias and dahlias, all planted and tended by Gertie over the years, bloomed amongst the last of the summer bedding. And by the door, a solitary yellow rose looked to the heavens, on a bush bought by Percy, for Gertie, on her seventieth birthday.

At ten minutes to two, a gleaming black hearse along with two limousines, pulled up in front of the house. Susan watched as it came into view over the top of a cotoneaster, laden with ripe, red berries. From it stepped the elegantly dressed undertaker, with whom the family had arranged their mother's funeral. He removed his hat and walked up the garden path.

Ned rode with the family in one of the limousines. Susan said it was what her mother would have wanted, and he was greatly touched. He sat beside Anne, along with John, Jess, Clive and Florence Anne. In the other car, Susan rode with her husband, Steve, and her brother, Tony, with his wife, Jean. Ollie was accompanied by Windflower.

At a steady pace the cars followed Gertie's coffin, hidden beneath a sea of flowers, through the village to the church where she had been christened and married, and where her late husband, Percy, was buried. She was then carried beneath the lichgate by six bearers, her two sons, Tony and John, her two grandsons, Ollie and Denzil, her granddaughter's husband, Clive, and her neighbour, Trevor Moore.

The mourners were few in number for, other than Ned, all of Gertie's contemporaries were gone.

After the service, Gertie was carried from the church, beneath the Virginia creeper covered tower, bearing red autumn leaves, along the gravel path and over the grass, still a healthy green due to the wet summer. Finally, amongst the newest graves, she was laid to rest beside Percy.

After the interment, the mourners made their way out of the churchyard and round the corner to the pub for refreshments. As they left, Ned, his arm linked with daughter, Elizabeth, paused to glance over the headstones of all those already gone, and Stella's in particular. He felt a lump in his throat. He wiped his reddened eyes. They continued to walk on, past the older graves, until Ned suddenly remembered, lost in a corner, tucked beneath the branches of a mountain ash, a grave, long forgotten.

"Hang on a minute, Liz."

He left her side and returned to the mound of flowers lying beside Gertie's yet-to-be-filled in grave. From a bouquet he plucked a single red rose and took it to the forgotten grave beneath the mountain ash. He stooped and lay it beside the headstone engraved with the name, Jane Hunt. The year, 1952. "A rose," he whispered, "for a dear girl I never knew, but who unwittingly changed the course of my life. Thank you, Jane."

When they left the churchyard, they walked beneath the lichgate and stepped onto the road where Ned was surprised to see the family standing in a group. He was puzzled. "Why haven't they gone in, Liz? It's too chilly to hang around in this cold north wind."

"They're waiting for you, Dad," said Elizabeth, calmly trying to keep the emotion from her voice. "Tally and Jim have a surprise for you."

"Surprise?" muttered Ned, nonplussed.

When Ned and Elizabeth reached the other family members they all walked together towards the pub. As they turned the corner and onto the cobbles, they all stopped.

"Dad, look up," said Elizabeth, pointing.

Ned raised his head. Hanging from the brackets where once the Jolly Sailor board hung, was a new board, but with an old name, The Ringing Bells Inn.

"Tally found all the old boards in the cellar," said Elizabeth. "They'd all got damp and were in a poor state of repair. We know you've always spoken with great affection for the days when the pub was the Ringing Bells Inn, and so Jim made a new board, and Anne painted it, exactly as it was painted before. It's a tribute to you, Dad. You, Gertie, and all those gone before you."

Inside the Ringing Bells Inn, Ned, emotional, moved and overcome with nostalgia, insisted on buying drinks for everyone. He then asked a favour of his granddaughter. "Tally, would it be alright for me to have a look round upstairs? I've not been up there for years, and now the Inn's in the family, I'd really like to see it again."

"Of course, Granddad. Would you like someone to go with you? The stairs are rather steep."

He shook his head. "No, no thanks. I'd like to be alone. I want to take a trip down Memory Lane and I'm used to stairs."

Tally smiled. "Of course, I understand. Help yourself then, Granddad. There's no-one up there."

Ned left the bar and walked into the passage. He passed by the closed doors of the dining room and kitchen, and on towards the foot of the stairs. He looked up. To his surprise the old painting of Saint Michael's Mount still hung where the stairs turned. He began to climb, slowly and thoughtfully, holding onto the banister until he reached the top.

The landing was much as he remembered it. But the doors were now painted brilliant white. Ned walked along the passage. The door leading to a small back stairway and the owner's downstairs living room, was now marked *Fire Exit*. Outside the last door on the right, he stopped. He opened it and peeped inside. It was the room in which he'd stayed sixty years earlier on his very first visit to Trengillion. He stepped into the room, surprised by the transformation. Gone was the old linoleum flooring. In its place lay a putty-coloured fitted carpet. The fireplace was also gone, and in its place hung a large radiator. The old iron framed double bed was replaced by a pine double, and a fitted wardrobe filled the corner where once the old wooden wardrobe and cumbersome chest of drawers had stood. But the windows, now Grade Two listed, were unchanged.

Ned closed the door, crossed the passage and went through the door opposite. It was the room in which his mother had stayed in 1952, and the room in which he and Stella had stayed in 1953 during their honeymoon. It too was much changed. The bed and carpet were as in his old room, the fireplace, likewise, was gone. Ned crossed to the window. But the sea was visible, just as he remembered.

Back downstairs, Ned went into the snug bar and sat at a table where the sun shone onto the polished surface. A fire was heartily burning in the hearth and the sweet scent of pine logs and lavender furniture polish lingered in the air. As Ned took a sip of his drink, Elizabeth came and sat by his side. “You alright, Dad? You look a bit peaky. Are you warm enough?”

He nodded. “Yes, thank you. I’m just feeling a bit nostalgic, that’s all. I’ve had a lot to think about lately, in London as well as here, and seeing the Ringing Bells Inn board has sent my mind spinning. I’ve got so many happy memories, Liz, and scores of them occurred within these walls.” He stroked the back of Elizabeth’s hand. “You can’t imagine how happy I am to know that this lovely place is now in the hands of young Tally. Jim too, of course. I’m very, very proud. I know they’ll do a good job here and I hope it’ll stay in the family for many years to come.”

“I hope so too,” said Elizabeth. “I’ve never seen Tally so happy. And as for Jim, I think he’ll make an excellent landlord, and I truly look forward to him being my son-in-law.”

Greg peeped inside the snug. “You’d better grab something to eat if you’re hungry, Liz. The food’s going very quickly.”

She smiled. “I’m not surprised. After all, Maurice said he was going to try out all sorts of new recipes on us.” She stood up. “Would you like me to get you something to eat, Dad?”

He shook his head. “No, thank you. I’ve no appetite. You go.”

Elizabeth leaned forward and kissed her father’s cheek. “Okay, I’ll pop back and see you in a minute.”

“No need to rush, Liz. I’m fine on my own.” He grinned. “It gives me a chance to think at my own pace.”

When she was gone he crossed to the fire and as he stood with hands behind his back enjoying the warmth of the flickering flames, he was able to see into the public bar. As he listened to the collective sound of muffled voices, his eyes narrowed and his heart began to race. Surely he could see a young Gertie standing at the far end of the bar. He sighed. No, of course not. How silly of him. It was Gertie’s granddaughter, Demelza, and the middle-aged man with dark curly hair, leaning on the bar was not Percy, but Percy’s son, Tony. Ned smiled. How much like Stella was their daughter, Anne. And Elizabeth, she resembled his mother, Molly in so many ways. Ned felt heartened. “People come and people go,” he whispered, “but their genes live on forever.”

Ned sat back down. He felt fatigued and his legs ached. He took a sip of whisky and leaned his head against the wall. His nose twitched and his eyes watered, both senses seemingly alerted by a waft of cigarette smoke. Ned sat up straight and glanced around the empty snug. He was obviously mistaken for he was quite alone. Furthermore, smoking was no longer permitted in British pubs. Tutting to himself, he again leaned his head back and closed his eyes.

From inside the public bar Ned thought he heard the deep tones of a man chuckling and the distinct merry laughter of a female. He opened one eye. Surely the chuckling and laughter flowed from the lips of Frank and Sylvia Newton? He sat up and sniffed the air. He could also smell the sweetly scented violets of his mother's favourite perfume. A black Labrador walked in and lazily curled up in front of the fire.

"Don?" whispered Ned, peering through a misty haze of dust speckled sunlight. But it wasn't Don, it was Valerie and Trevor Moores' dog, Gerald.

Ned smiled. His mind was playing tricks because his thoughts kept drifting back over the past sixty years. He took another sip of whisky and again closed his eyes.

A sudden strange sensation passed through his tired, aching body. His hands fell to his sides. Amidst the sound of the wind whistling down the wide chimney and the ticking of the old clock above the logs crackling on the open fire, voices were gently whispering his name.

In the public bar, John and Tony Collins asked Tally for however many bottles of champagne, she estimated, it would take to give everyone present a glass. They had decided, although some might think it inappropriate, to toast their late mother, and celebrate her life in a way they felt sure she would approve. Tally, in due course arrived with six bottles of champagne, and with Jim's help began to open them.

When all glasses were filled, Tony raised his glass. "To Mum. Thank you for the dedication, devotion and love you've given us over these many, many years. We shall miss you. Long may you rest in peace."

"To Gertie," chanted united voices, "long may you rest in peace."

After the toast, Elizabeth suddenly remembered Ned.

"Oh, no. We forgot Dad. How careless, especially when he knew Gertie longer than any of us."

"Take him my glass, Auntie Liz," said Jess, "I've only had a little sip and I don't really like champagne, anyway."

Elizabeth took the glass, along with her own, into the snug, intending that she and her father should toast Gertie together. She smiled when she saw him. His eyes were closed. He looked peaceful as he quietly slept.

But Ned was not in a sleep from which he might ever awaken. His aching heart had beat its last beat. His lungs taken their last breath and his lips spoken his last words.

Outside, the day drew to a fitting close. The fading light of the setting sun cast rich golden beams across the rippling waves of the dark, tranquil sea. An onshore wind, softened by the rising tide, gently blew around Trengillion, ruffling the petals of the flowers covering Gertie's grave, and rustling the autumnal leaves clinging to the tall trees which loomed around the old church tower.

And above the doorway of the Ringing Bells Inn, the new board gently swayed and softly creaked as though whispering a fond farewell.

THE END

Printed in Great Britain
by Amazon